Unexpected

by

Jana Richards

The Masonville Series, Book 3

Unexpected

COPYRIGHT © 2021 by Jana Richards

Cover Art by *Rae Monet, Inc. Design*

The Wild Rose Press, Inc.
PO Box 708
Adams Basin, NY 14410-0708
Visit us at www.thewildrosepress.com

Publishing History
First Edition, 2021
Trade Paperback ISBN 978-1-5092-3829-3
Digital ISBN 978-1-5092-3830-9

The Masonville Series, Book 3
Published in the United States of America

"Is there anything I can say to make you change your mind?"

"Say you'll marry me."

The words were out of his mouth before he knew he was going to say them. Jamie stared at him, eyes wide.

"What?"

"Marry me. You're the only woman I'd trust with my girls."

It suddenly made sense. If Jamie married him, he could keep his kids.

She jumped to her feet, waking one of the dogs who'd been sleeping on the couch next to her. "What kind of marriage do you want, Ben? Are you proposing something for show?"

"No... I don't know!" He stood and grasped her arms. "If you're asking me if we'll sleep together as man and wife, I don't know."

Her mouth twisted as if she was holding back tears. "You know I love the girls, but please don't ask me to pretend. The last few months of my marriage, I pretended I had a husband who loved me. I swore I'd never do that again."

Ben wanted to take her in his arms and hold her. He hated doing this to her, hated making her relive unhappy memories. He was asking too much of her, and he didn't blame her for saying no.

"Please, forget I said anything."

He'd stick to his original plan. He and the girls would disappear. He'd change their names, go someplace where no one knew them. A life on the run wasn't what he wanted for his children, but he'd do whatever he needed to do to keep them.

Praise for Jana Richards
and The Masonville Series

CHILD OF MINE
"Ms. Richards weaves the plot with sensitivity, eliciting sympathetic responses to both of the main characters."

~Bookophile

~*~

"This is the first book by Richards that I've read but I definitely doubt it will be my last!"

~Romantic Reads and Such

~*~

TO HEAL A HEART
"*To Heal A Heart* is a gut-wrenching emotional story about healing after a great loss and learning to cope with a disability… Highly recommend!"

~N.N. Light's Book Heaven

~*~

"If I had to choose one word to summarize this story then I'd choose the word 'heartwarming.' This was an inspiring and uplifting book."

~Long and Short Reviews

~*~

"*To Heal A Heart* is one of those page turners you will not forget soon…On a scale of 1-5, *To Heal A Heart* deserves a 7."

~Wild Women Reviews

Dedication

To my beta readers
—Ishbel, Melanie, and Alison—
thank you for saving me!
Couldn't have done it without you.

Chapter One

Ben Greyson froze as he stepped out onto his back porch. Where were his children? A minute ago, both girls were playing in the yard. Horrific scenarios sizzled through his imagination—they ran away, they were lured out of the yard by a predator.

Their grandparents made good on their threat to take them away.

Calm down. Don't panic. The Doyles wouldn't swoop in and steal them away without warning. Despite the problems between him and his former in-laws, they'd go the legal route.

And Masonville, North Dakota was a small town. Nothing bad happened in small towns.

Except when it did.

Ben hurried down the porch stairs. "Bella! Sophie! Where are you?"

He checked around the side of the house in case they were teasing him with a game of hide-and-seek. When they weren't there, he hurried to the storage shed at the back of the lot and unlatched it. In the fading October light, he could just make out the new rake he'd bought a week ago when they'd moved into the house. But there were no small blonde girls in puffy jackets, the youngest wearing her favorite glow-in-the-dark sparkly pink sneakers.

"Bella! Sophie!"

He couldn't lose anyone else he loved.

He struggled to focus, to push past the panic. They couldn't have gone far. They'd been playing outside alone for less than ten minutes while he made supper. They had to be nearby.

But they hadn't lived here long, and it was beginning to get dark. Maybe they were lost and afraid.

With his heart racing, Ben ran toward the gate that opened to the front yard. It swung free, the wind gently blowing it back and forth on its hinges. He'd latched it earlier, he was sure. He'd lived in big cities all his life and was meticulous about locking doors and securing gates.

On the front sidewalk, Ben looked up and down both ways. No sign of the girls. Panic bubbled up his throat, his stomach clenching in fear and indecision. Where should he go? What should he do?

He heard a sharp whistle and an anxious female voice. "Sammy! Rex! Get back here!"

A woman emerged from the back yard of the house next door and ran to the sidewalk, ponytail bobbing.

"Have you seen a couple of dogs? A black lab and a small brown terrier?"

Ben shook his head. "No, no dogs. I'm looking for my girls. They were playing in our back yard, and now they're gone."

She pointed at his house. "Are you the ones who just moved in next door?"

"Yeah." He checked the sidewalk both ways once again, not in the mood for a neighborly chat. "I've got to find my kids."

"Maybe they're with my dogs. The gate to my back yard was wide open, and—"

"You left your gate open? My kids must have run after your dogs. What kind of irresponsible idiot are you?" Ben gave his fear full reign, pointing an accusing finger at her. "Because of you and your damn dogs, I can't find my girls. If something happens to them—"

She pushed away his hand. "Hey. Hold on a moment, buddy. I closed that gate before I let the dogs out into the yard. What if your girls opened my *closed* gate to get into my yard, and the dogs ran out? Maybe you should consider that."

Ben focused his attention on the woman. She was tall and slim, with brownish hair pulled back into a ponytail. He got a sense of light-colored eyes assessing his character and finding him lacking. He knew he was being a jerk, but he didn't care.

"Supposing your theory is correct, where would your dogs go if they got loose?"

"I doubt they'd go far. We usually walk to the schoolyard and then over to the park. We could check there."

Ben hesitated. Should he trust this woman, this stranger? Or should he get in his car and patrol the streets?

Or call the police? *Dear God, don't let it come to that.*

She offered a tentative smile. "We'll find them. I promise."

Something in her smile calmed him and helped him focus. Her dogs were his only clue. What choice did he have but to follow her?

"Fine. Lead the way."

****

Jamie Garven puffed out a breath, doing a skip-run-step to keep up with her new neighbor. She stole a glance at him. Tall, dark blond hair, ridiculously good-looking. Something about him looked familiar, but she couldn't put her finger on it. In his elegant three-piece suit, he looked like he should be on Wall Street instead of Main Street in Masonville. Most of the guys she knew dressed far more casually.

And most of the guys she knew weren't nearly as rude.

She struggled to keep up, regretting her decision to give up her gym membership. Despite the exertion, she wouldn't ask her hot new neighbor to slow down. He was obviously anxious to find his kids. If she had children, she'd feel exactly the same way.

But I don't have any children and likely never will.

The thought provoked the usual stab of pain, but right now, she needed to focus on finding her dogs and Hot Neighbor's children. No time for wallowing in self-pity. She'd wallowed enough the last few years.

They reached the school, and he suddenly stopped, indecision and frustration etched on his handsome face. "Where do we go now?"

Jamie caught her breath before speaking. "The play structures are on the other side of the school. If they're not there, we'll go to the park. It's only a couple of blocks from here."

He hurried off, and Jamie ran to keep up with him. She was breathing so hard she almost missed the sound of dogs barking. Once they rounded the corner of the school, Jamie saw two little girls throwing sticks her dogs Sammy and Rex dutifully fetched. They dropped them at the girls' feet, tongues lolling and bodies poised for another throw. Jamie whistled for the dogs, and when they came to her, she attached their leashes to their collars and held them firmly.

"Isabella! Sophie! What are you doing here?" Hot Neighbor ran to the little girls and dropped to his knees to hug them, oblivious to the dirt messing up his fancy suit. Jamie blew out a sigh of relief. Thank goodness everyone was safe.

"We're playing with the puppies, Daddy." The smaller of the two girls flashed her father an adorable smile. "Aren't they cute?"

"Yeah, very cute. But did you ask permission to leave our yard?"

Her smile faded. "No."

He held her small face between his hands. "You know you're not supposed to wander off. I couldn't find you, and I was worried."

The older girl wrapped her arm around his shoulders. "We're sorry, Daddy. We forgot."

"Did you go into our neighbor's yard?"

The little one laid her head on her father's shoulder. The older one looked up at her father, her voice pleading. "We wanted to play with the dogs in their yard, but when we opened the gate, they ran away. So we followed them because we didn't want them to get lost."

When he glanced at her, Jamie arched a brow and sent Hot Neighbor an *I told you so* stare. His return expression was unapologetic. He turned his attention back to his children, his voice gentle but firm.

"What if the dogs, or you, ran out into the street and were hit by a car? You have to promise me you'll never leave our yard again without asking my permission first. And you're never to walk into a neighbor's yard on your own."

Both girls began to cry. Jamie's heart broke at their tears.

"You can visit Rex and Sammy any time, as long as you ask me first. And as long as the gate stays closed." The words were out of her mouth before she had a chance to think them through.

All three turned to stare at her, Hot Neighbor with a raised, imperious eyebrow. "And as long as *I* say it's okay."

Lifting her chin, she glared back at him. "Of course."

Controlling ass. She'd met his kind before. Hell, she'd been married to his kind.

Jamie sighed, knowing she should cut him some slack. He'd been worried about his kids, after all.

She pulled on her dogs' leashes, preparing to head home. In the future, she'd steer clear of her new neighbor, remaining polite but distant. She didn't need the aggravation.

"What's your name?"

Jamie glanced up at the sound of the child's voice. Her gaze connected with the older girl's. She considered walking away and pretending she hadn't heard the question, but it seemed like a rotten way to treat a child. She focused on the girl, not letting her gaze drift over to her father.

"I'm Jamie. What's your name?"

"I'm Bella, and this is my little sister, Sophie."

"Nice to meet you." Jamie scratched her Lab's ears. "This is Sammy, and the smaller guy here is Rex. They live with me, and so do my angel fish and my bird Hector."

The smaller girl lifted her head from her father's shoulder. "You have a bird?"

"I do. Hector is an African Grey Parrot. He's a cool guy, and he even talks."

"Birds can't talk."

"Some can. Hector definitely does."

Sophie's eyes widened. "What does he say?"

"My name, the dogs' names. All kinds of things."

"Can I see him?"

Jamie met Hot Neighbor's unsmiling gaze. "Sometime, if your dad says it's okay, you can meet Hector."

Sophie turned to her father. "Can we go now, Daddy? I want to hear Hector talk."

"No, we can't. Right now, we're heading home, and you two are going to be grounded for leaving the yard without permission."

She hung her head. "Sorry, Daddy."

He laid a gentle hand on her head. "I know you are, Sophie. Just don't do it again. My heart couldn't take it."

He wrapped his arms around both girls. Jamie watched, uncomfortable to be intruding on such a private moment. Something about the tender way this big man held these two tiny girls hit her square in the solar plexus.

Not every man behaved like her ex.

She cleared her throat. "I should get Rex and Sammy home. It was nice meeting you, Bella and Sophie. I'll see you around."

Her neighbor rose quickly and extended his hand. "Thank you for helping me find the girls. I'm Ben Greyson, by the way."

"Jamie Garven." She accepted his handshake. Again she had the sensation she'd seen him before. In the lights illuminating the playground, she could see his eyes were a mixture of green and brown and were framed by long, thick lashes. This close to him, she noticed the dimple in his cheek for the first time and caught the scent of a delectable men's cologne. For a moment, Jamie's heart wobbled like a washing machine with an uneven load.

Or a hormonal teenager with her first crush.

The embarrassing thought made Jamie tug on her hand. He released it immediately, and she forced herself to smile politely.

"It was nice meeting all of you. Goodnight."

Once she and the dogs rounded the school and were out of sight, Jamie urged them into a run. They raced all the way home. As if the hounds of Hell were on their tails.

Or perhaps her own unsettling thoughts were chasing her. Jamie stifled a groan. She was being ridiculous. She'd been momentarily dazzled by a pretty face. Any red-blooded woman with a pulse would have reacted the same way.

Anyway, there was likely a Mrs. Ben Greyson somewhere in the picture. Men who looked like him generally weren't single.

And men who looked like her hot new neighbor didn't give plain women like her a second glance.

Chapter Two

When she returned to her house, Jamie fed the dogs before starting on her own dinner. Tonight she was having poached salmon and a salad with avocado and cucumber. It was a far cry from her old diet. For the first couple of months after her ex-husband, Carson, moved out, she'd existed on a diet of ramen noodles and frozen pizza, when she bothered to eat at all. Gradually, she pulled herself out of the abyss and started eating more nutritious food. The high-quality vegetables, fruits, and proteins made her feel better physically and helped to improve her mental well-being as well.

As did her pets. There were days that, if not for having to feed and look after Hector and the dogs, she would have stayed in bed.

But it was behind her now. Two and half years ago she'd moved to Masonville to take a position as a veterinarian at the local animal clinic. She had a full life with plenty of friends and a career she loved. And a family who loved her. Even if that love sometimes felt strained.

As if on cue, her phone rang, and checking the screen she saw the landline number of her parents, Jack and Helen Garven. Suppressing a sigh, she hit the talk button.

"Hi, Mom. How are you?" She injected a note of

cheer into her voice, hoping it didn't sound fake.

"I'm fine. Dad's here with me, too."

"Hi, Dad. How's everything with you?"

"Things are good. Busy. Davis has decided to retire, and Zach and I are scrambling to keep up."

Davis Forbes had been her dad's partner in the veterinary clinic in Lewiston, North Dakota for over thirty years. About eight years ago, Jamie's brother-in-law Zach had joined the practice. "Oh, wow. I didn't think Davis would ever retire."

Jack Garven chuckled. "He just turned seventy and figured it was time. Birthing calves on midnight calls is a young person's game. Davis and Wanda are leaving Lewiston in a couple of weeks to spend the winter in Arizona. They bought a place down there."

"Tell them I wish a happy retirement for them. Do you plan to hire a new vet?"

"Yeah. We've been advertising for another large animal veterinarian to join the practice, but we haven't had any takers yet."

Jamie wasn't surprised. The life of a country vet wasn't for everyone. Finding the right person could take some time.

The talk turned to other subjects, like the goings-on in Lewiston and news about her parents' friends. Finally, her mother asked the question Jamie was sure was the point of this phone call.

"Are you coming home for Thanksgiving? We're planning a big dinner."

"I'm coming to Lewiston, but not on the Thursday. I'll be there on Tuesday and leave late Wednesday afternoon." She'd deliberately chosen to keep her visit short.

"We were hoping to have the whole family together for Thanksgiving." There was no mistaking the disappointment in her mother's voice. "I know Lisa was looking forward to seeing you. It's been a long time since you and your sister were together."

"I'm sorry, Mom, but I volunteered to be on call through the holiday. Everyone has plans with their families."

"You have a family, too, Jamie," her father said quietly.

Jamie closed her eyes and massaged her temple. "I know, Dad. But it's different for me. You know that."

Helen forced a cheerful tone into her voice. "Well, whenever you come, we're looking forward to seeing you."

They ended the call soon after. Jamie set down her phone and flopped onto her sofa, as exhausted as if she'd run a marathon. Every conversation between them was fraught with tension.

She wondered if her mother would try to get her and Lisa together while she was in Lewiston. She hoped not. She and her sister hadn't been chummy for some time.

Who was she kidding? They'd barely spoken in the last five years.

She knew her parents were disappointed she and Lisa didn't get along, and that they mostly blamed her for the rift. Lisa was the perfect daughter who always had time for her parents. She was in a loving relationship with Zach and had provided her parents with two beautiful grandchildren. In contrast, Jamie was divorced.

And barren. She'd never give her parents any

grandchildren.

Best not to dwell on it, or depression would follow. She'd learned that the hard way.

****

Mrs. Bonner's calico cat swiped at Jamie, making her displeasure known with an angry hiss. Luckily, her claws missed the mark.

"Lucy! Stop it!" Mrs. Bonner held her cat tighter. "Sorry, Dr. Jamie."

Jamie quickly injected the rabies vaccine just under the skin in Lucy's right rear leg. "No problem. I might get testy myself if someone poked me with this thing."

She listened to Lucy's abdomen and chest sounds and satisfied herself that the cat was in perfect health. After Mrs. Bonner wrangled Lucy back into her carrier, Jamie walked them out.

She stopped at the front desk. "Lauren, which examining room am I in next?"

Lauren and her veterinarian husband, Cole Walsh, had recently purchased the clinic and she'd taken over the role of practice manager. She had the place running like a well-oiled machine.

"You're in luck. Fred Baker had to reschedule Monty's appointment. You're done for the day."

"Oh. I guess I can start my weekend early."

"Got any big plans?"

Not a one. "Oh, sure. I'm cleaning Hector's cage. That's always a blast."

Lauren visibly shuddered. "Have a great weekend."

"You, too. See you Monday."

She made her way to the staff lounge, and as she slipped on her jacket, Blair Greyson came through the door. "Are you done for the day?"

"We had a cancelation. I'll probably regret it Monday when we're overbooked, but for now I'm going to enjoy the reprieve. Are you taking off, too?"

Blair pulled her jacket from the coat rack. "Yeah. I asked Lauren if I could leave early. We're having a big family dinner tonight. My brother and his kids recently moved to Masonville."

"That sounds like fun." A memory suddenly hit Jamie. *That's why he looked familiar.* She'd seen her new neighbor at Blair's grandfather's funeral that past summer. "Your brother is Ben Greyson, right? With two little blonde girls named Bella and Sophie?"

"Yeah, that's them. How do you know them?"

"Turns out they're my next-door neighbors. Unfortunately, we had a rocky first meeting." She told Blair about the incident with the runaway dogs.

"Please don't hold it against him." Blair wrapped a scarf around her neck. "They've had a tough year. His wife, Olivia, the girls' mother, was killed in a car accident about a year ago."

"Oh, my God." Her heart went out to the little girls. How awful for them to lose their mother. The enormity of their loss, especially at their young age, was staggering. Jamie and her mother had their issues, but she couldn't imagine Helen Garven not being in her life.

And her heart went out to Ben, too. She had some experience with losing a partner, though not in the way he had. But still, she understood loneliness. And grief.

"Our granddad left the house in Masonville to Ben and the kids in his Will. Ben didn't seem enthusiastic about leaving Chicago in the summer. But then, a few weeks ago, he phoned and said they were on their way here."

"Did he say why he changed his mind?"

"No. Maybe he found it too difficult raising the kids in Chicago without Olivia. At least here he has family, now that my brother Damon and I both live here. We'll help him any way we can."

"You're a good sister, Blair." Jamie experienced a pang of regret that she and her sister weren't as close.

Blair zipped up her jacket. "I feel guilty because I'm so happy with Garrett. It doesn't seem right when Ben's lost the love of his life."

"You deserve every happiness. Don't feel guilty about being in love."

"I know you're right. Still…"

Jamie hugged her tight. When she let her go, she held her at arm's length. "Go home and have a wonderful evening. Celebrate being in love and having your family together. That's a good reason to have a party."

Blair smiled. "You're right. Thanks, Jamie. Have a good weekend."

Jamie watched her leave the staff room. Overwhelming longing swamped her. Blair was off to celebrate with a family and a man who loved her, while she was off to clean poop out of a bird cage.

This wasn't the way she thought her life would go. She'd been married once, happy, and sure children were in her future. And then it all fell apart.

Jamie shook off the gloom before it could grab hold. She loved her life. She had a great career as a veterinarian, wonderful co-workers and friends, and pets she adored. It was a good life.

It just wasn't enough.

****

As Ben and the girls left their house, they saw Jamie Garven and her dogs walking down the sidewalk, with the smaller black-and-tan terrier in the lead. Sophie tore after them, waving madly at their neighbor.

"Jamie, Jamie, wait for me!"

He clasped Isabella's hand, refusing to let go when she would have run after her sister. Jamie stopped at the sound of Sophie's voice, turning around to look at her. Would she give her the brush off? He didn't want his daughter's feelings to be hurt.

Ben cringed in embarrassment as he remembered his behavior toward his neighbor four days ago. In his defense, he'd been worried sick about his kids, but he'd also been abrupt and rude and accused her of being irresponsible. Maybe he'd never truly fit into small town life, but he'd hoped for cordial relationships with his neighbors.

To his amazement, Jamie smiled at Sophie, looking for all the world as though his daughter was the person she most wanted to see. She knelt on the sidewalk and gave her dogs a command. Both sat obediently. Jamie introduced Sophie to her dogs once more, allowing her to pet their heads. The dogs patiently subjected themselves to Sophie's enthusiastic petting. They were obviously well-trained, contrary to what he'd believed on Wednesday evening.

As they approached, Jamie turned to Isabella and smiled warmly. "Hi, Bella. Would you like to pet Sammy and Rex, too?"

Isabella nodded but said nothing. She reached out tentatively to pet the dogs, then giggled when the Lab licked her. Ben loved to hear her laugh. His eight-year-old was cautious and careful when it came to new people and new situations. She'd been that way since he'd first met her when she was two years old. Conversely, Sophie dove into new adventures with carefree abandon. Their differences in personality amazed him and made him wonder how they could have originated from the same two parents. But even his gregarious five-year-old had been subdued in the last few months. The girls missed Olivia nearly as much as he did.

Pain shot through him at the thought of the girls' mother. How he wished Olivia were still alive. It had been eleven months and fifteen days since a drunk driver blasted through a red light and hit her car broadside, killing her instantly. People kept telling him his pain would ease, with time, but if anything, it had intensified.

Despite his grief, he carried on because Olivia's daughters needed him. They needed him sane and strong.

So that's what he'd be.

"Can I walk Rex, Jamie?" Sophie asked.

Jamie glanced up at him. "That's up to your dad."

Sophie turned to him, all hopeful innocence. "Can I, Daddy?"

Ben sighed. His younger daughter would likely test him for the rest of his days. "Sophie, you know you and your sister are still grounded for running off with the dogs the other day. That means you lose some privileges."

"But I've never had a chance to walk a dog before." Sophie turned sad eyes on him.

Ben blew out a breath. Though he should be used

to it by now, he hated playing the heavy. The role of disciplinarian had always fallen to him, even when Olivia was alive. He thought fast.

"If Jamie says it's okay, you can each walk a dog to the end of the street and back, but that's it. When it's over don't ask for anything more. After you're done, we'll go to the library like we planned."

"Can we walk them, Jamie?" Ben was amazed it was Isabella who asked the question in breathless anticipation.

Jamie rose to her feet and dusted off her knees. "Of course, you can."

"Yay." Sophie jumped up and down in elation.

Jamie offered each girl a leash. "If they start to pull on the leashes, pull back. They'll soon figure out who's in charge."

"The dogs wouldn't try to drag the girls into traffic, would they?" Ben asked, alarmed at the prospect.

"No, of course not. My dogs are well trained," Jamie said.

"Except when they bolt out of your yard."

He hadn't meant to bring it up again. Considering it had been his girls who'd opened her gate, he had no right to make any judgements. He was about to apologize when her face broke into a smile and she laughed.

"Okay, you've got me there. But generally speaking, Sammy and Rex *are* well behaved. And besides, you and I will be walking closely behind to keep an eye out. Will that make you feel better?"

"Marginally."

Jamie laughed again. "Have you ever been told you're a worry wart?"

"Once or twice."

Olivia had called him a worry wart all the time. She'd been a free spirit, always jumping head-first into projects that interested her. He'd always admired the way she could train her focus intently on a venture or a cause, without concern for what anyone thought of her.

And without concern for what was going on at home with the kids.

Ben pushed the disloyal thought away. He'd been happy to take care of things on the home front. He only wished she'd given the girls more of her time, more of herself. It had been a sore point between them.

Jamie grinned. "I can believe it." Her face softened into a reassuring smile. "Don't worry. It'll be okay, I promise. We'll be right behind them."

Her eyes are blue like a North Dakota sky. And when she smiles, her whole face sparkles.

The thought floated into his brain like a balloon drifting on a breeze, seemingly from nowhere. He cleared his throat and nodded. "Okay."

They walked a short distance behind, the dogs' tails wagging and the girls chattering happily. When Ben attempted to get closer, Jamie touched his arm to slow him.

"Give them a chance to prove they can control the dogs. It'll give them confidence." She gave him another sparkling smile. "Trust me on this, Dad."

Ben felt something lift inside him in response to her smile. The unfamiliar sensation made him dizzy.

With an effort, he turned his attention back to his girls and slowed his pace. Sophie had no problem with confidence, but Isabella struggled. If walking Sammy on her own provided her with much-needed self-assurance, he had to give her a chance.

"I appreciate you letting them do this."

There was a wistful quality to the smile she gave him. "It's my pleasure. They're beautiful children."

Ben tried to study her without being too obvious. She wasn't merely being polite. It *was* a pleasure for her to spend time with his kids. It made him wonder what, aside from kindness, motivated her.

They came to the end of the street and the girls obediently turned the dogs around and headed for home. Ben and Jamie followed, giving them space.

"We're having stew for supper," he said abruptly.

She glanced at him in confusion. "That sounds...nice."

Smooth move, Greyson. "I've made plenty. Maybe you'd like to share it with us tonight?"

She stared straight ahead. "That's very kind, but there's no need, really. Please don't feel obligated because I let the girls walk the dogs."

"I was rude to you the other day. There's no excuse for the things I said, but I'd like to apologize anyway. I hope you'll give me a second chance."

Jamie was silent until they were in front of their houses. Finally, she spoke. "Can I bring dessert?"

Ben expelled his breath, unaware he'd been holding it. "Sure, that would be great. Five o'clock okay?"

"Five is great." She paused, then looked up at him with an uncertain smile. "Thank you for the invitation."

"It's my pleasure."

Jamie nodded and, after taking the leashes from the girls and thanking them for walking the dogs, headed back to her house. Ben loaded the girls into the car and took them to the library to pick out some books.

Later, when they arrived home, new books in tow, he told them Jamie was coming for dinner. Their faces lit with excitement.

"Is she bringing Rex and Sammy?" Sophie asked.

"No. She's coming on her own." At least he hoped she wasn't bringing the dogs. "Can you help me set the table?"

"Sure!" Sophie immediately ran to the china cabinet. Ben helped her bring out their best dishes.

"Daddy, why did you invite Jamie to dinner?" Bella asked.

He could always count on his older daughter to ask the tough questions. "Well, because we're new in town and we don't know many people other than Auntie Blair and Garrett and Uncle Damon. We want to make friends. Jamie's our neighbor and we want to be…neighborly."

Bella nodded, and Ben was grateful his answer seemed to satisfy her. Sophie piped up. "I like Jamie. And I love Rex."

Ben laughed. "I bet you do."

As they continued to get ready for Jamie's visit, Ben contemplated Bella's question. Why had he invited her? He could have simply apologized, maybe brought her something as a peace offering. But to be truly honest with himself, he enjoyed her company. Aside from his business partner, Morley, and his siblings, he didn't know anyone in Masonville. It would be nice to have an actual adult conversation for a change.

Is that the only reason you invited her, Ben?

He refused to answer the question, even to himself.

Chapter Three

Jamie changed her clothes three times before finally settling on grey wool slacks and a soft pink sweater. The outfit was dressy without looking like she was trying too hard.

She hoped.

"How do I look, Hector?"

"Pretty Jamie. Pretty Jamie."

"Thanks, buddy." She'd take a compliment wherever she could get one. Even if she had taught her bird the phrase herself.

She drew in a nervous breath. Ben had likely invited her to dinner out of a sense of obligation—or maybe guilt. She probably should have declined with a polite excuse, but she'd wanted to accept. The girls were adorable, and Ben was…

Interesting. Yes, Ben was an interesting person. And he was her neighbor. For the sake of neighborly friendliness, she'd been obligated to accept his dinner invitation.

You're such a liar, Jamie.

Her stomach rumbled, though she didn't know whether it was from nerves or hunger.

What had Olivia Greyson been like? Was she beautiful? Had Ben loved her to distraction?

Of course, he had. After all, she'd given him two wonderful daughters.

It was ridiculous to be jealous of a dead woman, but Jamie envied Olivia for being able to give her husband children.

After putting Hector in his cage, Jamie grabbed a jacket and the pie she'd purchased at the Half Moon Bakery and walked the short distance to the Greyson house. Before ringing the doorbell, she smoothed her damp palm across her thighs, her heart pounding. The door opened immediately, and when she saw Bella's bright smile, she instantly relaxed. The girl appeared truly happy to see her.

"Jamie, Jamie! You're here!" Sophie raced toward her and grabbed her arm. "We set the table with Mommy's best dishes. Come see!"

Jamie found herself being pulled into the house, her nerves returning. *Mommy's best dishes?* The girls' mother was gone, but she acutely felt her presence.

Ben emerged from the kitchen wearing a chef's apron. He gave Jamie an apologetic smile.

"Sophie, I'm sure Jamie can make it to the dining room on her own. You can stop pulling her now."

Jamie held up the pie box. "I brought lemon meringue. I hope you like it."

He grinned. "It's one of my favorites. Thanks."

Jamie's brain momentarily turned to mush as two dimples played peek-a-boo in his cheeks. She'd always been a sucker for a cute pair of dimples.

And look where that got her. Dumped and divorced. The thought sobered her.

She cleared her throat and turned her attention to the children. "Your table is very pretty."

"Daddy helped," Sophie said.

"In that case, 'well done' to all three of you."

An embarrassed flush reddened Ben's face. "The girls insisted on the candlesticks."

Jamie tried not to laugh. The silver candlesticks were the epitome of tall, tapered elegance. But the orange-and-black Halloween candles emblazoned with pumpkins and witches dimmed some of their poshness.

"Very festive. Martha Stewart would be proud."

He relaxed his shoulders. "Well, if Martha approves, what more could I ask for?"

They smiled across the table at the shared joke. Maybe coming to dinner hadn't been such a bad idea.

"Can I get you something to drink?"

"I wouldn't say no to a glass of wine," Jamie said.

Ben gave her an apologetic smile, his gaze not quite meeting hers. "Sorry. We only have kiddie drinks in this house. How about lemonade?"

"Lemonade is perfect. Thanks."

Jamie relaxed and the rest of the meal passed amiably. She listened to the girls' stories about their new school and friends. Predictably, Sophie was a hit in her kindergarten class. But her heart broke at the expression on Bella's face when she asked how school was going.

"It's okay," she said without enthusiasm. "My teacher is nice, but most of the kids already have friends. They've known each other since kindergarten."

Jamie glanced at Ben. The pain in his return glance told her he was worried about Bella, too. It couldn't have been easy for him to uproot his kids and move them here.

Why had he moved here?

Like Blair said, maybe he'd decided he and the girls needed to be close to his brother and sister. She wondered if Ben had other family in Masonville. Had he grown up here? Did his parents live here? Jamie knew Blair had lived with, and looked after, her grandfather for some months until he passed, but she'd never heard her talk about her parents. She remembered seeing a couple she'd assumed were Blair's parents at Everett Branson's funeral, but she hadn't seen them since. She doubted they lived in the area.

After dessert and coffee, Jamie helped Ben and the girls clear the table. The girls brought the dishes to the kitchen and loaded the dishwasher with an efficiency that told her they regularly did this job. Ben was patient and gentle with the girls, but he didn't pamper them.

Once the kitchen was tidied and the food put away, Ben checked his watch. "You've got fifteen minutes before you have to get ready for bed, girls."

"Aw, Daddy, do we have to?"

Sophie's lip protruded in an adorable pout. Jamie coughed and attempted to hide her smile behind her hand. She supposed Sophie's pout wouldn't be so adorable if she had to deal with it every day the way Ben did.

"Yes, you have to." He sounded like he'd heard this complaint before.

They moved into the living room, and the girls sat on either side of her on the sofa, while Ben took the seat across from them in an upholstered chair.

"What do you do for a living, Jamie?" he asked.

"I'm a veterinarian. I work at the Masonville Veterinary Clinic, with your sister Blair."

"Oh." Ben's eyebrows rose.

"You know Auntie Blair?" Bella asked.

"I do. You'll find you'll get to know a lot of people

in a small town like Masonville. Soon you'll have lots of friends."

Bella didn't look convinced. Jamie squeezed her arm. "You will. I promise."

"What's a vet-ta-naron?" Sophie asked.

Jamie turned to her. "A veterinarian is a doctor for animals. I keep animals well and look after them when they get sick."

Sophie's eyes widened. "Like puppies and kittens?"

"Yes, and grown-up dogs and cats, and other animals."

"What kind of other animals?" Bella asked.

"People have all sorts of pets, like hamsters and gerbils and horses and snakes. And birds like my Hector. Would you like to see pictures of him?"

"Yes, please!"

Jamie pulled out her phone and scrolled until she found her latest pictures of Hector. With his soft grey body, black beak and red tail feathers, Hector was exceptionally handsome. "Here he is. Isn't he beautiful?"

Sophie scrambled onto to her lap to get a better look. "Where did you get him?"

"He was given to me. Hector belonged to one of my clients, and when he died, no one in his family was able to adopt him. So I took him in."

"What kind of bird did you say he is?" Ben asked.

"An African Grey Parrot." Jamie passed her phone to Bella. "Can you show your dad the pictures?"

Bella carried the phone to Ben and he scrolled through the pictures. "I think I read somewhere that birds like this can live for a long time. Is that right?"

"Yes, that's true." Jamie absently stroked one of Sophie's pigtails. "African Greys live forty to sixty years in captivity. Some have been known to live eighty years. It's a big commitment to own one."

"I can imagine." Ben gave the phone back to Bella. "How old is Hector?"

"He's about twenty-five." Jamie knew it was hard for someone who'd never been around a parrot to understand the bond a person could form with one. Her ex-husband had never understood. "When I first got Hector, about six years ago, he was terribly unhappy because he missed his former owner. It took some time before he accepted me."

Carson had resented the time she'd spent with Hector to ease his transition to his new life. Even a well socialized parrot needed a lot of attention and handling, but one like Hector, who was getting used to a new owner, required additional care. Hector's arrival had signalled the end of her marriage, though when she looked back with the advantage of hindsight, the cracks had been evident from the beginning.

Bella gave Jamie her phone. "I'd really like to meet Hector. Do you think I can?"

Sophie slung an arm around Jamie's neck. "Me too, I want to see Hector!"

She glanced at Ben before turning to Bella with a smile. "It's up to your dad, sweetie."

Ben got to his feet. "Jamie and I will talk, and I'll let you know. Right now it's time to get ready for bed."

Sophie hugged her neck. "Can Jamie tuck me in?"

"Sophie—"

"I'd like to, if it's okay with your dad."

"All right, fine." Ben didn't look happy with the

idea. "A quick tuck in and a goodnight, and then I don't want either of you to bother Jamie for anything else."

"Okay, Daddy. I promise." The angelic expression on Sophie's face made Jamie smile. She had a feeling Sophie would quickly forget her promise, and that Ben knew she would.

Once the girls got into their pajamas and brushed their teeth, Jamie came into their room. She pulled the covers up to Bella's chin.

"Goodnight, Bella. Sleep well."

"Goodnight, Jamie."

She turned to Sophie's twin bed and tucked the blankets around her. "Goodnight, Sophie."

"Can you read me a story?"

"Sophie, what did I tell you?"

Jamie heard the exasperation in Ben's voice. She turned to smile at him.

"What if I read a really short book?"

He rolled his eyes and reached for a well-worn copy of *Green Eggs and Ham* from the shelf above the bed. "Sophie, you're going to be the death of me."

Jamie tried not to laugh as he gave her the book, but she couldn't help the chuckle that escaped. The five-year-old obviously had her big, handsome daddy wrapped around her little finger. And she was well on her way to stealing Jamie's heart, too.

"When I was a little girl, my mom and dad read me this book, too. It was one of my favorites."

"When Daddy reads it to us, he does funny voices," Bella said.

Jamie glanced at Ben as he leaned against the door frame. On the outside he appeared serious, almost dour. It was hard to reconcile the dour man with the father who was prepared to do silly things to make his children laugh. But seeing him with the girls, she could imagine it.

She sat on the edge of Sophie's bed and read the book to the girls, doing her best to give the characters their own distinct voices. She was rewarded with giggles from both girls. After reading "The End" she closed the book and rose.

"Now it really is time to go to sleep. Goodnight, girls."

"Goodnight, Jamie."

"Thanks for the story!"

Jamie left the room and watched from the hallway as Ben kissed each child. There was something so tender in his actions, and so full of love that she had to turn away. She felt like an intruder, the way she had on the playground. She headed for the living room, intending to make her way home.

Ben joined her a minute later. "Would you like another cup of coffee? I can make decaf if you like."

It was on the tip of her tongue to decline, but something in his eyes stopped her. There was a loneliness there, an emotion she recognized all too well.

She made herself smile. "Sure. Decaf would be great."

"Can I interest you in another piece of pie?"

She laughed. "You really know how to tempt a girl, don't you?"

The laugh died in her throat when the double meaning of her words hit her. Ben Greyson was certainly tempting. But he was a grieving widower who was completely off limits.

And out of her league.

But she couldn't help feeling he needed a friend right now.

"Maybe I could manage another small sliver of lemon meringue."

Jamie saw relief in the smile that lit his face. "Great. Why don't you join me in the kitchen? You can cut the pie while I make coffee."

The kitchen was bright and cheery with a definite country vibe Jamie didn't associate with Ben. From his stylish haircut and fancy suits to his Italian leather shoes, he was a city boy from head to toe.

"Pretty kitchen. Did you decorate it?"

"No, nothing in the house is my style." He put grounds in the coffee maker. "My grandmother decorated the place. She and Granddad were all set to move in, and then she passed away suddenly. Granddad didn't want to move without her."

He'd suffered too many losses recently, Jamie thought. Blair had told her about her grandmother's sudden passing. Olivia died a few months later, followed by Ben's grandfather, Everett, a few months after that. She couldn't imagine the pain of losing three family members in such quick succession.

"What is your style? If you could live in your perfect house, what would it be like?"

Ben leaned against the counter, arms folded across his chest, his expression wistful. "I had my perfect place. In Chicago. It was a loft in a converted warehouse with exposed brick, high ceilings and stainless-steel ducts running throughout. It was amazing."

"It sounds great."

"It was." He pushed himself away from the counter

and turned to retrieve coffee cups from the cupboard. "But this place is better for the girls. They have lots of room and a big yard to play in. My brother and sister are here, and Masonville is a safe place for them to grow up."

"It is."

Masonville might be better for the girls, but Jamie wasn't certain it was the right choice for Ben. He'd sacrificed a lot for his children.

"What about you? What brings you to Masonville? Or did you grow up here?"

"No, not Masonville, but I did grow up in North Dakota. In Lewiston, about two hundred miles from here." She clutched her hands together. "I was living in Minneapolis, but after my divorce I decided to take the job at the Masonville clinic. I've been here almost three years."

"You decided to come home," Ben said.

"Yeah, sort of. I wanted to be closer to my parents but not too close." She tried to make a joke. "Can't live with them, can't live without them. You know?"

His whole demeanor darkened. "I prefer living without my parents."

They stared at one another, and Jamie held her breath. What had happened between him and his parents?

Gradually, Ben's face relaxed, and the storm in his eyes passed. When the coffee was ready, he poured them each a cup. Jamie stirred in milk, then set down her spoon.

"I have a confession to make. Blair told me about Olivia and how she was killed in a car accident. I'm really sorry, Ben."

"I appreciate your concern." His voice was clipped. "But we're doing okay. It's easier here with family close by."

Jamie nodded, not knowing what else to say. Silence stretched between them.

"They're not mine," Ben said suddenly.

Jamie blinked, confused. "Excuse me?"

"The girls. They're not my biological children." His eyes turned fierce, as if readying for an argument. "But dammit, nobody could love them more. And nobody's going to take them away from me."

Chapter Four

Ben had no idea why he'd told Jamie about his children's parentage. Jamie was practically a stranger. He was sure she didn't want to get involved in his problems, and he certainly didn't want anyone poking into his private business.

Jamie's face and voice were calm. "It's obvious you love the girls very much. I think you're an amazing father."

He stared at her, not sure how to respond. Sometimes he felt like he was doing everything wrong, that he was failing his girls. But when they put their arms around his neck and told him they loved him, the doubts disappeared and all he knew was they needed him as much as he needed them.

"Who do you think is going to take them away?" she asked.

Ben busied himself by wiping the counter. "Olivia's parents are concerned. Even when she was alive, they didn't like the idea of the girls growing up in a big, scary city. They're small town people from a safe little town in Wisconsin. But after she died, they started making noises about Sophie and Bella coming to live with them. I decided the right thing to do, for all of us, was to move to Masonville. They seemed happy with the decision."

"Then, you're the girls' stepfather?"

"Yeah. Olivia's first husband, Rob, was the girls' father. He died of cancer a few weeks before Sophie was born. Rob and Olivia and I worked together. We were friends."

It was a much abbreviated, and sanitized, version of the facts. But giving voice to even a small portion of his concerns was a relief. He'd been very alone with his fears. He hadn't told his brother and sister the real reason they'd moved to Masonville because he hadn't wanted to worry them. They already worried about him enough.

"What about your parents? Are they glad you and the kids moved out of the city, too?"

"I don't give a damn what they think. The girls and I don't have anything to do with them." Ben couldn't keep the note of bitterness out of his voice.

Jamie's eyes widened, but she made no comment. Instead, she passed him a piece of the pie and sat at the kitchen table. "Masonville is a good town. You and the kids will like it here, and their grandparents can rest easy knowing the girls are in a safe place."

Ben slipped into the chair across from hers and raised his cup in a toast. "To Masonville."

With a grin, Jamie clinked her cup against his. "To Masonville."

****

Morley Walker lowered himself into the chair across from Ben's desk. "Have you heard any more from Olivia's parents?"

At just over seventy, Ben's law partner might look like everyone's favorite grandfather, but he was no doddering old fool. The man was as sharp as a shiv and about as lethal. That's why Morley was his lawyer.

"No." Ben tapped his pen against the wooden desk. "Not since the letter we received the other day from their lawyer."

"Have you considered their request?"

He'd done little else. His stomach was permanently tied in knots because of the letter. "I've considered it."

"And?"

"I don't want them telling me how to raise the girls. They say they want to maintain contact with their grandchildren, but I think it's simply a pretext to gather information to use against me."

"They're not making outrageous demands. If they can assure themselves the girls are happy and well-adjusted, they'll concede they're better off here with you in Masonville than being uprooted again to live with them in Wisconsin."

Morley removed his glasses and wiped them with a tissue. "Not everyone is like your parents, Ben. Not everyone has an ulterior motive for their actions. There are people you can trust."

Ben found his statement hard to believe. There were few people in his life he could truly trust.

"How about this? The girls can write letters to their grandparents and they can write back. I'll send them school photos every year. But I get to read the letters first, both incoming and outgoing."

Morley sighed and slipped his glasses back on. "Do you have any idea how paranoid you sound?"

"I don't care. I'll do whatever I have to do to keep my girls safe."

"The Doyles aren't planning to sell them into slavery. They're good people. They only want what's best for the kids."

"So do I! Russ and Elizabeth are over seventy. What if they got custody and a few months later one of them died or became incapacitated by illness or dementia? What would happen to the girls then? Would they be forced into foster care? I won't risk it, Morley."

"Allowing them a few visits with their grandparents is a far cry from putting them into foster care. You have to be reasonable. I believe you're doing Bella and Sophie a disservice by not letting them get to know their mother's side of the family."

Ben experienced a twinge of guilt at the thought. The girls had the right to know their history. But fear outweighed the guilt. He shook his head.

"When they're older, they can ask their grandparents all the questions they want."

Morley snorted. "By then the Doyles will be dead. But that's probably your plan, isn't it?"

He didn't want to deprive his children of their heritage. He didn't want to deprive them of anything.

But if Olivia's parents ever learned the truth about him…

Cold dread settled in his heart. If they discovered the truth, they'd take the girls away.

They could never discover the truth.

"Getting letters from the girls should be enough for them," he said.

Morley sent him a challenging look. "If the situation was reversed, would it be enough for you?"

Ben conceded it wouldn't be. But it was the best he could do.

****

After talking to Morley, Ben needed to get out of the office. He asked their receptionist, Carmen, to take a message if anyone called for him, then put on his coat and walked outside.

It was a brisk afternoon in late October, and although the sun was shining, it was cold. He pulled a knitted hat from his coat pocket and pulled it over his ears.

He had no idea where he was going. He walked toward the edge of town where he was less likely to meet anyone else out walking. Ben thought of the work he'd left sitting on his desk. Routine Wills and real estate transactions. He was grateful for the work Morley had given him, but it bored him to tears. If the girls were happy in Masonville, he'd endure boring jobs for the rest of his life. But was coming here truly the right decision? The Doyles obviously weren't placated by their move to a small town, and Isabella was having trouble settling in. He wished he knew how to make things easier for her.

When he looked up, he realized with a start that he in was in front of the Masonville Veterinary Clinic where his sister worked. Where Jamie worked.

Ben was assailed by an overwhelming need to talk to someone. Jamie had been a good listener. He'd told her more about his circumstances, and his feelings, than he'd shared with either his brother or sister. He wasn't sure why he'd opened up to her. He only knew she'd been kind to the girls. And to him.

Before he could talk himself out of it, he was looking up the number for the clinic on his phone. A moment later he listened to the phone ring.

What the hell am I doing? She didn't want to hear from him, especially in the middle of a busy day at work. He was about to end the call when someone answered.

"Masonville Veterinary Clinic. How can I help you?"

Ben cleared his throat. "Can I speak to Jamie, I mean Dr. Garven?"

"I'm sorry, she's with a client right now—oh, wait, she just left the examining room. Can I tell her who's calling?"

Again, he considered hanging up. Instead he heard himself say, "It's Ben Greyson."

"One moment, please."

The line went silent as she put him on hold. Ben paced back and forth on a small patch of gravel road in front of the clinic. He stared at his shoes, noting the dust covering the smooth leather. He didn't know what he was going to say to Jamie. Why was he even calling her?

"Hello, Ben?"

The moment he heard her voice, his whole body relaxed. "Hi. I'm sorry to bother you at work. I know you're busy."

"No problem. What can I do for you?"

"Well, the girls have been asking about meeting Hector. Do you think it would be all right if I brought them over some time?"

"Yes, of course. I'm not working on Friday. Why don't you guys come over for dinner?"

"I wasn't angling for a dinner invitation."

"I know. I'm offering. I'm a fantastic cook, if I say so myself."

That made him smile. "Now I'm intrigued. Thank you. What time should we be there?"

"Come a few minutes before five and I'll introduce

Bella and Sophie to Hector."

"Okay. See you then."

"See you. Bye."

Ben grinned as he put his phone in his pocket and began walking back to his office.

Everything was going to be okay.

****

Jamie opened the door of her parrot's cage and cooed to him softly, holding out her arm.

"Come on out and meet the girls, Hector."

Hector stepped out onto the ledge protruding from the birdcage before opening his wings for the short flight to her outstretched arm. Jamie scratched the back of his neck, and Hector bent forward, closing his eyes in ecstasy.

"Oh, you like that, don't you, fella?" Jamie crouched, allowing the girls to get a better look at Hector. "He likes to be scratched and petted. You can try it, but you have to be very gentle."

Sophie was first to reach for the bird and stroke his back. "Like this, Jamie?"

"Yeah, soft and gentle. For now, let's speak quietly to give Hector a chance to get used to having you around."

"Okay, I will," Sophie replied in an exaggerated whisper that made Jamie smile.

"Can I touch him?" Bella asked.

"Of course." She turned to Sophie with a smile. "Let's give Bella a turn."

To her credit, Sophie didn't argue. "Okay. Your turn, Bella."

Bella hesitated a beat before touching the bird. "Will he bite me?"

"I won't let him." She tightened her hold on Hector, prepared to accept the wrath of his beak if he took a notion. He hadn't bitten her since the first few months after he'd come into her care, when he was confused and grieving the loss of the only handler he'd known. He'd mellowed a lot since then, but she wasn't exactly sure what he'd do in this situation. She hadn't introduced him to many people, and he wasn't used to being handled by anyone but her, especially not a child.

She needn't have worried. Hector accepted Bella's gentle strokes with closed eyes and a blissful expression.

"He likes you girls." She turned to Ben, who watched the proceedings from a safe distance. "Would you like to pet Hector?"

"No, thanks. I'm good."

She threw him a teasing smile. "Coward."

"You bet."

He stood three feet away, looking both concerned and nervous. But he was letting his daughters meet her bird, even though he obviously wasn't keen on the idea.

"Birds like Hector are very smart. They have to have things to play with and keep them occupied or else they might get into trouble. Just like little girls."

Sophie giggled. "What does Hector like to play with?"

"Sometimes I give him wooden popsicle sticks to chew on. They keep his beak strong. And he loves ripping paper to shreds. Makes a mess, though."

After more stroking from both girls, Jamie rose to her feet with Hector on her arm. "We'll give Hector some time to fly around the house before we put him back in his cage. He needs exercise to keep his wings strong."

"Wait a minute. The bird is going to fly around? Loose?"

Jamie wanted to laugh at the look of horror on Ben's face, but she managed to keep her expression neutral. "Sure. We do this every evening. Like I said, he needs the exercise."

"What if he, you know, makes a mess on something while he's out of his cage?"

This time she couldn't stop her grin. "Don't worry. Hector is trained to poop in one spot in his cage. He rarely has accidents."

The girls giggled at the word poop. Ben eyed the bird warily. "I don't know about this."

"I don't know! I don't know!" Hector squawked, making the girls giggle even more.

"He *can* talk," Sophie cried. "Make him say something else, Jamie."

"How about if we politely ask him to say a few words?"

"Okay."

Jamie turned to Hector. "What's your name?"

He bobbed his head. "Hector, Hector. Pretty bird."

"Yes, you are a pretty bird. What's your favorite food, Hector?"

"Care-ot. Care-ot."

"You love carrots, don't you? Can you say Bella?"

The bird hesitated and Jamie repeated Bella's name several times. Hector gave it a try.

"Bell. Bell."

Jamie tried again. "Bell-ah. Bell-ah."

Hector bobbed his head and flapped his wings. "Bell-ah. Bell-ah."

"He did it!" Bella cried.

"Can he say Sophie, Jamie? Please?"

"We can try, but sometimes it takes him a while to learn a new word." She turned her attention to the parrot. "Say Sophie. So-fee."

Hector only stared at her. He wasn't used to having this many people around, and he certainly wasn't used to performing on command. She'd leave it for now and teach him to say Sophie's name when they were alone.

"I think Hector's had enough for one day," Jamie told the girls. "Why don't we make some hot chocolate? Would you like some, Sophie?"

Hector flapped his wings. "So-fee! So-fee!"

"He said my name! Did you hear, Daddy?"

Ben grinned at her. "Yeah, I—"

"Da-dee! Da-dee!"

Hector launched himself from Jamie's arm and landed on Ben's shoulder. "Da-dee! Da-dee!"

"Jamie." Ben's voice was calm but carried a note of urgency. "A little help here, please?"

"Hector, come." Jamie held out her arm. "Hector. Come."

The bird ignored her, choosing instead to run his beak through Ben's thick hair. The girls dissolved in giggles.

"Daddy, he likes you," Sophie said.

"Da-dee. Da-dee."

"Jamie, get your bird off me before he bites my ear off." Ben's voice was less calm now.

"He wouldn't do that." At least she didn't think he would. She plucked Hector carefully from Ben's shoulder and carried him back to his cage, giving him a wooden spool to play with to keep him occupied for a while.

"You're a naughty boy, Hector." She kept her voice low as she closed the cage door. "You're not exactly making friends here."

"Da-dee. Da-dee."

The girls played with the dogs while Jamie put on the kettle for hot chocolate. Ben followed her into the kitchen.

"I'm really sorry about Hector," she told him. "I've never seen him react like that to anyone."

"It's okay. No harm done, but it was unnerving to have a parrot stick his beak in my ear."

Jamie couldn't stop her giggles from bubbling to the surface. She burst into helpless laughter. "You should have seen the look on your face!"

Ben's icy glare chilled her. "It's cruel to laugh at another person's discomfort."

The bottom dropped out of her stomach. "You're right, Ben. I'm so sorry…"

She spotted a twinkle of humor in his eye. Then a slow, wicked smile spread over his face. Jamie's breath caught. The man's smile was lethal.

"Gotcha," he said with a wink.

Jamie expelled a relieved breath. She was glad he wasn't angry with her and Hector, and more importantly, she was tickled to discover that despite the grief following him the last couple of years, Ben was a man with a sense of humor, a man willing to laugh at the ridiculousness of life. A man who didn't take himself too seriously.

That made him very attractive.

And dangerous to her peace of mind.

Chapter Five

Jamie's stomach rumbled as she kicked off her shoes and flopped onto her sofa. Though she was starving, she couldn't muster the energy to cook. She wondered if she had some canned soup she could heat up.

The prospect of watery chicken noodle didn't excite her taste buds.

A knock sounded at her front door, and with a groan, she hauled herself from her comfortable seat and answered it. Ben and his girls stood on her front step.

"We brought pizza," Sophie announced.

Ben carried a large pizza box bearing the logo of her favorite pizza restaurant. The smell of pepperoni and melted cheese wafted on the air, making her salivate.

"The pizza place sent us an extra-large by mistake," Ben explained. "We've got way too much and thought you might want to share with us."

"Thanks, guys. That's really generous of you. Come on in."

They gathered around her kitchen table and Jamie distributed plates and utensils and napkins. She passed Ben a lifter.

"You can do the honors. But hurry up. I'm starved."

Ben chuckled as he set pieces on the plates. "I'm

working as fast as I can."

Jamie accepted her piece and sank her teeth through the gooey cheese and thin, crisp crust. "So good."

"Mmmm. So good," Sophie said, chomping into her pizza.

Ben shook his head, but he gave his daughter an indulgent smile. "Don't talk with your mouth full, Sophie."

Since Sophie was mirroring her behavior, Jamie attempted to exhibit some proper etiquette. She swallowed her pizza and wiped her mouth with a paper napkin.

"How did you guys know I was hungry and didn't feel like cooking tonight?"

"Probably because we felt the same way." Ben took another bite before continuing. "I hate cooking. Actually, I don't mind the cooking itself. It's the coming home at five o'clock and trying to figure out what to make for dinner I hate."

Jamie polished off her first piece and reached for a second. "The planning and shopping is my favorite part. I love going through cookbooks and websites for new recipes."

"And yet, here we are, eating pizza."

Jamie grinned. "I didn't say it was a fool-proof plan."

"I like to cook." Bella gave Jamie a shy smile. "Daddy lets me help him sometimes."

"I help, too," Sophie exclaimed.

"Yes, you do." Ben smiled fondly at his younger daughter. "You and your sister are a big help."

"I like your kitchen, Jamie. It's pretty," Bella said.

"Thank you. I think it's pretty, too. It was the main reason I bought this house."

Ben glanced around the room. "It's nice and big. The three of us tend to bump into each other a lot in our little kitchen."

The idea of bumping into someone in the kitchen sounded good to Jamie. She had all this space and no one to share it with. The house was bigger than she needed, but she'd loved the newly remodeled kitchen so much she'd bought it anyway.

Ben reached for more pizza. "I meant to ask if you had a recipe for a sweet potato casserole that doesn't involve mini marshmallows. We're going to Blair's for Thanksgiving in a couple of weeks, and I promised to bring the sweet potato dish."

"Sure. I've been making my mom's recipe for years. It has a topping of chopped nuts, fresh herbs and a splash of maple syrup. It's fabulous."

"Sounds interesting. Are you doing anything for Thanksgiving? I'm sure Blair would love to have you."

She didn't want to impose herself on a holiday dinner meant for family. "Actually, I'm spending part of Thanksgiving week with my parents in Lewiston and then I'm on call for the rest of the holiday."

"Are you looking forward to your visit?" he asked.

"Yeah, of course." She couldn't manage to sound enthusiastic about it.

Ben cocked an eyebrow. "Are you sure?"

Jamie glanced at the girls, who listened avidly to their conversation. "It's just...family stuff. You know?"

"Oh, yeah. I know."

Ben's voice held a touch of...something. Anger? Was he thinking of Olivia's parents or his own?

Time to change the subject. "What if we made the casserole together on the weekend? Then you'll be a pro when you make it for Blair's dinner. I'll give you a list of ingredients."

Ben thought it over as he finished his pizza. "That's a good idea. Thanks."

They talked about favorite Thanksgiving foods until it was time for them to go home. After they left, she wondered again about the emotion she'd heard in Ben's voice when he spoke of family.

****

Jack Garven raised his wine glass in a toast. "To an early Thanksgiving and to having our daughter with us to celebrate."

Helen touched her glass to his. "Hear, hear."

After joining in the toast, Jamie sipped her wine. She'd arrived in Lewiston, a three-and-a-half-hour drive from Masonville, a couple of hours ago, and had been greeted by the scents of good home cooking.

"Thanks for making all my favorites, Mom."

"It's my pleasure. I love a good roast beef as much as you do."

Jamie had never been a fan of turkey, the traditional Thanksgiving staple. But Lisa loved it, so her mother had always cooked a turkey for the holidays.

Just another illustration of the differences between her and her sister. And how their parents treated them.

Jamie pushed the thought away. She wanted this short visit to pass without any unpleasantness.

"Any news about a replacement for Davis at the clinic, Dad?"

"No, nothing yet. But we're hopeful. We've got a couple of leads."

Helen laughed. "Davis and Wanda sent a postcard from Arizona with a picture of the swimming pool at their condo complex that said, 'Wish you were here!' "

"Talk about rubbing it," Jack said with a grin. "It's not exactly swimming pool weather here right now."

Jamie cut her roast beef into bite-sized pieces. "Is spending the winter in a warm location something you'd like to do one day?"

"I'm not ready to retire just yet," Jack replied. "But the idea is tempting. Especially on the coldest days."

Helen tilted her head. "I'm not sure. I know people who spend five or six months in the southern states every winter. I can't imagine being away from my grandchildren that long."

Helen went on to talk about Lisa's children, Todd and Shannon, and how much she enjoyed watching them play hockey in the winter and volunteering in the kitchen at the local arena. Jamie pushed the food around her plate, her appetite deserting her. Each word reminded her she'd never have a child of her own.

She knew her mother wasn't trying to be deliberately cruel, and she also recognized she was being over-sensitive. But the conversation reminded her why she didn't visit often. It was simply too painful.

She couldn't wait to get back to Masonville.

****

When Jamie answered the knock on her door and saw Ben on her front step, her heart made an involuntary flip. No matter how much she fought against it, seeing him always affected her. The man was simply too…everything.

A couple of weeks had passed since he and the girls had brought over pizza. After practicing his sweet potato dish with her in her kitchen, it seemed natural for the four of them to get together to cook. Jamie looked forward to those occasions.

He gave her his crooked grin. "Guess who forgot to buy spaghetti for spaghetti night?"

She shook her head and laughed. "I think I've got some extra. Come in."

Ben followed her to the kitchen. "I've been meaning to ask how your trip home went over Thanksgiving, but I didn't want to say anything in front of the girls. I had the feeling you weren't looking forward to it."

"It went fine. It was short and sweet." She didn't want to get into the many reasons her parents were disappointed in her. She found an unopened box of spaghetti in her pantry and passed it to him. "You should make a grocery list."

If Ben wondered about the abrupt change of subject, he didn't comment on it. "I did make a list. And then I forgot it at home."

Their usual teasing banter was far more comfortable. And safe. "It's a wonder you and the kids don't starve."

"Not everyone is as super organized as you. Some of us mere mortals forget things now and then."

Jamie was a planner by nature. Making lists and organizing gave her a much-needed sense of control over her life. "I'm grocery shopping on Saturday. Do you want me to pick anything up for you?"

"I appreciate the offer, but I can't ask you to shop for me. I'll go. Eventually."

"Why don't you and the girls come with me? I'll give you some of my best shopping tips."

His expression sobered. "I feel like I'm taking advantage of you. We're over here too much as it is."

"That's ridiculous. You're not taking advantage of me. You're bringing most of the food when we cook together."

"Still…" He lifted the box of spaghetti as if to illustrate his point. "I'm always imposing on you."

Something like panic rippled through Jamie's chest at the thought of Ben and the girls staying away. "If I thought you were imposing, I'd tell you."

"You're far too nice to tell me to take a hike."

"I'm not that nice."

Ben simply laughed. "Right."

She opted to go with a version of the truth. "I enjoy seeing you and the girls and having the three of you here to eat. Even with all my pets, this house can seem empty sometimes."

They stared at each other for several long minutes. Finally, Ben nodded.

"What time are we shopping on Saturday?"

Jamie released a breath. "How about two in the afternoon?"

"Sounds good. I have one condition. We shop in Bismarck."

She nodded, understanding. Masonville was a small town, and if people saw them shopping together, they'd assume something was going on between them.

Was there something going on between them? Jamie rejected the idea. Ben was a grieving widower who still mourned his late wife. To him, she was simply a helpful friend.

Did she want there to be something going on between them?

Her breath hitched at the thought. It was a question too far out of the realm of possibility to even consider. Ben placed her strictly in the friend zone, and that's where she'd stay.

Even if it killed her.

****

Ben loved Jamie's kitchen. It was spacious and efficient with plenty of storage and counter space. The white cabinets and their white quartz countertops kept the room bright and airy. A window over the sink and another next to the eating area let in plenty of natural light. It was a good kitchen to work in. Modern, but homey.

It made him...happy.

He contemplated the unfamiliar feeling, rolled it around in his mind, while he sliced red bell peppers for fajitas. In the last six weeks he'd become comfortable cooking in Jamie's kitchen. And he'd become comfortable with her.

Cooking was now fun, instead of the chore it had been before. He and Jamie sparred over recipes and ingredients, debated the merits of various cooking shows, and even shopped for food together, though never in Masonville. They'd become friends. Jamie was only the second woman he could give the title to. He and Olivia had been friends. If it hadn't been for her and Rob and the lifeline they'd offered to help him get sober, he'd likely be dead. He'd forever be grateful.

"That's a very pensive look on your face," Jamie said. "Care to share?"

He made himself smile. "Just contemplating the merits of preparing our own fajita seasonings as opposed to using the pre-packaged kind."

The raised eyebrow she gave him told him she didn't believe it for a moment, though she didn't push for answers. But he owed her more than a glib response.

"Actually, I was thinking how much I enjoy cooking in your kitchen. I'm happy here." The vulnerability in his admission made him uncomfortable. He tried to cover it with a laugh. "It's kind of a foreign concept for me."

"I'm glad you're happy." She touched his shoulder, her blue eyes full of compassion. "You know you can talk to me about anything that's on your mind, don't you?"

"Yeah, I know." Her touch sent shivers of awareness up and down his arm. "It goes both ways, you know. If you have something on your mind, you can talk to me, too."

Their gazes met and held. Panic flared in her eyes before she withdrew her hand and turned her attention back to the salad she was preparing. "I'm fine. My life's an open book."

"An open book, huh? Then why are you afraid to live close to your parents?"

"I'm not afraid."

"Really?"

He heard her sigh. "I've disappointed my parents. It seems to be a recurring theme in our relationship."

He couldn't believe Jamie could disappoint anyone. "What do you mean?"

"They were upset when Carson and I divorced. They expected grandchildren and happily ever afters. I think my mother started knitting baby booties the day after my wedding."

Ben chuckled. Jamie's humor in the face of

adversity was something he most admired about her. "You have the right to live your own life."

"Yeah. I know. But it's never easy to feel like you've let down the people you love."

Her statement hit him in the gut. He was well acquainted with being a disappointment. At least she could say her parents loved her.

He needed to change the subject. "Did you hear about Blair and Garrett's engagement?"

Jamie's smile was genuine. "Yes, Blair came into the clinic today wearing her beautiful diamond. She deserves to be happy. I don't know Garrett well, but he's Lauren's brother, and she thinks the world of him."

"They're good together. I think they'll be happy."

"They deserve some happiness."

Her voice was wistful. Had she been unhappy in her marriage? She must have been, since it ended in divorce. But she'd never told him the reasons for its demise.

No, Jamie wasn't as open as she claimed.

He found himself wishing she'd share her secrets with him. He wished she could trust him the way he trusted her.

The idea stunned him. He didn't trust easily, but he trusted Jamie. There was something honest about her. Real. Maybe someday he'd take her up on her offer to listen to his story. Jamie was the only person, aside from his siblings, to whom he could imagine telling the truth.

She put the finishing touches on the salad and heated tortillas while he stir-fried chicken with peppers and onions and spices. When they were ready to put the food on the kitchen table, he called the girls to dinner.

Sophie arrived with Hector on her arm. The bird took one look at him and headed for his shoulder. Ben automatically stiffened.

"Da-dee! Da-dee!"

"You'd think I'd be used to this by now." Hector nuzzled his hair.

"Sorry, Ben. He doesn't do this with anyone else. The only thing I can think of is you remind him of his former owner. Maybe it's something about the texture of your hair or your scent. He was really attached to Mr. Johnson."

"I guess it's not the worst thing in the world to be Hector's object of adoration."

"That's the spirit," Jamie said with a grin.

Jamie removed Hector from his shoulder and, after putting the bird back in his cage, they sat down to eat. The girls told them about their day and their friends. He wasn't surprised about Sophie's popularity, but he was relieved and thankful Bella was making friends, too. If his kids were happy, he was, too.

He was flooded with gratitude for his family. And as his gaze connected with Jamie's, he realized how profoundly thankful he was to have her in his life. He was lucky she was his friend.

Maybe moving to Masonville hadn't been such a bad decision after all.

Chapter Six

The next morning, Morley was waiting in Ben's office after he'd dropped the girls off at school. The look on the older man's face made his heart jump into his throat.

"What is it? You weren't planning to be in the office today. What's going on?"

"Close the door, Ben."

Ben did as he asked, his stomach making an ominous swoop. Morley pushed himself to his feet. "There's no easy way to say this, so I'm going to jump right in. The Doyles have decided to seek sole custody of the children."

For a second the room whirled, and Ben thought he'd be sick. He grabbed hold of the back of a chair to steady himself.

"They know you're an alcoholic. They say that makes you unfit to raise Bella and Sophie."

The room started to spin again. This was his greatest fear coming true. He was going to lose his family.

"What do we do?" Ben didn't have much hope. He *was* an alcoholic, plain and simple.

"We'll argue that you've changed. You've been clean and sober for five years, and you regularly go to AA meetings. You do go, don't you?"

"I've been in contact with my sponsor in Chicago,

but I haven't found any meetings here yet."

"Well, find some, quick. We need to show you're committed to your sobriety and you're a fit parent."

"Okay." Everything he loved was slipping through his fingers.

"Then we argue that the Doyles are too elderly to be raising two small girls. They need someone young and vital and in good health."

"Right." Ben felt a thousand years old. With a heart about to break.

"It's unfortunate you never got around to legally adopting the children while Olivia was alive. It would make your claim stronger, and it would have shown Olivia wanted you to be the girls' father."

"She *did* want that."

"You know as well as I do that without any sort of documentation, it's hard to prove." Morley paced the small office. "Are you involved with anyone right now? Showing the court two parents and a stable family is preferable to a single father."

A picture of Jamie popped immediately into his mind. She'd be the perfect mother to his children. Warm, kind, funny, stellar reputation in the community. He already knew she loved his kids and they loved her. And he and Jamie were friends. They got along great.

Ben wasn't sure he wanted their relationship to go any further. He liked it the way it was—safe, uncomplicated, and predictable. But every now and then he'd look into Jamie's eyes and see…something. Something he was afraid to explore.

It wouldn't be fair to drag her into this mess. "No, I'm not involved with anyone."

"Too bad. I'm afraid we could be in for a fight."

Ben nodded. He wouldn't let Olivia's parents destroy his family. He'd do whatever it took to keep them together.

****

Jamie's doorbell rang, surprising her into full wakefulness. Her watch said 9:15 p.m. She yawned and stretched. She'd had a long day, beginning at four o'clock in the morning when she'd been called to the clinic to treat a sick cat. Blinking the sleep from her eyes, she opened the door and saw Ben on her doorstep. Her heart made its usual leap at the sight of him.

"I know it's late, but can I come in?"

Jamie stepped aside and waved him in. "Yeah, of course. Come in."

Ben walked into the living room but didn't sit. Instead, he paced the room like a caged animal.

"You look tired. Did I wake you?"

Jamie smoothed her hair, knowing it was probably a mess. "I was on call last night. What's going on? Are the girls okay?"

"Yeah, they're fine. They're having a sleepover at Blair's. I…I need to talk to you."

"Okay. Let's sit down."

"I can't sit." He paced between the dining room table and the couch. "There are some things you need to know about me."

"Okay." She sat on the edge of the couch, confused. "Like what?"

He stopped pacing to look directly at her. "Like the fact that I'm a recovering alcoholic."

"Oh." She couldn't keep the shock out of her voice, couldn't think of anything else to say.

"I started drinking when I was a teenager, but I

kept it more or less under control. It was mostly binge drinking on weekends, but even back then I knew if I took one drink, I wouldn't be able to stop."

He resumed his pacing. "Things got worse in college. There was a lot of pressure to succeed, to get good marks, to be accepted into law school. The more pressure I felt, the more I drank. Did I tell you I met Olivia in college? At Northwestern?"

"No." There were a lot of things he hadn't told her.

"We had classes together as undergraduates, hung out with a lot of the same people. We both got accepted into law school at the same time." He stopped pacing, rubbed his eyes and stared at the floor. "She witnessed my drunken behavior on more than one occasion. It's not something I'm proud of."

Jamie didn't respond. Even if she'd known what to say, the words couldn't get past the giant lump in her throat.

"Law school was a pressure cooker." He shook his head. "So, I did what I always did when things got tough. I drank.

"Olivia and Rob found me passed out in the law library. They dragged me home, sobered me up, and then told me some home truths. If I didn't quit drinking, I was going to kill myself. They scared me enough that I was able to work up the courage to go to student services and get some help. I managed to stay on the wagon long enough to finish law school with distinction and get a job with the best corporate law firm in Chicago."

Jamie sensed this wasn't the end of the story. She forced out her words. "Then what happened?"

He began pacing again. "My dream job turned into

a nightmare. It was all about billable hours. They didn't care if their clients were polluting the earth or treating employees like indentured servants. As long as they made a buck, everything was A-Okay.

"I started drinking again and ended up in rehab. Olivia and Rob were the only people, aside from my brother and sister, who came to see me. My colleagues from the firm sure as hell wanted nothing to do with me."

"When I was well enough, Olivia and Rob offered me a job. They'd opened a law firm providing services to people who had little or no money for lawyer's fees. It was the kind of law I wanted to practice because I could really help people. I started going to AA and seeing a therapist because I had to be clean and sober if I wanted to keep the job.

"And then Rob got sick. It was unbelievable how fast the cancer progressed. Olivia was overwhelmed with his illness, and work. Bella was less than three and Sophie was on the way. I stepped in at work and took over Rob's clients and some of Olivia's. And I stepped in to help with the kids. I figured it was the least I could do after everything they'd done for me.

"Rob died a couple of months after he was diagnosed. Olivia was eight months pregnant, and a total wreck. I helped as much as I could, staying overnight at Olivia's house to watch over her and Bella.

"Sophie came early, probably because of all the stress Olivia had been under. I took her to the hospital and stayed with her through the birth. When the nurse put Sophie in my arms, I fell in love with her the way I'd fallen in love with Bella."

Jamie smiled at that. Seeing him with the girls

now, she could imagine it.

"I helped out with the kids as much as I could. Eventually Olivia started back to work and began taking clients again. We set up Sophie's portable crib and a play space for Bella in my office. It was tough, but I managed.

"Olivia and I grew closer and eventually I moved in with her and the girls. I finally convinced her to marry me, about six months before she died."

He blew out a breath, signaling the end of his story. He lowered himself into the armchair and sat with his elbows on his knees, his head downcast. Telling her this story appeared to take everything out of him.

Questions raced through Jamie's mind. Blair had told her Olivia was the love of Ben's life, but he'd never once mentioned the word love. And he made it sound like he'd been Sophie's primary caregiver since birth. Where was Olivia in her children's lives?

But those questions would have to wait. Right now, only one thing needed to be asked.

"Why are you telling me this now, tonight?"

He lifted his head and let out a shaky breath as he looked into her eyes. "Because Olivia's parents have discovered I'm an alcoholic and they're planning to sue for custody. And I wanted to let you know."

"Know what?"

"That I'm running away with the girls."

Chapter Seven

Jamie stared at him, her eyes wide with shock.

"Are you serious?"

"Yes, very." He'd die before he'd lose his children.

And they *were* his children, dammit. For over five years he'd changed diapers, wiped noses, patched skinned knees. He'd stayed up nights when they were sick or teething, and soothed them when they were frightened. He was their father in every possible way. He loved them.

"You think you'll lose custody, but you don't know for sure. You've been raising them for five years. Doesn't that count for something?"

"I'm the only father they've ever known, especially Sophie. But I don't have any legal claim to them. I never formally adopted them. I wanted to, after Olivia and I married, but we didn't get around to it before she died. She didn't leave a Will saying who she wanted to raise the girls, either."

Olivia had dragged her feet about updating her Will the same way she'd put off the adoption. Ben had understood why, but it hadn't hurt any less.

"What about Rob's parents? Do they support you?"

Ben shook his head. "Rob never knew his father. His mother raised him alone and he didn't have any siblings. She died a couple of years before Rob did."

"Olivia's parents wouldn't have any legal right to

them either, would they?"

"The girls didn't live with them, but they are related by blood. There's two of them and that's always preferable to one parent. And they'll bring up my past to show the court I'm an unfit parent."

"But that's in the past. It's not who you are anymore."

"Jamie, I'm an alcoholic. I'll always be an alcoholic. It's not like it goes away. I work hard to keep from sinking back into a bottle, but I can't make any guarantees."

Jamie's brow furrowed with worry. "Ben, you can't run away. Is that what you want for the girls? A life on the run?"

"No, of course not, but I don't have any other choice."

"There's got to be another solution. What does Morley say?"

"I haven't told him." He didn't want to make Morley choose between protecting him and upholding his professional ethics. "I didn't want you to worry when we disappear. I wanted you to know the girls will be okay."

"What about Blair and your brother? Have you told them what you plan to do?"

"No." They'd likely try to talk him out of leaving, too. Especially Damon.

"When do you plan to leave?"

"Soon." Today he'd researched online about how to disappear. He'd taken a few tentative steps and even contacted someone about creating false identifications. Then he'd withdrawn a large sum of cash from the bank and purchased a prepaid phone he could use without it being traced back to him.

"Is there anything I can say to make you change your mind?"

"Say you'll marry me."

The words were out of his mouth before he knew he was going to say them. Jamie stared at him, eyes wide.

"What?"

"Marry me. You're the only woman I'd trust with my girls."

It suddenly made sense. If Jamie married him, he could keep his kids.

She jumped to her feet, waking one of the dogs who'd been sleeping on the couch next to her. "What kind of marriage do you want, Ben? Are you proposing something for show?"

"No... I don't know!" He stood and grasped her arms. "If you're asking me if we'll sleep together as man and wife, I don't know."

Her mouth twisted as if she was holding back tears. "You know I love the girls, but please don't ask me to pretend. The last few months of my marriage, I pretended I had a husband who loved me. I swore I'd never do that again."

Ben wanted to take her in his arms and hold her. He hated doing this to her, hated making her relive unhappy memories. He was asking too much of her, and he didn't blame her for saying no.

"Please, forget I said anything."

He'd stick to his original plan. He and the girls would disappear. He'd change their names, go someplace where no one knew them. A life on the run wasn't what he wanted for his children, but he'd do whatever he needed to do to keep them.

"Ben—"

"I'm sorry, Jamie."

Ben was out the door before he could hear anymore of her objections.

****

Jamie didn't sleep the rest of the night. The logical part of her brain told her if Ben lost custody, it wasn't her fault. Circumstances beyond her control, and Ben's, had conspired against them. But worry wouldn't let her rest.

The crazy thing was she could see the four of them together as a family. And she could see herself with Ben. She'd been fighting her feelings for him since the day they met. Learning he was a recovering alcoholic was a shock, but she knew he was much more than that. He was kind and funny, and a loving father.

But he didn't love her.

She remembered what it was like to watch, day by day, as Carson fell a little more out of love with her. Every day another piece of her soul withered. To the outside world they probably still looked like a happy couple. But she could feel Carson pull away bit by bit, like water trickling out of a broken vase. It was in the awkward silences between them, the unexplained absences, the times he didn't reach for her in the night.

Eventually the slow trickle turned into a torrent, and he was gone. It had nearly destroyed her.

Could she live with a man who didn't love her— for a second time? Could she willingly step into a relationship, knowing it would likely end the same way her relationship with Carson ended?

Thoughts and emotions whirled in her brain,

making her dizzy.

At four in the morning she gave up all pretense of sleep. She went to the kitchen for a drink of water, and as she ran the tap, she saw the lights were on in Ben's house. He probably couldn't sleep either.

What must he be going through? She couldn't imagine losing a child.

The old longing ache she'd worked so hard to dispel pressed on her heart. *This is your chance*, her heart whispered. *Maybe your only chance to have children.*

Jamie groaned out load. She couldn't say no. Ben and the girls needed her.

Yet how could she say yes and expose herself to almost certain heartbreak?

Maybe some things were more important. Maybe it was enough to be a mother to the girls and create a family with them. She couldn't expect Ben to love her as well. It was asking too much.

She couldn't let him lose the girls. And she couldn't let her one chance to be a mother slip away.

She grabbed a coat and boots from the closet and threw them on over her pajamas. Before she could change her mind, she hurried out of her house and ran next door. A moment later she knocked on Ben's door. Surprise registered on his face when he opened it. She held up a hand to stop him when he opened his mouth to speak.

"There's some things about me you should know," she said.

****

"Do you want coffee?" Ben asked after Jamie kicked off her boots and tossed her coat over a chair.

She was wearing flannel pajamas in a pink print decorated with puppies and kittens, and her feet were bare. The fact she didn't take time to dress told him she had something urgent to say.

"No. Yes. No, no coffee. Let me say what I need to say first."

"All right."

He sat on the couch and Jamie followed him, sitting beside him. She ran distracted fingers through her hair, and Ben noticed for the first time how it hung loose around her shoulders rather than being confined in its usual ponytail or bun. It was much longer than he'd imagined, falling below her shoulder blades, the strands honey-colored and shiny. He wondered what it would feel like. Would it be as silky as it looked? Sometimes when they worked together in the kitchen, he'd catch Jamie's sweet floral scent and he'd want to bury his face in her hair and drink her in.

Stop. He swallowed those thoughts and concentrated on listening to what she had to say.

She folded her hands in her lap and stared at them. "I can't have children. I have something called Polycystic Ovarian Syndrome, which means I rarely ovulate. It makes it difficult to conceive. My ex-husband and I tried to have a baby for several years with no success. Not being able to have children contributed to my divorce." She let out a shuddering breath. "When it became clear I couldn't have his child, Carson, my ex, found a woman who could. He came home one day and told me he wanted a divorce. He was in love with someone else and she was having his baby."

Ben's fists clenched. She hadn't deserved to be

treated like garbage by her ex. Knowing how much she loved kids, not being able to have a baby would have been more than painful enough for her. "I'm sorry, Jamie. I truly am."

She lifted her head and met his gaze, her blue eyes flashing. "I didn't tell you this because I wanted your pity. I'm telling you because I want you to know you're not the only one who has a disease with a profound effect on your life. And I want you to understand I still very much want to be a mother. I love Bella and Sophie, and I think they like me, too. Perhaps you and I each have something the other needs. I think we should get married."

His heart stopped beating. "Are you serious?"

She swallowed and nodded. "Yes. I think we can be good parents for the girls. Perhaps, once they meet me, Olivia's parents will see we have the best interests of the girls at heart. I can't imagine them being taken away from you. They adore you, and you're a wonderful father."

"I don't want you to feel pressured into this. After I talked to you this evening, I did a lot of thinking. Marriage isn't only about raising children. It's about two people sharing their lives, caring about each other. Do you honestly feel you could live with me?" He glanced away. "Care about me?"

"I already care about you, Ben."

He turned abruptly back to her and examined her face. Her eyes were clear, her voice steady. His heart filled with hope, but he had to be brutally honest with her.

"I care about you, too." He shook his head. "Jamie, I'm an alcoholic. I've been sober five years, but I can't guarantee anything. I want you to understand what you're getting into if you marry me."

Jamie took a deep breath, then slowly released it. "I understand. There are no guarantees. When I married Carson, I thought we'd be together forever, with a house full of kids. But it wasn't in the cards. I'm going into this with my eyes wide open, Ben."

"Okay." Hope surged once more. "I'm glad we're friends, Jamie."

She smiled. "Me, too. If we start as friends, maybe this marriage thing can work." She sobered. "I know you loved Olivia, and I know I could never replace her. I wouldn't even try. But I promise I'll do everything I can to make you happy."

A vision of Jamie in his bed, her naked body pressed to his, slid through his thoughts.

"And I promise I'll be true to you. Always. I'll honor you as my wife."

"And I'll honor you. I would never cheat on you, Ben. I know how hurtful infidelity is."

He nodded, knowing he could believe her. If he understood anything about Jamie, it was her honesty. She kept her word. Maybe honor and respect were enough between them. He'd been in love with Olivia, and it had only brought him pain.

"You asked earlier what kind of marriage I wanted, if marriage meant we slept together as man and wife. I want that, but we'll take it slow. I won't push you into anything you're not ready for. Okay?"

"Okay." She swallowed. "Are we really doing this?"

"Only if you're sure."

A smile slowly transformed her face. There was

something magical about Jamie's smile, as if her soul lit from within. Despite the worry and uncertainty, an answering smile tugged on his lips.

"I'm sure." Her smile widened. "Let's get married."

Chapter Eight

As soon as Ben dropped off the girls at school on Monday morning, he and Jamie drove to Bismarck to get a marriage license. After presenting their identification along with Jamie's final divorce decree and Olivia's death certificate, they obtained the license and booked a time for the ceremony at the Recorder's Office on the following Friday afternoon. Then they drove back to Masonville.

"Bennington, huh?" Jamie gave him a teasing grin.

Ben rolled his eyes. She'd seen his full name for the first time when they applied for the license. "Yep. I was named after my father's father. Blair is named in honor of our Grandmother Greyson's maiden name. And Damon is named for Grandfather Greyson's only brother, who died in infancy."

"No names from your mother's side of the family?"

"Hardly. My mother was trying to win brownie points with her in-laws, but I'm not sure she ever succeeded."

"I think Ben suits you better. Not so pretentious."

"Nah. Pretentious is my middle name."

Jamie laughed, and Ben joined in. It was good to share a laugh. He hoped it bode well for their life together.

Soon, they were back in Masonville. He waved

goodbye to Jamie as he pulled out of her driveway, and she waved back. Not the most romantic gesture for a couple planning to get married in less than a week.

He rejected the thought. He didn't need romance. He needed a wife and a friend. Honor and respect and trust were far more important than romance.

Tonight he'd go to the farm to tell his brother and sister about his upcoming nuptials. They'd likely be shocked, and would probably voice objections, especially Damon. But he and Jamie had made their decision, and he'd back down only if she changed her mind.

He hoped she wouldn't. She'd been the first person he'd wanted to talk to, even before his brother and sister, when he got the news about the upcoming custody battle. Something about Jamie's good humor, common sense, and kindness calmed him and made him believe things would be okay. She was his rock.

Speaking of rocks. Ben headed back to Bismarck and found a jewelry store. The least he could do was to get Jamie a nice ring. He found one that spoke to him, a golden band with four diamonds, two large ones flanked by two smaller stones. He stuck it in his pocket and headed to his office in Masonville, feeling good about the purchase.

Jamie was in his kitchen starting supper with the girls when he arrived home from work. Earlier, they'd decided to cook at his house tonight so Jamie could stay with the girls and put them to bed while Ben went out to the farm. He listened with half an ear through dinner as the girls told stories about their day, a part of him obsessing about Damon's and Blair's reactions. They'd likely try to talk him out of marrying Jamie, and if he'd been in their shoes, he'd probably do the same. He imagined they'd tell him he was rushing into a loveless marriage, one that didn't stand a chance of lasting.

He couldn't argue against those statements. He *was* rushing into marriage. But despite the odds against them, it felt right to be marrying Jamie. They were friends, and they cared about each other. She loved the girls without reservation.

But he worried about Jamie. Did she really understand what marrying him would mean? He wasn't the easiest person to live with. Growing up in a dysfunctional family had made him distrustful and suspicious and probably a number of other negative things he didn't fully recognize.

Were they doing the right thing?

When the time came for him to leave, Jamie walked him to the door. "I'll bathe the girls before I put them to bed. I promise to tuck them in at their regular time, even if they beg me to let them stay up."

"They probably will. Stay strong." He pulled his jacket from the closet. "Do you think your parents will be able to make it to the wedding on such short notice?"

Her smile faded. "I think it's best if I don't invite them. They'll just try to talk me out of it. Or my mother will insist on having a big wedding. I want to keep things simple. I'll call them after we're married. Trust me, it'll be better that way."

He didn't want to cause a rift between her and her parents. "Are you sure? We could postpone—"

"Absolutely not." She lifted her gaze to his. "I don't want to be a bundle of nerves on my wedding day, and I'm afraid I will be if my parents are there."

"Okay, if you think it's best. I don't want you to be

nervous either. Maybe we can invite them for a visit later."

"Maybe." She didn't sound sure she wanted her parents to meet him. They probably wouldn't be thrilled to learn their daughter was marrying an alcoholic.

Jamie likely wasn't thrilled either.

Ben swallowed. "Jamie, listen to me. We don't have to go through with this marriage if you don't want to. It's not too late for you to back out."

Her eyes were steady on his. "Do you want me to back out?"

"No, of course not! But I'm asking too much of you."

She laid her palm against his heart. "I haven't changed my mind, and I don't want to back out. I want to be a mother, to have a family. With you."

"Okay." He rested his forehead against hers and exhaled in relief. Silently, he swore to be a good husband to her. Jamie deserved nothing less.

"I found an AA meeting tonight in Bismarck. Would you be able to stay with the girls till I get back? I thought I might need to go after I see Damon and Blair."

"Of course, I can stay." She placed her hand over his. "It'll be fine, Ben. Your brother and sister might be shocked at first, but they'll understand. My parents will too, eventually. One thing is for sure, though. Once they get over the shock, my parents will be thrilled to be grandparents. You'll see."

He turned over his hand and linked her fingers with his. He didn't know how she did it, but she always managed to make him feel better.

"Thanks. I needed to hear that." He leaned in to

kiss her cheek, drinking in the sweet scent of her. He let his lips linger against her soft skin for a beat, then pulled away. "I need to go."

Jamie smiled. "I'll see you later."

His car barely had time to warm on the short drive to the farm. He parked in front of the house and turned off the ignition, hesitating a moment before getting out of the car. Then he summoned his courage and headed to the front door.

Blair answered his knock with a broad smile. "Hey, you, I didn't know you were coming over. Where are the girls?"

"At home. A friend is staying with them." Ben glanced around the room. The kitchen was full of people and activity. He knew Garrett's friends Chris and Alison and their children were living at the farm, but it didn't occur to him until now how difficult it would be to have a private conversation.

Ben waved hello to Chris and Alison. Garrett and Damon joined them in the kitchen. Garrett extended his hand in a shake. "Hi, Ben. Have you eaten? I can put a plate together for you if you like."

"No, I'm fine, Garrett, thanks. I was hoping to have a word with Blair and Damon. And you." He knew Blair would want him included in any family business.

"Sure," Blair said. "What is it?"

Ben glanced toward the sink where Alison and Chris were washing dishes. "Is there some place we can talk?"

Damon scrutinized him. His younger brother had always had the uncanny ability to sense turmoil in another person. "How 'bout we go to the barn to check on the horses?"

Blair looked between him and Damon. "Okay. I'll get my coat."

They walked to the barn in silence, under the illumination of the yard light. Garrett slid open the barn door and turned on the interior lights. Blair turned to Ben as soon as they were inside.

"What's with all the secrecy? What's so hush-hush you can't talk about it in front of Alison and Chris?"

"I'm getting married."

They all stared at him, eyes wide and mouths open. No one appeared able to speak. Somehow it caught Ben as funny, and he laughed.

"I see I've got your attention."

Blair swatted his shoulder. "Don't even joke about getting married. It's not funny."

He stopped laughing. "I'm not joking. I *am* getting married, and I'm hoping you'll stand up for us at the ceremony."

"I don't understand. You've been in Masonville for two months. Who are you marrying?"

"Jamie Garven. We're neighbors, and we've become good friends these last few weeks."

"Jamie told me you'd met, but I didn't realize how close you'd become." Blair blew out a breath. "Okay. I like Jamie. She's a great person. Have you set a date? Maybe next summer?"

"The wedding will happen this Friday."

"Friday? Ben, that's crazy!"

Damon tilted his head and examined him in his unnerving way. Ben tried not to squirm under his brother's scrutiny as he said, "Blair, I think the question to ask is why. Why are you marrying Jamie Garven in such a hurry, Ben?"

He wouldn't lie to them. He owed his brother and sister, and now Garrett, some honesty.

"Olivia's parents are suing for full custody."

He told them about the battle he was about to face and how having Jamie as his partner would increase his chances of winning the fight. Blair shook her head.

"Yeah, but getting married? It's a drastic step to take, one you've never taken lightly before. You knew Olivia for ages, and you lived with her before getting married. What's different with Jamie?"

Everything, he wanted to say, but he kept the thought to himself. "Time. I don't have time. The Doyles are moving forward with their suit, and we have to act now."

"Jamie is a caring, compassionate person. But you barely know her."

"You and Garrett only knew each other a short time before you decided you belong together."

Garrett put his arm around Blair and kissed the top of her head. "He's got you there, sweetheart. When you know, you know."

"Jamie and I aren't some great love story. We've become friends, and we like and respect each other. She loves the girls and wants to be a mother to them, and they love her. We both believe our friendship will carry us through."

"Yeah, but you loved Olivia so much." Blair shook her head in disbelief. "I don't want you to settle because you're scared."

"I'm not settling. Not at all. I'm doing what's right for my family."

Blair nodded, though she didn't look convinced. "If you're sure, then I guess the only thing to say is congratulations."

He expelled a relieved breath. "Thanks, Blair. I appreciate it. Does that mean you'll stand up for us at the ceremony?"

"Of course I will."

"We'll both be there," Garrett added.

Ben nodded, grateful for their support, however doubtful they might be. He turned to Damon. "How about you? Will you be at the ceremony?"

"I won't tell you I'm not concerned, but if you think marrying Jamie is the right thing to do, I'll back you all the way."

Ben pulled him into a hug and laughed, relief making him giddy. "I can't tell you how much that means to me."

****

The next day, Ben and the girls ate dinner at Jamie's house. They had decided the previous evening to tell the girls they were getting married. Even though she knew the girls liked her, Jamie's stomach fluttered with nerves all through the meal. What if they didn't want their father to remarry? They might be afraid she'd take his attention away from them. Or maybe they didn't want anyone trying to replace their mother. It hadn't been long since they'd lost her, poor babies.

Once the meal was done and the dishes cleared, Ben turned his attention to the girls. Jamie thought he looked as nervous as she felt.

"Why don't we go into the living room? Jamie and I have something we want to tell you."

"Are we getting a puppy?" Sophie asked, eyes wide.

Ben's amused gaze briefly locked with Jamie's as

he tried to hide his grin. "No, we're not getting a puppy. Come on."

Once the girls were seated on the sofa, Ben sat in the armchair across from them and leaned forward with his elbows on his knees. Jamie remained standing, too keyed up to sit.

"We've all become friends with Jamie since we moved to Masonville."

"Jamie's my best friend," Sophie declared. "Except for Stacey Wright."

"Jamie's my best friend, too." Bella's shy smile melted Jamie's heart.

"And you're my best friends." Jamie clasped Ben's shoulder. "And your dad, too. We like each other very much."

Ben reached for her hand. "Because we like each other so much, Jamie and I have decided to get married. Jamie's going to be part of our family."

For a second neither child said anything. Then Sophie asked, "Will Hector and the dogs and the angel fish live with us?"

"Actually, you'll all come to live here in my house," Jamie said. "This house is bigger than yours, and your dad and I decided it's easier for you to move than to move my pets. Will you be okay with that?"

"Yes! Bella, we're going to live with Sammy and Rex and Hector," Sophie cried, clapping.

Bella sat quietly staring at her lap. Jamie sat next to her. This was what she was afraid of. They were moving too fast for her.

"Is there something you want to say?"

Bella looked up at her. "You can't be my mother."

Jamie's heart stopped. If Bella was opposed to

marriage between her and Ben, she wouldn't go through with it. This marriage was all about the girls, and if Bella was unhappy with the idea, what was the point?

"Bella—" Ben began, but Jamie shook her head to stop him.

"I know I'll never replace your mother, Bella. No one ever could because she's so special to you. I want to continue to be your friend and live with you and Sophie and your dad. And maybe someday you'll think of me as your stepmom. That's someone who hasn't given birth to a child but loves them and chooses to live with them." She smoothed Bella's silky, blonde hair. "I choose you and Sophie because I love you very much."

"Can I call you Mommy?" Sophie asked.

Jamie reached out to the five-year-old and cupped her cheek, loving her so much her heart nearly burst. "Of course you can."

"Okay." Sophie hopped off the sofa. "Can I play with the dogs now?"

Jamie looked up at Ben. He gave her a shrug, as if to say *One down. One to go.* "Sure, but no throwing the ball inside the house."

"Okay." Sophie hurried off to find Sammy and Rex. Bella remained where she was, her expression contemplative, as if she was taking in all the information and trying to make sense of it in her eight-year-old brain.

"Do I have to call you Mommy, too?" she asked.

"Not if you don't want to. You can call me Jamie, the way you do now."

Bella nodded. "We're going to move here to live with you and Hector and the dogs?"

"Yes, and don't forget the fish. Their tank is too heavy to move. Are you okay with that?"

"Do I have to share a room with Sophie like I did at our house? She's messy."

Jamie's heart lifted. If Bella was thinking about a new bedroom, maybe she was okay with the idea of moving.

"You and Sophie could each have your own room." Her house had three bedrooms on the main floor and one in the basement.

"Can I paint it pink?"

"Sure. We can go to the hardware store together and pick out the shade of pink you want." She glanced at Ben once more, silently asking him for help. He leaned forward.

"Bella, are you okay with me marrying Jamie?"

"Yeah." She looked down into her lap, not meeting their eyes.

"You don't sound happy," he said. "Can you tell us why?"

Bella looked up at Jamie, fear in her eyes. "You won't die, will you?"

Jamie's heart broke for her. "Oh, baby, I hope not. I can't promise I'll never die because sometimes accidents happen like they happened to your mom. But I want you to know I plan to be around for a very long time. I want to see you and Sophie grow up."

Bella threw her arms around her and buried her face against her shoulder. "I want you to be around for a long time, too."

Jamie held her tight and rested her chin on top of her head. Her eyes met Ben's. There was so much at stake. They had to make this marriage work.

Chapter Nine

Ben paced in front of the Recorder's office, nerves dancing. He checked his watch—4:52 p.m. In exactly eight minutes he'd marry Jamie. Bella and Sophie, decked out in their prettiest dresses, watched him pace.

"We get to be flower girls, right, Daddy?" Sophie said, holding up the small bouquet of silk flowers he'd purchased for her.

"You bet." Was he doing the right thing? He had no doubt this marriage was the right thing for his children. But was it right for Jamie? What if sometime down the road she met the man she was actually meant to be with? Would she leave them? Or would she stay for the children's sake and deny herself a chance at happiness?

What the hell was he doing?

Jamie walked in with Blair and Garrett on either side of her and Damon bringing up the rear. Their eyes met and held. Her hair was down around her shoulders the way he liked it best. She gave him a reassuring smile, and his whole body relaxed.

Sophie ran to her. "Jamie, look, I have flowers— I'm going to be a flower girl!"

Jamie bent over to hug her, then reached out to embrace Bella when she joined them. "Yes, you are. And Bella, too. You'll be perfect flower girls."

"I can take your coat," Ben said. "We can leave our

things in the cloak room across the hall."

"Thank you." Jamie unbuttoned her coat and shrugged out of it before handing it to him. She wore a slim, pale pink skirt with a matching jacket that hugged all her curves and emphasized her long legs. It occurred to him he'd never seen her legs before, since she usually wore jeans or scrubs. He had to tell himself not to stare.

But damn, if the woman didn't have first-class legs.

"You look beautiful," he blurted.

She blinked at him, clearly startled by his compliment. "Oh. Thank you. You look pretty amazing yourself."

He grinned. "This old thing?"

She smiled back at him. "You wear it well."

The truth was he'd changed his clothes three times before settling on the charcoal gray suit, white shirt, and blue patterned tie. Nothing in his closet had seemed fitting for the gigantic leap of faith they were about to take. But seeing the approval in Jamie's eyes made everything feel right.

He hung Jamie's coat in the cloak room, and when he returned, he held out his hand to her. "It's time. Are you ready?"

She clasped his hand in hers, her eyes clear and calm. "I'm ready."

The ceremony itself was mercifully short, less than ten minutes. Ben barely heard the Recorder's words. He stared into Jamie's eyes and clung to her hands. As the ceremony reached its conclusion, he loosened his hold, not wanting her to think he was afraid she'd bolt.

"You may now exchange rings," the Recorder said.

Jamie turned to Blair, who opened a jeweler's box and passed her a ring. Jamie slipped it on his ring finger and looked up at him with a shy smile. The gold band was beautiful and classic, much like the woman who gave it to him.

He pulled the ring box from his pocket and removed the ring. His hand trembled as he slid it on her finger. Once again nerves jangled. There was so much riding on this marriage. They couldn't fail. What if they failed?

Her gaze met his. "Four diamonds. For the four of us."

He relaxed and smiled, pleased she understood what the ring meant to him. Four diamonds for the four of them and the family they were trying to create.

"I now pronounce you husband and wife. You may kiss your bride."

Ben brushed a kiss across Jamie's soft lips. He lingered there, drinking in her sweet scent. They'd only talked briefly about intimacy and sex. He didn't know if she was interested in him in a sexual way. He could only pray she was. It had been a long time for him...

Damon let out a whoop and Blair clapped. "Congratulations!"

Ben looked into the eyes of the woman who had just become his wife and prayed he could make her happy.

****

When Jamie entered Blair and Garrett's farmhouse, she was greeted by the delicious smells of home cooking. Much to her and Ben's surprise, his family had arranged a dinner party to celebrate their marriage. Cole and Lauren, who was Garrett's sister, and their baby, Piper, were already there. Her co-workers from the clinic, Dr. Waverley and Audrey and Evelyn, and their respective spouses, greeted them. Morley Walker, Ben's law partner, was there, along with Charlotte Saunders, who was helping Blair and Garrett's friends Alison and Chris with the food. Bella and Sophie enthusiastically greeted Alison and Chris's girls.

"Chris and Alison have been cooking all day," Blair said as she took Jamie's coat.

Jamie offered Alison a warm smile. "Thank you. This is wonderful. And so unexpected."

"A wedding calls for a celebration," Alison said as she set a bowl of mashed potatoes on the kitchen table.

Ben put his arm around Jamie's shoulders. "Thank you. This means a lot to us."

The small caress warmed her. He made it feel natural, as if she belonged in his arms. But she couldn't help wondering if he touched her for show, to convince his family they were more intimately connected than they really were.

Ben had hired movers to bring over the girls' beds and their belongings earlier in the day so they could all start married life together under one roof tonight. But she'd noticed the movers brought a third bed, a queen-sized one, that they'd set up in the empty basement bedroom. Did Ben intend to sleep there rather than with her?

Steam rose from the platter of sliced roast beef Chris set on the table. "Food's ready, everyone. Get it while it's hot."

Guests sat at the extended kitchen table while the children ate at their own little table in the living room. There was much chatter and laughter and good food.

Jamie joined in, enjoying the fun and friendship.

"Have you figured out which house you're going to live in?" Lauren asked.

"In Jamie's," Ben answered. "It's bigger, and it's easier for the girls and me to move than to move all her pets."

Cole chuckled. "How are you and Hector getting along?"

"Hector adores Ben," Jamie said with a grin. Ben rolled his eyes.

Halfway through the meal, Garrett got to his feet and clinked his knife against his glass. "We weren't going to say anything tonight because we didn't want to steal Ben and Jamie's thunder. But I can't hold it in any longer."

He grinned at Blair, and she rose to stand next to him. "We've decided on a date for our wedding—next spring, on June sixth."

Blair and Garrett sealed their announcement with a kiss amidst claps and hoots and calls of congratulations. As they ended the kiss, Garrett tenderly brushed Blair's curly hair from her forehead, the look on his face telling the world she was the only person he saw. The only person he wanted to see.

Jamie swallowed hard as she stared down at her plate. That's what she wanted. To have a man look at her like she was the most important person in his world. To know he would love her no matter what happened, through the good and the bad. Through hardships and infertility.

She glanced at Ben. He'd risen to his feet to clap for Blair and Garrett, his smile broad. She'd told him about her infertility, but he'd never said if he wanted another child. She wished now they'd talked about it. She wasn't sure she could put herself back together again if he eventually decided he wanted more children and went in search of a woman who could give them to him. Like Carson had.

She was getting ahead of herself. Ben said he wanted a real marriage, one where they shared a bed as man and wife. But was he attracted to her in that way? They hadn't talked much about that either. Maybe, despite what he'd said, their marriage was strictly for show.

The thought made her lose her appetite.

Ben lifted his glass in a toast. "To my beautiful sister Blair, and to Garrett, the man who captured her heart. May they have much happiness together."

"To Blair and Garrett."

Ben resumed his seat. Jamie smiled and talked and pushed food around her plate, hoping no one would notice she wasn't actually eating.

Ben leaned over to whisper in her ear, his breath warm on her neck. "You're not hungry?"

"Sure, I am." She stuck a forkful of cold mashed potatoes into her mouth to illustrate her point. They tasted like sawdust. She swallowed hard and grabbed a glass of water to wash them down.

Worry wrinkled Ben's brow, his hazel eyes troubled. "Are you okay?"

The last thing she wanted to do was upset him, especially tonight. And she didn't want anyone to think there was already trouble in paradise. She laid her palm on his cheek. "I'm fine, really," she whispered.

Ben stared into her eyes. *I could look at him forever*, she thought. Strong chin, perfect cheekbones, glorious thick lashes surrounding incredible green-brown eyes. He was beautiful.

Finally, his lips curved into a smile. "Okay."

It took Jamie a moment to realize everyone had stopped talking. She tore her gaze away from Ben's to glance around the table at the grins staring back at her.

Blair lifted a wine glass filled with sparkling grape juice. "To my big brother Ben and my new sister-in-law Jamie. May they be happy together always."

****

It was past ten p.m. by the time they arrived back in Masonville to Jamie's house. *Correction*, he told himself. *Their house*. It would take some time to get used to calling this place home. He and the girls hadn't put down strong roots in the house he'd inherited, which made the move easier for them than it would have been for Jamie. Considering the enormity of what he'd asked of her, it was the least he could do.

She'd been quiet on the drive home, and he wondered if she was already regretting her decision to marry him.

Ben pulled up to the house and turned off the ignition. A glance in his rearview mirror showed two sleeping children.

"That's gotta be a record. Asleep in less than five minutes. They must have been tired."

Jamie twisted in her seat to look at them. "It was a big day for them."

"For us, too."

She smiled. "Yes. For us, too."

"Let's get them inside."

They each carried a sleeping child into the house and tucked them into bed in their new rooms. Both

86

roused briefly but were sound asleep again as their heads hit the pillows. Ben paused in the hallway before closing the bedroom doors.

"Sleep tight, girls," he whispered. Love for his daughters swelled in his heart. He'd do whatever it took to keep them safe.

He found Jamie in the kitchen with the dogs. They sat at her feet, the picture of obedience, looking up expectantly. Ben stood back and watched unobserved.

"Okay, guys. One treat and it's time for bed. No whining."

Sammy, the black lab, made a sound in his throat, not taking his eyes off the treat.

"Was that a whine, Sammy?"

The dog immediately stopped, trying his best to look innocent.

"Much better."

She reached out a hand to each dog to deliver the treats, and they grasped them daintily with their teeth.

"Good boys." She petted them affectionately, laughing when they licked her face.

Jamie was a woman with much to give, to her pets, her clients, her friends. In a short time, she'd shown his girls more attention and love than they'd ever received from their biological mother.

Ben winced. He was being unfair to Olivia. She loved her daughters, he knew that. But her grief had prevented her from showing them the depth of her love.

Jamie lifted her head and her gaze collided with his. "Oh! I didn't see you."

"Sorry. I didn't mean to startle you. I was watching you with the dogs. You have them well trained."

"Mostly. We're still working on it." She went to

the sink and washed her hands. "I was about to make some tea. Camomile, I think. Would you like some?"

He wasn't ready to say goodnight either. "Sure."

Jamie filled the kettle with water and set it on the stove to boil. Ben pulled up a chair at the kitchen table and watched her bring out a teapot and drop in a couple of teabags. Her movements were graceful. It occurred to Ben that Jamie did everything with grace.

Including marrying him.

"Are you sorry you married me?"

He hadn't meant to blurt out the words. Jamie lifted her gaze to his, her eyes wide.

"I wouldn't blame you if you were." Ben rose to his feet, too nervous to sit. "I rushed you into this marriage. And let's face it, I'm not much of a prize."

She stunned him by laughing. "Come on, be serious. Have you looked in a mirror lately?"

"The looks are meaningless, simply the outside shell. I've learned it's what's inside that counts more." He shook his head. "My insides can be pretty ugly sometimes."

"You're so hard on yourself." Jamie set a couple of mugs on the table.

"I'm an alcoholic, Jamie. I have to be hard on myself."

"But it's not everything you are. You're a dad and a brother. And you're amazing in those roles."

He was also a husband again. He wondered if Jamie would come to believe he was amazing in that role as well. "You haven't answered my question. Do you regret marrying me?"

"No, I don't. The reasons I married you are still valid. I'll do whatever I can to help you keep the girls.

They belong with you. And I still want to be their mother."

Such clear-headed logic. Her answer should have pleased him, but he found himself wishing she'd said she didn't regret marrying him because she wanted to be with him. Because she felt something for him.

She'd told him she cared for him, and he cared for her. For now, it had to be enough.

He watched as she poured hot water into the teapot and set the kettle back on the stove. "What about you? Do you regret marrying me?"

"No. Absolutely not." Ben stepped forward to take her hand. "I have no regrets."

She bit her lip and stared into his eyes. "I'm glad. The girls need us. I want this to work."

"Yeah, so do I."

He tugged her closer. The scent of her perfume intoxicated him with its sweetness. As he raked his fingers through the silky strands of her hair, her eyes drifted closed. Slowly, Ben lowered his mouth to hers, kissing her softly, tentatively.

He couldn't explain what happened next. She made a sound in her throat and gripped his shirt, bringing him closer. A switch snapped on in his brain and desire roared to life. Ben ravaged her mouth, sliding his tongue over hers again and again until he was dizzy. He gripped her hips and pressed against her, letting her feel how much he wanted her. All he knew was he needed her like he needed his next breath.

"I want you, Olivia."

The minute the words left his mouth he realized the enormity of his mistake. He immediately felt Jamie's withdrawal. She stiffened, dropped her grip on his shirt, and took a step back, her gaze averted.

"Jamie, I'm sorry. I don't know why I said that. Please forgive me."

"It's all right. I understand." She took two more steps away, still not looking at him. "It's been a long day. I think I'll go to bed. Goodnight."

"Jamie—"

"Please, don't apologize. I understand, I really do." She glanced up, giving him a wan smile, her gaze somewhere over his shoulder. "When you love someone that much, it's hard to let go. Goodnight, Ben."

She hurried from the room and a moment later Ben heard the bedroom door down the hall softly close. Ben swore under his breath. What devil had prompted him to utter Olivia's name in a moment of passion with Jamie?

He wanted to hit something, break something, rage at the world.

She understood, she'd said. She probably thought she did. But how could Jamie understand his relationship with Olivia when he'd never understood it himself?

It was hard to understand a love that only went one way.

Ben threw back his head and groaned. Then he made his way down the stairs to the room in the basement and the cold bed waiting for him there.

Chapter Ten

Jamie's fingers trembled as she punched her parents' number into her phone. She almost hoped they wouldn't be home. But it would only delay the inevitable. She'd have to steel herself all over again to tell them about her marriage to Ben.

Her mother's voice came on the line. "Hi, Jamie! It's good to hear from you. We haven't talked since Thanksgiving."

A flood of guilt immediately swamped her. "Hi, Mom. How are you? Did you get over the cold you had at Thanksgiving?"

"Yes, I'm fine. Just a few sniffles left. How about you? What have you been up to?"

Jamie wiped sweaty palms against her jeans.

"Actually, I have some news." She did her best to inject a note of cheer into her voice. "Is Dad there?"

"Yes, he's right here. I'll put you on speaker phone."

There was a momentary delay while her mother adjusted the phone. The wait seemed interminable. She needed to get this over with, to rip off the bandage quickly with a minimum of pain. She already knew they'd be upset. They wouldn't like the fact she barely knew Ben, and they especially wouldn't like not being invited to the wedding.

"I'm here, Jamie," her father announced. "Your

mother says you have some news."

"Yeah, I do. I got married yesterday."

Silence greeted her announcement. Jamie heard her mother cough and mutter something about needing water. Her father was the first to find his voice.

"Who the hell did you marry?"

"His name is Ben Greyson. He and his children moved into the house next door to me this fall, and we became friends."

"Sounds like you're more than friends now." Her father didn't attempt to hide the sarcasm in his voice. "This is a man you've only known a short time? And he has children?"

"Yes, two little girls, eight and five. Bella and Sophie." Jamie paced an examining room in the clinic while she spoke. "They're wonderful kids. Ben and I want to make a family together."

"Does he know about your infertility?" her mother asked.

Trust her mother to bring up the most painful subject of her life. "Yes, he knows."

"Are you sure he isn't going to want more children at some point?"

"Yes, I'm sure." Jamie spoke confidently, even though she wasn't sure at all. "His family is complete."

"Is he divorced?" her father asked.

"Widowed. His wife died about a year ago."

"A year ago? Jamie, what were you thinking? He's probably still grieving."

She was well aware. The point had been driven home last night when he'd called her by Olivia's name as he was kissing her. She was forever destined to be a pale imitation of Ben's dead wife.

"He needs a wife and the children need a mother. And I want a family."

"Oh, honey, I hope you know what you're getting yourself into. I don't want you to be hurt again. I'm worried you've let your desire for children blind you to the dangers of marrying someone you barely know."

"He's not a stranger. I know Ben. And I work with his sister. He's a good man and a good father." They didn't need to know he was also an alcoholic. "You're going to like him. And I know you're going to adore the girls."

"I'm sure we will." Her mother tried to sound upbeat. "Did you have a wedding celebration?"

"No, the ceremony was at a municipal office in Bismarck. It lasted maybe ten minutes."

"Even so, I would have liked to be there."

Jamie closed her eyes against a tsunami of guilt. She'd known her parents, especially her mother, would be hurt by not being included, but still, it was painful to hear.

All her life she'd tried to be a good daughter, to make her parents proud. Sometimes it hadn't been easy to even get their attention. For years they'd been consumed with her sister's illness, making Jamie feel like an afterthought.

"When do we get to meet them?" her mother asked. "How old did you say the children were?"

"Eight and five." Jamie scrambled to come up with an answer to the first question. "Give us some time to get settled."

"Is there some reason you don't want us to meet your new husband?" Her father's voice carried a note of suspicion.

"I'm not trying to stop you from meeting them. This is all new and a little overwhelming for the girls. They've suddenly got a new house and a new stepmother. I'd like to give them a few days to get used to me and their surroundings before I spring new grandparents on them, too. You're going to love them, Mom. They're the sweetest little girls. I'll send you some pictures."

"That sounds wonderful, Jamie." Her mother's voice was over bright. "I look forward to meeting them. Please don't make us wait too long."

"I won't, Mom. I have to run. I'm at work, and I've got to check on a dog we operated on yesterday. I'll talk to you soon."

"Be sure you do. Goodbye, Jamie." She heard the disappointment in her father's voice loud and clear.

"Bye, Dad."

Jamie ended the call and squeezed her eyes shut. Their conversation went about how she'd expected. Their disappointment weighed heavily on her, crushing her with guilt.

****

Ben opened the door of the house with the key Jamie had given him and was immediately welcomed by the barking of dogs and Hector's squawks.

Good God. The place was a zoo. Every neat fiber in his body recoiled in horror.

The girls squealed and laughed as they ran to greet him. Sophie launched herself at him and hugged him around the legs, nearly throwing him off balance.

"Daddy, Daddy, Daddy! Jamie came to pick us up from school today, and then we walked the dogs when we came home."

"Da-dee. Da-dee." Hector eyed him from his perch on top of the china cabinet. After five days living in Jamie's house, Ben was beginning to get used to a bird flying around the house. But he was positive he'd never get used to one landing unexpectedly on his shoulder. The thought made him shudder.

Bella tugged on his arm. "Daddy, we made cookies with Jamie. Come see!"

Ben normally picked up the girls after school, but today Jamie had rearranged her schedule because he had a meeting with a client who could only meet with him in the late afternoon. He knew it wasn't easy for her because she'd had to move around appointments, but she'd made it happen.

He let himself be led into the kitchen where Jamie was spreading frosting on sugar cookies. She looked up at him with a smile.

"Hi. How was your meeting?"

"It was fine. Another senior couple wanting to draw up a Will."

She nodded. "I hope you're not too hungry, because I haven't started dinner yet. I thought it would be fun to make Christmas cookies with the girls and time got away from me. Fortunately, we're not too hungry because we've eaten a few cookies. In the interest of quality control, of course."

Ben chuckled. "Of course. How about if I make scrambled eggs and toast for dinner? It's one of the girls' favorites."

"Sounds great. Thanks."

"Look at the cookies we made, Daddy," Sophie said.

Bella pointed to a group of cookies covered in blue

icing and decorated with happy smiles made of mini chocolate chips. "Jamie let me decorate these cookies all by myself. I even got to make the color of the icing."

Ben squeezed her shoulders. "You did a great job, honey. You both did."

The kitchen table was covered with sugar cookies frosted in several colors of icing and decorated with candy sprinkles, bits of chocolate, and gummy bears. The trimmings were lopsided and definitely not perfect, but they were beautiful to him. His daughters' efforts made him smile.

He had a sudden memory of Christmas in his parents' house. His mother had never baked cookies with him and his siblings, opting instead to purchase fancy Christmas treats from a high-end bakery. Victoria would never have tolerated a mess like this in her kitchen, or these imperfect results. She would never have served guests cookies her children had helped to bake.

Maybe that was why Christmas in his parents' house was never happy. Or joyful. A little mess, a little imperfection, could be a pleasure.

Ben scrambled eggs while Jamie and the girls packaged the cookies in containers and cleaned the table. By the time they finished and returned from the bathroom where they washed their sticky hands, he was dishing eggs and toast onto plates with a side order of carrot sticks.

"Come and get it."

The girls kept up an excited, sugar-driven stream of conversation through dinner. Jamie listened attentively to their stories and laughed often, obviously enjoying their company. Every once in a while, his gaze met hers and they shared a smile over something one of the girls said.

Ben's mind drifted back a week to the kiss that had knocked his world off kilter. They'd been polite to each other since then and had scrupulously avoided talking about what happened. If he hadn't blown it, if he hadn't uttered Olivia's name, would he be in Jamie's bed now?

But he'd made the mistake and he couldn't take it back, as much as he wanted to. He still didn't understand what had come over him. He'd known he was kissing Jamie, known it was her he'd held in his arms. He hadn't fantasized about being with his former wife. He'd wanted Jamie, not Olivia.

Acknowledging the fact came as a shock to Ben. Since Olivia's death, he hadn't thought he'd desire another woman again.

After dinner they all pitched in to clean the kitchen. The girls performed their usual job of putting dishes in the dishwasher, and Jamie gave Bella a cloth to wipe the kitchen table and showed her how to use it.

"Scrub hard. I hate it when sticky bits are left. It's gross." Jamie made a disgusted face that had the girls laughing.

Bella wiped vigorously at the table. "I'll do a good job, Jamie."

"I know you will, sweetheart."

After helping Bella with some homework, the nightly ritual began, with baths, brushing teeth, pajamas, and story time. Finally, the girls were safely tucked into bed, and Ben and Jamie were on their own. Over the past week, he'd found he enjoyed this quiet time with her. Sometimes they watched TV, but more often they talked, usually about the girls, or the schedule for the following day. But occasionally Jamie gave him a glimpse into her life by telling a story about a funny incident at work with a client. Sad things must have happened at work too, but if they did, she preferred to focus on the happy.

Jamie's evening ritual was a cup of camomile tea. He wasn't as big a fan as she was, but because he wanted to spend time with her, he had a cup as well.

She brought two mugs of tea to the living room and set them on coasters on the coffee table. "How's work going?"

"It's all right. Most of it is routine."

"You sound bored." Jamie tucked her legs beneath her and turned to him as if settling in to hear a story.

"I was used to more challenging work. I have a penchant for taking on difficult causes. Some might say hopeless causes. After I got out of corporate law and went to work with Rob and Olivia, I took on cases that pitted little guys against big business. Renters evicted by landlords, employees unfairly dismissed by their employers, things like that."

"As long as there's injustice in the world, there'll always be work for white knights like you."

Her words took him aback. "I'm no white knight."

"Really?" She grinned at him over her mug. "Sure looks that way to me."

Ben was uncomfortable with this topic, so he changed it. "Right back at you. You're the one who looks after the welfare of animals. You even bring them into your home if you have to."

"I know it can't be easy for you living in a house full of pets, especially when you're not used to them. I appreciate how you upended your life to move into this house."

He linked his fingers with hers. "I'll admit I'm still getting used to your pets. But as long as the girls are happy here, and as long as you're happy having us, I'm good."

She tilted her head and smiled. "Yeah. You *are* good."

Ben stared into her eyes. It was an unfamiliar experience to be looked at as something special, and he wasn't sure how to feel. A part of him was thrilled to know Jamie thought of him as a hero. But another part was terrified he'd eventually disappoint her.

He changed the subject again. "I had Morley contact the Doyles and tell them about our marriage."

"Oh. How did they react?"

"They were surprised. Maybe shocked is a better word. They said they want to meet you and assure themselves you're not an axe murderer."

She laughed. "I'm sure they did not say that."

"Well, maybe not the axe murderer part, but they do want to meet you." He brushed a curl from her forehead. "You don't have to if you don't want to."

"Of course I want to. The whole point of us getting married was to convince them their granddaughters were safe and well taken care of. Let's show them."

His head knew she was right, but his heart was terrified of losing his family. "I know, but…"

She brought his hand to her mouth and kissed the back of it. "Don't be scared. I promise it'll be all right."

His breath caught, making it hard to take in air. He was scared all right but not only because of the Doyles. Jamie terrified him. In a short time she'd managed to get inside his head and decipher all his weak spots and fears. Her perception unnerved him.

So he did what he did best. He avoided and deflected.

"Did you talk to your folks?"

Her demeanor immediately grew guarded. "I called them a few days ago. They were astounded to hear I got married again, to say the least. And—no surprise—they want to meet you and the girls."

"I'm sorry to put you in this position with your parents."

"No," she said with a shake of her head. "Things have been tense between us for a while."

He nodded but said nothing more, sorry he'd pushed her on a painful subject.

After one last squeeze, Jamie let go of his hands and reached for her mug of tea. "Do you know when the Doyles are going to visit?"

"Not exactly, but Morley said they'd like to see the kids before Christmas. They'll contact him with dates."

"Whatever happens, I don't want you to worry. We'll work through this together. Okay?"

"Okay."

Ben was grateful to have someone in his corner. Someone who cared. It was a new and unfamiliar feeling.

Chapter Eleven

The next day, Morley heard from the Doyles. Providing the weather cooperated, they planned to drive to Masonville the following Friday. They'd stay the weekend in order to deliver Christmas gifts to the girls and spend time with them. Ben dreaded the visit.

In the meantime, he did his best not to think about it. One day after school, he and the kids brought home a live Christmas tree that filled the house with the fresh scent of pine. Once Jamie got home from work, they set it up in the tree stand, and after supper the four of them decorated it together as Christmas music played in the background. While they decorated, Jamie told the girls their grandparents were coming for a visit. They were excited, especially Bella, who remembered the Doyles better than Sophie did. Seeing her excitement, Ben felt guilty for keeping them apart.

Friday arrived and the knot in Ben's stomach tightened as the day wore on. Around three o'clock, Morley got a call from the Doyles announcing their arrival. As Morley set down the phone he turned to Ben.

"They're here. They'd like to see the girls this evening and meet Jamie. Seven o'clock work for you?"

He preferred they didn't visit at all, but he didn't have a choice in the matter. "I'll let Jamie know."

He sent her a text and a few moments later she

replied.

—*Okay. I'll make sure the dogs and Hector are on their best behavior. I'm not sure if I can do anything about the girls though. They've been so excited. I expect much giggling.*—

Ben answered, —*Maybe you should worry if I'm going to be on my best behavior.*—

—*I have faith in you. You'll be the perfect gentleman.*—

Her words calmed him. Knowing Jamie believed in him eased the tension in his gut.

As usual, he picked up the girls from school. Later, when Jamie got home from work, they ate dinner together, though Ben was too keyed up to eat much. While he cleared the table, Jamie helped the girls put on pretty dresses and brushed their hair into shiny blonde waves. In the kitchen, she got a plate of Christmas cookies ready and filled the coffeemaker with water and coffee grounds. She clearly wanted to make a good impression on the Doyles. Ben hoped her charm offensive paid off.

The doorbell rang at precisely seven o'clock. The girls ran to the door and the dogs barked hysterically. Hector squawked from his cage.

"Doorbell. Doorbell."

Jamie grinned at Ben. "So much for best behavior. At least the fish are quiet. Are you ready?"

No, not at all. But he nodded anyway.

Ben opened the door, and before he could say anything, the girls rushed toward their grandparents, ignoring the cold as they threw their arms around them.

"Grandma! Grandpa!"

"Goodness, look how much you've grown! And

how pretty you are," Elizabeth Doyle exclaimed.

"Girls, let your grandparents get in the house. It's cold out there," Jamie said with a smile.

Mr. and Mrs. Doyle stepped inside, and Ben closed the door behind them. Mr. Doyle turned to him.

"Thank you for having us. It means a lot to Elizabeth and me."

Ben simply nodded. None of this had been his choice, but seeing how excited his daughters were to see their grandparents, he knew it had been the right thing to do.

"I'd like to introduce you to my wife." He reached for Jamie's hand, and she held it tightly. "Mr. and Mrs. Doyle, this is Jamie."

Jamie smiled warmly. "I'm happy to meet you, Mrs. Doyle."

"Please, call me Elizabeth. And my husband is Russ."

"It's nice to meet you, Elizabeth and Russ. The girls have been looking forward to your visit."

As Ben listened to Jamie's conversation with Elizabeth, he was suddenly struck by how much Olivia had resembled her mother. They shared the same fine bone structure, the same blue eyes and determined chin. Though Elizabeth's hair was now gray, Olivia had inherited her blonde hair from her mother as well.

As had Bella and Sophie. Though Sophie's features reminded him more of her father's every day, Bella looked more like Olivia. There was no denying genetics.

Bella tugged on her grandmother's arm. "Grandma, come see my room. Jamie let me pick out the color, and I helped her paint it. It's beautiful."

"My room is beautiful, too," Sophie declared. "Come see!"

"Girls, give your grandparents a chance to take off their coats first," Ben said.

While he hung the coats in the closet, Sophie and Bella dragged their grandparents down the hall, followed by the dogs. They showed them the whole house, introduced them to the angel fish, and then brought them to Hector's cage.

"Grandma, Hector can talk," Sophie said.

"Oh, my goodness. What a smart bird."

Hector perked up with the attention. "So-fee, So-fee. Pretty bird."

"Sometimes Jamie lets Hector out of his cage, and he flies around the house. Sometimes he lands on Daddy's shoulder," Bella said with a giggle.

"Da-dee! Da-dee!"

Elizabeth stared at the bird. "Oh, my."

"Hector's taken quite a liking to Ben," Jamie said with a smile.

"So, he's your pet?" Russ asked.

"Yes. As well as the dogs and the fish. Ben's been very understanding about my animals. He knows they mean a lot to me."

"Jamie's a veterinarian," Ben said.

"You work at the clinic here in town, don't you?" Elizabeth asked.

"Yes, that's right."

Ben's suspicions immediately flared. "How did you know where Jamie works?"

"I think Mr. Walker must have mentioned it."

Elizabeth gave him an innocent look, making Ben even more suspicious. Had they been checking her out?

He wouldn't put it past them.

Jamie gestured toward the sofa. "Why don't you have a seat? Would you like some coffee?"

"We'd love some, thank you."

"Come on, girls. You can help me with the Christmas cookies."

Sophie and Bella skipped alongside Jamie as they made their way to the kitchen. Jamie set her arm on Bella's shoulder as she spoke to Sophie. Russ smiled.

"The girls certainly seem to have taken to your new wife."

"The girls adore her. And she adores them."

"Will Jamie feel the same way about our granddaughters if she has a child of her own?" Russ asked.

Anger bubbled through his veins like hot lava. How dare they disparage Jamie? "That won't happen."

Before either of them had a chance to respond, Sophie and Bella returned to the living room, each carefully balancing a plate of cookies.

"We made these, Grandma!" Sophie declared.

"Did you? Well, then I must taste them."

A cookie slipped off Sophie's plate. It barely had a chance to hit the floor before Rex snapped it up and gobbled it down in one bite. Russ laughed.

"Looks like your dog likes your cookies, too."

Sophie's mouth turned down and tears welled in her eyes. "I didn't mean to drop the cookie."

"It's all right." Jamie spoke soothingly as she set a tray with a coffee carafe and mugs on a side table. "I guess Rex needed a Christmas treat, too. But just to be safe, I'll put the dogs in the back bedroom before they help themselves again."

Ben jumped to his feet. "I'll do it."

Jamie blinked at him. She was likely surprised because in the two weeks he'd been living in her house he hadn't offered to do anything with her pets.

Ben herded the dogs down the hallway and into Jamie's bedroom. He closed the door behind him to keep the dogs from escaping, and to give himself a minute to calm down. He'd nearly lost it with Olivia's father. His remark about Jamie struck a nerve, especially knowing she couldn't have children of her own. He hoped she hadn't overheard.

Ben studied the sturdy oak furniture and queen-sized bed. Everything was neat and tidy. Her scent lingered in the air, something floral with undertones of spice he'd come to associate with her. It was the first time he'd been inside her room, and he couldn't help wishing it was under much different circumstances.

The dogs sat at his feet, looking up expectantly. He blew out a breath. "I'd better get back. Behave yourselves."

Ben returned to the living room and resumed his place on the sofa next to Jamie. She handed him a mug of coffee, the café au lait color telling him she'd added milk, just the way he liked it.

"Did the boys give you any trouble?"

"No, but they asked me to save them a couple of cookies."

Her lips curved upward and her eyes twinkled in amusement. "I think we can make that happen."

Ben's heart lifted to see her smile. For a few precious moments, he forgot about his former in-laws and the looming custody battle and enjoyed her happiness.

Sophie wiggled her way onto Jamie's lap and wrapped her arm around her neck. "Can we give Grandma and Grandpa our gifts now?"

"Sure. They're under the tree. Bella can read the tags."

She scrambled off Jamie's lap and ran to the tree with Bella. Ben exchanged a look with Jamie. *Gifts?* He hadn't even thought of buying gifts from the girls to their grandparents. She gave a slight shrug, like it was no big deal.

The girls pulled two gifts from under the tree and brought them to their grandparents, the bows askew and the wrapping paper crooked.

"We wrapped these ourselves," Sophie said proudly.

"Jamie helped," Bella added.

"I wonder what it could be," Elizabeth said. She ripped open the paper to reveal a picture of Sophie in a silver frame. When Russ opened his present, he lifted a picture of Bella in a matching frame to show his wife.

"Well, aren't these two pretty pictures of two pretty girls," he said.

"They're this year's school photos, taken soon after the girls started at Masonville school," Jamie said.

Elizabeth smiled at her. "This is very thoughtful. Thank you."

"You're welcome."

"We've got some presents for you girls as well. Is it all right if I pop back out to our car to get them?"

Russ turned to Ben, waiting expectantly for his answer. Jamie also turned to him, giving him an encouraging smile. He turned his attention back to his former father-in-law.

"Yes, of course." Did they all believe he'd forbid the girls from accepting gifts from their grandparents?

The older man's face brightened. "Great. I'll only be a minute."

Russ hurriedly put on his coat and boots as if afraid Ben would change his mind. Ben hated being treated like the heavy. But perhaps he deserved it. He'd been the one who'd done his best to keep his children away from their grandparents.

Not everyone is like your parents, a voice in his head told him. *Not every child needs to be shielded from the adults in her life.*

Part of him knew this was the truth. But another part, the part containing remnants of the little boy hurt by his parents' indifference, needed to protect his daughters.

They were all he had.

Ben pushed down the fear and sipped his coffee, willing his hands not to shake. While he listened to Bella and Sophie talk excitedly with their grandmother about Christmas, he realized with a start that Jamie was watching him. She frowned, and he made himself smile for her. Her frown slowly eased. Had she been worried about him? She touched his arm in silent support, as if she understood how much this meeting worried him.

For a few fleeting seconds, Ben didn't feel so alone. Could he count on her to always be on his side?

Russ returned to the house bearing several gift-wrapped packages. With excited cries, the girls ran to him.

"Grandpa! Grandpa! There's so many boxes," Sophie exclaimed.

"Well, we added an extra present for each of you

since we missed your birthdays this year." He slid Ben a quick look before turning his attention back to the girls. "Let me take off my boots and coat, and then you can open your presents."

Jamie got the girls settled on the sofa while Russ removed his outerwear. Sophie vibrated with excitement.

"Daddy, we get a Christmas present and a birthday present!"

"Wonderful, Sophie."

"I love Grandma and Grandpa," she said sweetly.

Ben felt like a dagger had been thrust into his chest. Were they trying to buy his children's love? If they were, it appeared to be working.

The rest of the evening dragged on. The girls opened their presents, and Jamie served more coffee. Sophie was thrilled with the dress-up chest filled with outfits that let her pretend to be a princess. She also received crayons and markers and coloring books, along with a plush dog toy. Bella loved the board games and Lego set she received, but she was especially thrilled with her kit for making friendship bracelets. Finally, around nine, Russ checked his watch.

"It's getting late. We should let these little ones get to bed."

Elizabeth reluctantly nodded. "Yes, I suppose we should. They need to be ready for our big day together tomorrow."

Ben's jaw clenched. What kind of ideas would they put in the girls' heads over the course of a whole day? His inclination was to forbid them from seeing the girls tomorrow. But he'd given his word to go through with the visit, and Bella and Sophie were excited. And if he backed out now, Jamie would be disappointed in him.

Somehow that was the strongest argument.

Jamie and the girls walked them to the door while Ben hung back. After some hugs from the girls, handshakes from Jamie, and a curt nod from him, the Doyles said goodnight and left. Ben exhaled, relieved.

"Come on, girls. Let's get you ready for bed," Jamie said. "Go brush your teeth, and then Daddy and I will tuck you in."

"Okay, Jamie." They raced down the hall, giggling, Sophie with her new plush dog under her arm.

Jamie turned to him with a smile. "I think we might have a hard time settling them down to sleep tonight. They had an exciting evening."

"Yeah." Ben was unsettled, too. Nervous energy made his heart race. His fists clenched and unclenched, seemingly on their own accord.

"This must have been a difficult evening for you. Do you want to talk about it after the girls are in bed?"

Her eyes were full of concern and empathy. For a moment he wanted to unburden himself, to tell her his every fear for the future of his family, to confess every hurt of his past.

Guilt held him back. It wasn't fair to lean on Jamie, to burden her with fears that were his alone. And if he was honest, shame stopped him, too. She already knew about his alcoholism. He didn't want her to know about his past, his childhood, as well.

It was too humiliating.

"I'm fine. Let's see what the girls are up to."

She hesitated, as if wanting to say something more. Finally, she nodded, her smile not reaching her eyes.

"Okay, but if you ever change your mind, I'm

here."

She walked down the hallway to the bathroom, and Ben heard her voice and the girls' excited giggles. Jamie was right about them being hard to settle tonight.

He closed his eyes. His wife and children were right here, yet he felt more alone than ever.

****

Jamie stood in the open door and watched the girls scramble into their grandparents' car. As promised, Russ and Elizabeth arrived promptly at ten. They had a full day planned with the girls—skating at the ice rink, shopping in Bismarck, and lunch at a fast-food restaurant. Jamie had no doubt Bella and Sophie would have a ball.

Ben hadn't come to the door when the Doyles arrived. Instead, he'd stayed out of sight in the kitchen and said his goodbyes to the girls there. Though he put on a happy face for his kids, anxiety flowed from him in waves that practically smacked Jamie in the face. Fortunately, the girls were too excited to notice.

After the Doyles' car pulled away from the curb, Jamie shut the front door. She made her way to the kitchen where Ben was washing the breakfast dishes. She watched him for a moment. His broad shoulders were bunched with tension, and she was sure if she looked into his face, she'd see that his jaw was clenched.

"I'm supposed to work this afternoon, but I could see if Cole would be willing to trade a shift with me."

Ben kept his attention on the dishes in the sink. "I don't need you to babysit me, Jamie."

"I wasn't planning to. But I thought maybe you'd prefer not to be alone."

He stilled. After a brief hesitation, he turned his head to look at her. "It's not necessary, but thanks. I appreciate the thought."

"But you're upset—"

"I said I'm fine. I don't need you."

Jamie froze, his words hitting her like a slap to the face. She was immediately whisked back in time to her marriage to Carson, to some of the hurtful things he'd said to her.

Though she'd known from the beginning her marriage to Ben was mostly for show, she hadn't expected such an emphatic rejection. At least, not so soon.

"I'll get out of your way." Jamie hated the hurt in her voice. She'd never been any good at disguising her feelings. She turned blindly, needing to get out of the house.

Dishes rattled. "Jamie, come back. I shouldn't have said—"

She didn't wait to hear him finish. Grabbing her jacket, she ran out the door, not bothering to put it on. Even the bitter north wind didn't hurt as much as Ben's *I don't need you.*

Chapter Twelve

As promised, the Doyles returned at five o'clock with the girls. Bella and Sophie were tired but full of stories about their exciting day. Ben was thankful the day was finally over. Maybe now, after satisfying themselves that the girls were fine, Olivia's parents would go home and leave him in peace.

Shortly after the girls entered the house with their grandparents, Jamie arrived home from work. Ben's eyes met hers across the room. He'd hurt her this morning, and he deeply regretted it. Jamie was the last person he wanted to cause pain. But he'd learned a long time ago it was better not to lean on someone, to depend on them. In the end, they'd let him down.

Yet he found himself wanting to lean on Jamie. To matter to her. She gave him a slight nod and a brief smile before averting her gaze. Ben hoped it meant she'd forgiven him.

Russ Doyle cleared his throat as he addressed him. "We'll be leaving tomorrow, but we were hoping to take the girls out for breakfast before we leave. About nine?"

Ben didn't want to allow it. The weekend had been long enough, and he was ready for the Doyles to get out of Masonville and out of their lives. He didn't want them filling the girls' heads with negative things about him.

The word *no* was on the tip of his tongue when his gaze connected with Jamie's. She stood hugging herself, her curly hair escaping the confines of her ponytail to form a halo of ringlets around her tense face. Ben sensed her worry. She was afraid he'd say something to offend the Doyles.

And he found he didn't want to disappoint her. Not again.

"Why don't you come here for breakfast?"

Bella squirmed with excitement. "Daddy, can we make pancakes?"

"Sure."

"Can I put in the blueberries?" Sophie asked.

Ben grinned and lifted her into arms. "Of course you can. How could I cook without my two helpers?"

"Daddy makes the best pancakes, Grandpa. You'll see."

"I guess we will, Sunshine." Mr. Doyle extended his hand. "Thank you for the invitation. About nine?"

Ben shifted Sophie to accept the older gentleman's shake. "Nine is perfect."

After some hugs and kisses, the girls' grandparents left. Ben breathed a sigh of relief. One more day and they'd be gone, and life could get back to normal.

Normal? He had no idea what normal looked like anymore.

Shortly after dinner, he and Jamie put the girls to bed. Their busy day had left them tired, and though excited about their breakfast with their grandparents the next morning, they fell asleep quickly.

After closing Sophie's bedroom door, Ben made his way to the kitchen where Jamie was clipping the dogs' leashes to their collars.

"Going for a walk?"

"Yeah. They need to blow off some steam."

Her voice was friendly, but she avoided his gaze.

"Jamie, I'm sorry for this morning. What I said—"

"It's okay, Ben. I understand you've been upset about this visit."

"Yeah, but I shouldn't take it out on you. I hope you can forgive me."

The dogs whined in anticipation of their walk, their hindquarters shaking with their wags. Jamie looked up at him with a smile that was too cheery.

Too fake.

"Apology accepted. I'd better go before the boys have an accident." She hurried out the back door. She may have accepted his apology, but it didn't mean she'd forgiven him.

It was his own fault. What did he expect after the way he'd rejected her offer of help this morning? Disappointment swamped him. Though this was a marriage in name only, a part of him had hoped for more.

****

The next morning the dogs woke Jamie in the pre-dawn to be let out. While they were doing their business in the back yard, she padded barefoot in the dark to the kitchen to make coffee, only to find a full pot already made.

"Good morning."

Jamie started at Ben's deep voice. "Geez! You could warn a person. Why are you sitting in the dark?"

"Sorry. I couldn't sleep."

Jamie filled a cup with coffee and slid into the chair next to him at the kitchen table. "Are you worried about this breakfast with Olivia's parents? Is that why you can't sleep?"

He gave her a wry grin. "Having them in town probably doesn't help my sleep."

"They only want to see the girls, Ben."

He sipped his coffee, his eyes downcast. "I know. But I keep waiting for the other shoe to drop, for them to tell me they're taking the girls away and never bringing them back."

"Oh, Ben."

She linked his fingers with hers. Sitting in the semi-dark of the kitchen felt intimate and private, as if they were the only two people awake on earth, or at least in Masonville.

"I'm sorry. I know I've been hard to live with this weekend." He lifted his gaze to look into her eyes. "You've been nothing but supportive, and I've been an ass."

"You're being hard on yourself again."

"Okay then, a heel. I've been acting like a heel this weekend. Is it a better body part analogy?"

Jamie laughed. "Yes, much better."

Ben gently stroked his thumb over her upper lip. "You have a beautiful smile. You light up from the inside every time you smile."

"There's nothing special about my smile." Her voice hitched as his fingers traced the delicate skin beneath her eye. "Aside from my mouth being too big."

"Now who's being hard on herself?"

She stared into his eyes, mesmerized by his words. And confused. Yesterday he didn't want her around, but today... Well, she didn't know what he wanted today. Was it possible...?

The dogs barked, wanting to be let back in. With a sigh, Jamie tugged on her hand and Ben released her, breaking the spell that had descended upon them. She got to her feet and went to the back door, using the towel she kept there to wipe the dog's feet. By the time she returned to the kitchen, Ben had turned on the lights. The room now appeared stark and bright, no longer the intimate retreat of mere moments ago.

Just as well, she thought. Those kinds of feelings weren't real, at least on Ben's part. He was still mourning Olivia. Only stress and exhaustion had prompted him to say the things he had in the last few minutes.

Jamie fed the dogs and gave them fresh water, then checked the clock on the stove. Seven thirty-five. Time to get ready. "I'm going to shower before the girls wake up." She groaned as she reached up to touch her hair and found a curly, tangled mass. "And I'll need to deal with this bird's nest on my head. I don't want to scare small children and old people."

"Why do you do that?"

"Do what?"

"Put yourself down."

His observation made her uncomfortable. "Come on. My hair's a mess. I could hide a flock of geese in there."

Ben brought out a couple of bowls from the cupboard. "You're a beautiful, intelligent woman, Jamie. Cut yourself some slack."

She didn't believe for a moment he thought of her as beautiful. But still, it was nice to hear. "I've always believed it was better to laugh at myself before someone beat me to it."

Ben laid his palm against her cheek. "Anyone who laughs at you sure as hell doesn't see what I see."

For a moment she couldn't breathe. His eyes bored into hers and she couldn't look away.

He's simply being kind, she told herself. *He's grateful for my help with the girls. Nothing more.*

Jamie backed away. "I'd better shower."

She escaped to the bathroom. By the time she emerged, with her unruly mane brushed and braided into submission, the girls were awake and dressed. Ben had a bowl of pancake batter ready for the griddle and bacon frying in a pan. Jamie hugged the girls.

"How about we set the table? Grandma and Grandpa will be here soon."

Sophie twirled in an excited circle. "Yay!"

"I can't wait!" Bella said.

Jamie laughed. It was very easy to love these beautiful little girls.

The doorbell rang at precisely nine a.m. Sophie and Bella ran to the door, followed by the two barking dogs. Jamie took a deep breath, pressing a palm against her nervous stomach.

"It's show time. Act happy."

Ben grinned wryly. "I'm not that good an actor."

Neither was she. But for the girls, she'd try.

She joined the girls at the door and greeted their grandparents, taking their coats and hanging them in the closet. "Good morning. How are you this morning?"

"Good morning. We're well, but oh, my goodness, it's cold out there," Elizabeth said.

"Grandma, Daddy's making pancakes," Sophie exclaimed.

"Oh, I love pancakes. Good thing I brought my

hungry tummy this morning."

"Come on into the kitchen, and I'll pour you some coffee," Jamie said.

Russ Doyle rubbed his hands together. "Sounds great. I need a hot drink for a cold morning like this."

Ben said good morning to the Doyles as he dropped spoonfuls of batter onto the heated griddle. Jamie hid her smile. It looked as though his plan was to feed them quickly and get them out fast. But at least he was making the effort.

Jamie motioned Elizabeth and Russ to take a seat at the table while she brought them coffee. "I hope the weather holds for your drive home."

"According to the weather channel, it's going to be sunny and cold with no wind for the next couple of days. Perfect winter driving weather," Elizabeth said.

"We won't drive the whole way in one day. It's too far for an old driver like me, especially on these short winter days. I don't like to drive after dark," Russ said.

Jamie poured orange juice for the girls. "The important thing is to be safe, no matter how long it takes."

Ben brought a stack of pancakes and a plate of bacon to the table. "Dig in while it's hot."

Jamie took her seat at one end of the table and helped herself to a pancake. It was fluffy and light with just the right amount of sweetness. "Oh, my goodness, Ben, these are delicious!"

He grinned at her from across the table. "Glad you like them."

"We told you, Jamie," Bella said around a mouthful of pancake.

"Boy, were you right." She pointed her fork at Ben

and grinned. "What other culinary talents are you hiding?"

"I make a mean grilled cheese." He winked at her over his coffee cup.

"You've never tasted Ben's pancakes before?" Elizabeth asked.

"No, this is the first time he's made them since he and the girls moved in."

"Then you haven't known each other long?"

Ben's smile disappeared. Jamie struggled for the right thing to say. "No, not long. We were neighbors. Ben's grandfather left him the house next door." She smiled across the table at Ben. "But even after a short time, it felt right to be together."

A corner of Ben's mouth turned up in an answering grin. "It was definitely right."

"Does it mean your drinking is under control?"

Ben turned to stare at Russ, and he stared back. With sudden clarity, Jamie realized this was what Russ and Elizabeth had come to Masonville to find out and what Ben had been dreading since they'd arrived.

"Yes, it's under control. It has been for nearly six years."

Russ began to speak, but Jamie interrupted. "I don't think this is a conversation for little ears."

Russ sighed and nodded. He picked up his fork once more.

The rest of the meal was completed in silence except for Sophie's questions to her grandparents. Bella glanced nervously between Ben and her grandparents, picking up on the sudden tension in the room. Jamie tried to reassure her with a smile, but Bella was a perceptive child and she knew something was wrong.

As soon as the kids were done eating, Jamie rose to her feet. "Girls, I think the dogs need to go outside. Why don't you play with them in the yard for a while?"

She bundled the girls into their snowsuits, then whistled for the dogs and ushered them all outside. Expelling a deep breath, she returned to the table and stood beside Ben's chair, one arm looped around his shoulders. His muscles were bunched with tension.

"Ben is an amazing father and the girls adore him. Everything he does, he does for them." Jamie struggled to keep the tears out of her voice. "Alcohol hasn't been an issue since I've known Ben. He told me about his past, but that's the thing. Alcohol is in his past. I know he'll do anything to make sure his girls are safe and happy. Ben is the strongest person I know."

He looked up at her, surprise in his expression. She willed herself not to cry. She hated confrontations, but she had to make the Doyles understand.

Russ toyed with his coffee cup. "Forgive me, Jamie, but I had to know. Our granddaughters are the only family we have left. We need to know they're safe."

"Olivia told us about Ben's history with alcohol, and we were concerned when they married. But now that she's gone..." Elizabeth's voice trailed off to a whisper, her expression revealing the depth of her grief.

"Olivia told you?" Jamie heard the shock in Ben's voice.

"Yes," Elizabeth said. "She never kept secrets from us. She told us about your alcoholism and recovery, and she also told us you loved the girls and they loved you. We were willing to give you a chance because of it." Her voice broke. "She never would have kept us from seeing the girls."

Russ sighed. "I think we should go, Lizzie."

Elizabeth nodded and pushed herself to her feet. With a squeeze to Ben's shoulder, Jamie stepped away. "I'll get your coats."

While the Doyles got ready, Jamie called in the girls to say goodbye. She glanced at Ben as she went to the back door. He was still sitting at the table, his head bowed. She wanted to go to him, but at the moment the girls took priority.

She helped them remove their outerwear. "Grandma and Grandpa have to leave. Come say goodbye."

After many hugs and kisses, Russ and Elizabeth left. Jamie breathed a sigh of relief. She helped the girls stow their snowsuits and boots in the closet, then set them free to play downstairs in the blanket fort they'd constructed. Jamie made her way to the kitchen where Ben was loading the dishwasher.

"Can I help?" she asked.

He looked up briefly and gave her a nod. "Sure."

They worked together in silence, putting away leftovers, wiping the counters, and washing dishes too big for the dishwasher. As they finished, Ben turned to her.

"Thank you for what you said earlier. I appreciate it."

"It was the truth. They needed to know."

"They're never coming here again. I won't allow it. They won't stop until they take the girls away from me."

Jamie heard the barely repressed anger in his voice. "Come on, Ben, don't say that. Once you have a chance to calm down, you'll feel differently."

He shook his head. "No. This is the end. The only contact they'll have with my kids from now on is through my lawyer."

"Ben, be reasonable—"

"No!" He whirled to face her. "I'll do whatever I have to, to save my family, and if it means keeping them away from their grandparents, I'll do it. I expect you to respect my wishes."

"What does that mean?"

"It means I don't want you inviting them here, and I don't want you to talk to them."

Her gut twisted at the anger in his words. "Are you seriously forbidding me from speaking to them?"

His jaw tensed. "If you were on my side, I wouldn't even have to ask."

Jamie blinked, taken aback by his words. "That's not fair. I've always been on your side."

"The very fact we're having this conversation makes me wonder if it's true."

Jamie stared at him. He talked about saving his family, but it didn't sound like he was including her in his circle. It hurt.

She lifted her chin. "I'll always support you. But you're wrong about this. Very wrong."

Jamie hurried out of the kitchen and grabbed her coat and car keys at the back door before leaving the house. She was going to cry, and she didn't want Ben or the girls to witness it.

Chapter Thirteen

Ben leaned back in his office chair and twisted his pen between his thumb and forefinger, his work unable to hold his attention. His thoughts flew to yesterday's events. Moving to Masonville was a mistake. And he was afraid marrying Jamie had been a mistake, too.

For her.

I'll always support you. But you're wrong about this. Very wrong. He hated being on the outs with her, disappointing her. Her approval was important to him. Maybe more than it should have been.

He'd acted like a dictator. He had no right to tell her what she could do.

He might as well admit it. He needed her. She was an island of calm in his turbulent life.

What if he was forced to disappear with the girls? He couldn't ask her to give up her whole life to come with him. But how could he leave her?

The door to the outer office opened and Morley walked in, brushing the snow from his coat as he closed the outside door behind him.

"It's really coming down out there." Morley removed his coat and scarf and hung them in the closet. In the reception area, he chatted with Carmen about the weather, their conversation the amiable banter of colleagues who'd worked together many years. A few moments later, he walked into Ben's office and closed the door behind him.

"Good morning, Morley. I didn't think you were coming in today."

Morley lowered himself into the chair in front of Ben's desk. "I hadn't planned to, but I got a call from an old friend and I wanted to run a couple of things by you."

Ben sighed inwardly. Probably another old friend who needed a Will drawn up. "What things are those?"

"I know you're being under utilized. Estate planning is good, necessary work, but I can see you're bored. You need more. Just like I did when I was your age."

Ben sat up straighter. "What do you mean?"

"Back in the day, I was the go-to lawyer around here for hopeless causes. Anytime a little guy wanted to go up against a big corporation or big government, people came to me. I tilted at a few windmills in my time."

This was news to Ben. He looked at the old man in a new light. "Granddad never mentioned it."

"That's probably because my crusading days are long past. It's a young man's game. Besides, crusading didn't always pay the bills." He grinned as he gestured to the beat-up wooden desk and fading wallpaper. "You may have noticed the less then palatial accommodations around here."

Ben returned the grin. "I've noticed. Who's this old friend you're talking about?"

"The chief of a Sioux reservation a couple of hundred miles from here. McDowell Energy wants to frack for oil on their land and build a pipeline to transport it. Some members of the community are eager for any industry that promises to bring jobs and prosperity. But others, like my friend, are concerned about the effects of fracking. In other places, it's destroyed underground sources of water. He doesn't want that to happen on his land."

"What does your friend want us to do, exactly?"

Morley leaned back and steepled his fingers. "If it was completely up to him, McDowell wouldn't be allowed on reservation land. But he recognizes they need the jobs fracking can bring. He wants a lawyer to ensure they aren't taken advantage of. They want to compel McDowell to hire a certain number of workers from the reserve and provide training for them. They want to make sure they're adequately compensated and all environmental standards are upheld. I thought you'd be a perfect fit for the job."

It sounded exactly like the kind of work he enjoyed, something he could sink his teeth into. But he had questions.

"Does your friend expect me to work *pro bono*?" He had a family to support, and he wouldn't work for free if it meant his girls went without.

"We'll work out an arrangement with the reserve to give you adequate compensation, perhaps based on the agreement you work out with McDowell."

Ben nodded. It was exactly what he was looking for. But if he had to run, he'd be leaving his client in the lurch. His conscience wouldn't allow him to begin a job he might not be able to finish. After the weekend visit with the Doyles, running looked more and more inevitable.

The thought of running, of leaving Jamie, caused a knot in his gut.

"Let me think it over for a couple of days."

Ben turned his attention back to his work, or at least tried to. Morley remained seated, his gaze focused on him.

"What do you have to think about?" he asked.

"The work you're proposing is all-consuming. I have to weigh helping the reservation against the time I'll be away from my family."

Morley's gaze drilled into his, making Ben fidget. "Is there anything else you're concerned with?"

Ben tried to think of a reasonable objection. "I'm not sure the job's a good fit for me."

Morley folded his arms across his chest. "This is exactly the sort of work you did in Chicago. You told me you loved it."

"This is different."

"Is it?"

"I'm thinking about moving back to Chicago." The lie tasted bitter.

"How does Jamie feel about moving?"

"She…" Ben turned away from Morley's intense scrutiny. "She doesn't know."

"She doesn't know? Are you thinking about leaving without her?" Morley's eyes widened as comprehension dawned. "You're thinking about running away with the girls, aren't you?"

Ben didn't know how he'd guessed his plans, but for Morley's sake, he had to deny it. "No, of course not."

Morley ignored him. "How far do you think you'd get? What kind of life could you make for your children?"

"I told you, I have no plans to run away." The

words sounded empty even to his own ears.

"Maybe, if you were on your own, you could disappear. But with two small girls? Not so easy." Morley gave a disgusted snort. "When you're caught—and you *will* be caught—you'll never see your children again. Is that what you want?"

"Of course not!" Ben jumped to his feet, and his chair crashed against the wall behind him. "I only want to save my family. Is that so wrong?"

"Wanting to preserve your family is commendable. But to do it by running won't get you what you need. In the end, you'll lose everything."

He was afraid Morley was right. His deepest fear was if he went into hiding with the girls, they'd grow to hate him for taking them away from everything familiar and everyone they loved.

Including Jamie.

But what choice did he have? The Doyles hadn't withdrawn their custody suit. After the way they'd parted this past weekend, he was sure they'd be in contact about the suit very soon.

"I'm a damn fine lawyer, Ben. Trust me. I can help you keep your family together."

He trusted Morley. Still…

"What about Jamie?" Morley asked.

"What about her?"

"She doesn't deserve to be abandoned."

His friend's words hit hard. And they shamed him. Jamie had been abandoned once before, and she'd been hurt. She deserved nothing but good things. She deserved a family and a man who loved her with everything he had.

He was staggered by how much he wanted to be

that man. And by how much the thought of leaving her hurt.

****

Lauren waved as Jamie left the examining room. "Jamie, wait. You've got a phone call on line two."

Jamie hesitated with her hand on the doorknob of examining room one. She had a German Shepherd with a cut on his paw waiting inside, and an aging Rottweiler with a failing liver up next in examining room three. "Can you take a message?"

Lauren shook her head. "I tried, but this woman is adamant she speak to you. She wouldn't give me her name, but she says it's an urgent personal matter."

She groaned. It was likely her mother, though she couldn't imagine what was so important it couldn't wait until after work. Unless her sister was sick again… She stuck the German Shepherd's medical record file back into the holder on the door.

"All right, I'll take the call in the break room. What line did you say it was?"

Lauren gave her a sympathetic smile. "Line two."

Jamie was relieved no one was in the break room when she arrived. She closed the door and went to the phone, punching the line two button as she lifted the receiver.

"Hello?"

"Hello, is this Jamie?"

The voice on the line was not her mother's. "Yes, it is."

"Jamie, I'm sorry to bother you at work. This is Elizabeth Doyle."

"Oh. Hello." She pulled out a chair and sat. This couldn't be good news. "What can I do for you?"

"Russ and I were upset about the way we parted the other day. We didn't intend to antagonize Ben, but we need to know what's going on. We need to know our granddaughters are safe and well cared for."

"I can assure you Bella's and Sophie's welfare is a priority for both Ben and me."

"It was good to meet you and to see the way you are with the girls. It's obvious they care about you very much."

"I care about them, too."

"Yes, I believe you do." Jamie heard the older woman inhale, then slowly exhale. "That's why I'm hoping you'll help us. Ben's made it quite clear he doesn't want us to be part of our granddaughters' lives. We won't be excluded, especially since we know his past history with alcoholism. We're afraid he could start drinking again."

"I can assure you, he won't. Ben works hard on his sobriety."

"I know you want to believe in Ben, and we do, too. But we have no way of knowing what he's doing to keep himself sober because he shuts us out. It's the reason we launched our custody suit. We felt we had to force him to pay attention to us."

If it had been their intention to grab Ben's attention, it had certainly been successful. Ben was totally focused on the custody of his children. To the point he'd almost run away with them.

Was running still on his mind? Elizabeth Doyle wasn't the only one in the dark.

"Perhaps if you'd withdraw your suit he'd feel more comfortable giving you access to Sophie and Bella."

"We can't do that. Launching this suit is the only way we're going to be able to see our granddaughters."

Jamie was afraid she might be right. Ben's stubbornness bordered on the obsessive. She didn't understand the deep-seated fear driving him, because he wouldn't talk about it. Would he ever trust her enough to confide in her?

"We're glad you're part of their lives," Mrs. Doyle continued. "You're good for the girls, and I think you're good for Ben, too. We believe you have their best interests at heart."

"I do."

"I'll be honest with you, Jamie. Russ and I know we're too old to raise two little girls. But if push came to shove, if we believed Ben's drinking put them at risk, we wouldn't hesitate to fight for them. We hope it never comes to that. All we want is to be involved with our granddaughters, to talk to them, to see them grow, and know they're happy."

It wasn't an unreasonable request, and she'd told Ben so. But he'd been adamant in his refusal.

"Why are you calling me, Mrs. Doyle?"

"Because we need your help. Maybe you can let the girls talk to us over the internet. Then we can see their faces and hear their voices. Maybe you can let us know how things are going in your house."

"You're asking me to spy for you. You're asking me to go against my husband's wishes." Jamie pinched the bridge of her nose.

"I know we're putting you in an awkward position, but if we have no access to our granddaughters, we'll have no choice but to bring our custody suit to court. Do you really want to subject the girls to such a battle?"

"No, of course not."

"It's not what we want either. I'd hoped we could work out an amicable solution, but Ben has refused to even speak with us."

"Let me talk to him one more time. I promise I'll be in touch with you soon."

"All right. I'm sorry to put you in this position, but Ben's left us with no other choice."

Once they exchanged phone numbers and said goodbye, Jamie hung up the phone. She needed to tend to her patients but couldn't bring herself to move. What was she to do? Did she go behind Ben's back to do something she knew he'd hate her for, or did she do nothing and watch as his life was torn apart?

Chapter Fourteen

By the time Jamie got home, Ben had already started dinner. The girls were at the kitchen table, Bella doing homework and Sophie coloring a picture. Jamie kissed them before grabbing an apron from a drawer.

"Sorry I'm late. The operation took longer than we expected." She tied the apron around her waist. "What can I do to help?"

Ben shook his head. "I've got it under control. Why don't you sit down and relax for a minute? Sounds like you've had an eventful day."

Jamie thought of the phone call she'd received from Elizabeth Doyle. It had indeed been an eventful day. She felt disloyal for even thinking about going against Ben's wishes.

But after their fight yesterday, she wasn't sure she had a choice.

Now he was being sweet to her. Did it mean he was sorry about their fight? Yesterday, she'd driven around for an hour, until her tears were under control. When she got back, neither of them brought it up again. Ben blew hot one minute and cold the next, making it hard to know where she stood. What would it be like to walk into his arms and know she belonged there? To know she was truly wanted?

"Are you sure I can't help you?"

"Absolutely." He rubbed her shoulder, his gaze not

quite meeting hers. Then he dropped his hand and went back to slicing vegetables. "It's nothing fancy, just a stir-fry, but it's one of the girls' favorites. How about a cup of tea? I could put the kettle on."

Jamie sat beside Sophie. "Thanks. That would be great."

He filled the kettle with water and set a cup and spoon and a box of camomile tea in front of her. "How's the Dalmatian doing after his big operation?"

Late in the afternoon, she and Dr. Waverly had performed an emergency operation on a Dalmatian who'd eaten things he shouldn't have.

"About as well as a dog who just had half a dozen Legos surgically removed from his abdomen can be expected to do. Dr. Waverley and I and Audrey are taking turns checking in on him this evening and overnight." She checked her watch. "I've got the ten-to-midnight shift, and then I'm back at four a.m. to take over from Dr. Waverley."

"All the more reason for you to relax while you can."

Rex hopped into her lap, and Sammy stood next to her chair waiting for a scratch to his ears. Jamie blew out a breath. "I guess I should take these guys for a walk."

Ben filled her cup with hot water. "No need. After I got your text about the emergency, the girls and I walked them because we knew you'd be late. They've been fed, too."

"That's a relief. Thanks."

Ben gave her a quick grin before turning back to his work. "No problem. I didn't do anything with Hector, though. Him I will leave to you."

"I'll see to Hector in a bit."

She watched Ben move around the kitchen with graceful ease. He was like a dancer, tall, lithe, beautiful. Jamie closed her eyes. How could she deceive him?

"Do you like my picture, Jamie?" Sophie asked, sliding her paper in front of her. Jamie pushed her disloyal thoughts away to concentrate on the child.

"I do. It's very colorful." She took another, closer look. "Why is the sun pink, sweetie?"

"Because it's just coming up in the sky."

"Oh, I get it. It's a sunrise."

"This is my bestest picture. I'm going to send it to Grandpa and Grandma. Can you mail it for me, Daddy?"

Jamie caught his momentary hesitation and the stiffness in his shoulders before he answered his daughter's question. "Sure."

"Do you miss Grandpa and Grandma?" she asked.

Sophie sighed dramatically. "I wish they didn't live so far away. I wish they lived with us and we could see them every day."

Jamie glanced at Ben, who had his back turned to them. "You love them, don't you?"

She sighed again. "I do."

Bella looked up from her math homework. "I love them, too. They remind me of Mommy."

Jamie reached over to rub her back. "I know, honey."

Ben soon had dinner on the table, and the subject of the children's grandparents was dropped. Time flew by after dinner with clean up, baths, and preparing lunches for the following day. Jamie let Hector fly around for a while to get some exercise and then spent some time petting him. He had a spot behind his ear he loved having scratched. He closed his eyes, totally relaxed and submissive.

Ben returned to the living room after tucking in the girls. "How's Hector this evening?"

"Da-dee!" Hector croaked, his eyes still closed.

"Still your biggest fan." Jamie gave him one last scratch before putting him back in his cage and covering it to give Hector the darkness he needed to sleep. She turned to Ben when she was done. "Can I make you a cup of tea this time?"

"Sure."

"I'll be right back."

Jamie prepared a pot of tea and placed it on a tray along with a small jug of milk for Ben's tea. She brought it into the living room and set it on the coffee table. Ben folded the newspaper he'd been reading and set it aside.

"Something interesting happened at work today," he said.

"Oh, yeah?"

"An old friend of Morley's, a Sioux chief, wants our help." He explained some of the details of the job.

Jamie sipped her hot tea. "Is this a job you'd be interested in?"

"Yes, definitely."

She studied his somber expression. "For someone who claims to be interested in a job, you don't seem excited."

He set his teacup back in the tray. "I'm concerned that getting involved in this project will take me away from home a lot. I don't want to spend too much time away from the girls. They've had enough upheaval in their lives."

Jamie set down her cup as well. "For what it's worth, I'm here to back you up. I'll do whatever I can to support you and the girls."

"It's worth a lot." He reached for her hand and linked his fingers with hers. "I'm sorry about our fight yesterday. I acted like a jerk. Can you forgive me?"

Relief flowed over her. "Yes, of course."

"Thank you." He frowned. "Seems I'm always asking for your forgiveness."

Jamie tried to make a joke of it, though it was no laughing matter. "I'm getting used to it."

"I'll try to do better, Jamie. I promise. I want our marriage to work. And I want you to be happy."

Jamie stared into his hazel eyes, noting the bits of turquoise circling his pupils. Perhaps she was being naïve, but she believed him. It meant the world to know her happiness was important to him.

"I want our marriage to work, too."

His smile lifted her heart. "I'm glad."

He gripped her fingers one last time before letting go, leaving her bereft and craving his touch. It took all her willpower to keep from reaching for him.

Ben poured more milk into his tea and stirred. "You have your own work to consider. You've got a busy practice. Tonight is a perfect example. You're going to spend half the night with a sick dog."

"It's not like it happens all the time. I'm usually able to be home in the evenings." She considered her next words carefully. "You're not on your own. If you let them, I'm sure the girls' grandparents would be willing to help out, too."

Ben's relaxed smile vanished. "That's not going to

happen."

"I know the Doyles upset you by suing for custody, but maybe it was the only way they felt you'd pay attention to them."

"I don't want them filling my daughters' heads with lies about me."

"What makes you think they'd do that?"

"If I can't trust my own parents, how can I trust Olivia's?"

Jamie stared at him, shocked by his response. He averted his gaze, his clenched-jaw expression telling her he regretted revealing this much. He sat on the edge of his seat as if getting ready to run.

Was he still thinking of running away? Of leaving her? Her chest ached at the thought.

"I'm sorry you feel you can't trust your parents," she whispered. Had he always felt that way? Her parents had their faults, but she'd never doubted their trustworthiness.

Ben appeared embarrassed by his admission. He lifted his cup, his eyes not meeting hers.

"Can you tell me about them?" she asked.

He sighed, his tea forgotten. He remained quiet for so long Jamie thought he would continue to hold onto his secrets. But then he began to speak.

"My parents only ever cared about power and money. My mother had political ambitions for my father. He came from a prestigious Minnesota family, and she believed they could exploit his family's money and well-known name all the way to the White House. Dad's father and grandfather had represented Minnesota in the House of Representatives for years and were well respected. Dad was elected into the

Minnesota state legislature, but he has a drinking problem." He paused and shook his head. "No, let's call a spade a spade. My father is an alcoholic, like me. The only difference between us is that he's never seriously tried to get sober."

Jamie held her breath, afraid to say or do anything that might make him stop talking. She wanted to know everything about him, to understand how he thought. Perhaps understanding his relationship with his parents was the key.

"When my mother finally realized Dad wasn't going to give her the power and status she craved, she turned her attention to me. By the time I reached high school, she was grooming me for a future in politics. My mother said it was important to build my resume and to associate with people who could help me in the future. My father went along with whatever she said. I did whatever they asked. It was the only way to get their attention. Their love."

He paused and sipped his tea again. Jamie's head reeled. What kind of people were his parents?

"I got into Northwestern University, where I met Olivia and Rob. The pressure really ramped up then. I had to keep my grades up so I could get into Harvard law like my mother wanted. Drinking became the only way I could cope."

He stopped talking and stared into space. Jamie touched his arm. "What happened then?"

He blew out a breath. "I found out I didn't get into Harvard. My whole world crashed around me. My mother let me know how worthless she thought I was, but she wasn't prepared to give up. I still got into law school at Northwestern. It wasn't Harvard, but she was going to make it work.

"I studied hard, but by now my drinking was out of control. I told you how Olivia and Rob took me to student services to get me help, and for a while it worked, at least long enough for me to graduate."

"They were good friends."

A corner of Ben's mouth lifted briefly. "Yeah. After graduation Olivia and Rob went one way, and I went another. My mother insisted I get a job in corporate law, so she used family connections to get me a job at the biggest corporate law firm in Chicago. I told you before how much I hated it. But I stayed because, for once, my parents seemed pleased with me. To cope, I slipped back into my old ways. I drank.

"My mother began talking about my political future. She'd even decided I would run for the House of Representatives in my grandfather's former voting district in Minnesota in the election two years away. She'd already begun putting the machinery in place to ensure I won the nomination. I panicked. For the first time I realized if I stayed on this course, if I didn't do something, I would be under my mother's thumb for the rest of my life. I finally understood I would never win their love, no matter what I did. I was simply a pawn to them, not a son."

He scrubbed a hand over his face. "I hit rock bottom and quit the firm. If it hadn't been for Olivia and Rob, I'd probably be dead by now. The only bright spot was that my parents finally left me alone. I'm of no use to them any longer."

Jamie wondered if the relationships Blair and Damon had with their parents were as dysfunctional as Ben's. "Not everyone's parents are like yours. I have issues with mine, but I know they love me. Olivia's parents loved her, too. From everything you've told me, she was a remarkable person. Part of it must have come from her parents."

"I know what you're trying to do, Jamie." Ben's voice became anxious. "Can't you see the Doyles want to take my daughters away from me? I can't let them."

Oh, Ben. He was so afraid that he couldn't see the big picture. If he didn't give a little, the girls would be lost to him. She'd never convince him otherwise.

Jamie checked her watch. "I've got to leave. Audrey's probably ready to go home."

Ben sighed. "Better go check on your Dalmatian."

"Yeah." On impulse she cupped his cheek. "Will you be all right?"

His warm hand covered hers. "I'm fine."

"You're not alone, you know. I'm here for you." *Always. Forever.*

Ben leaned forward to kiss her. His lips were warm and soft and sweet, his kiss full of unspoken need. Jamie pulled him closer, deepening the kiss. She wanted him, but she couldn't force him to have those kinds of feelings for her. Either he had them or he didn't.

She was the first to pull away. She rose on shaking knees. "I should go. Try to get some sleep."

He nodded. "I will."

Jamie hurried out of the house and drove to the clinic, where she relieved Audrey. After checking on the Dalmatian and assuring herself he was doing well, she pulled out her phone and silently prayed that one day Ben would forgive her for what she was about to do. As much as it pained her to admit, his relationship with his daughters was more important than her relationship with him. She'd do whatever it took for them to stay together as a family. Even if she wasn't included.

Despite the late hour, Elizabeth Doyle answered after the first ring. "Jamie, hello."

Jamie didn't waste time on niceties. "I'll help you stay in touch with your granddaughters."

Chapter Fifteen

Since there was no school on Christmas Eve, Jamie took the day off to be with the girls while Ben was at work. After picking up the last of the groceries they'd need for Christmas Day, she drove the girls to her clinic. Her stomach pitched as she parked her car in front of the building, knowing she was about to betray Ben's trust.

Pushing the thought away, she got out of the car and helped the girls from their car seats.

"Let's go inside and say hello to my friends."

"Will there be puppies?" Sophie asked hopefully.

"I don't know. We'll have to see."

Inside, Lauren greeted them at the reception desk. "Hey! There's two of my favorite girls. Are you ready for Santa to visit tonight?"

"We made cookies for Santa," Bella told her.

"And we bought carrots for the reindeer at the grocery store," Sophie added. "Jamie said they get hungry flying around all night."

"Oh, dear, I hadn't thought of the reindeer," Lauren said, with a wink in Jamie's direction. "I'll have to make sure to pick up some carrots, too."

"Is Blair in today?" Jamie asked.

"No, she took the day off to cook Christmas Eve dinner for us all tonight. I told her not to make a big fuss, but she was determined to cook for her family and friends." Lauren smiled. "I know exactly how she feels. Last year I was excited to host Christmas dinner for the first time."

Jamie knew both Lauren and Blair had gone through difficult times before finding the loves of their lives. She was happy for both of them, she truly was. She only wished she could find the security and happiness they'd found.

And the love.

She remembered the way Ben had kissed her yesterday and burned from the inside out once more. She only wished she knew what it meant. Was Ben beginning to care for her, or was it only wishful thinking on her part?

After they petted Mrs. Mitchell's Shih Tzu in the waiting room, Jamie steered the girls to an empty examining room and closed the door. She pulled her tablet from her purse and booted it up.

"Would you like to say Merry Christmas to your Grandma and Grandpa?"

Sophie jumped up and down. "Yes!"

Bella was more subdued. "Are you sure we should?"

Bella had picked up on the tensions between her father and grandparents. Jamie did her best to reassure her.

"They'd like to hear from you, and I know you'd like to say hello, too. Right?"

Though she nodded, she still appeared unsure. "Will Daddy be mad?"

"Your daddy will never be mad at you. I promise."

She was sure he'd save all his ire for her.

Jamie inputted the Doyles' information, and in

seconds their faces appeared on the screen. Sophie squealed with excitement.

"Merry Christmas!"

"Merry Christmas to you, too, Sophie and Bella!"

The girls told the Doyles about Christmas preparations and about going to their Auntie Blair's house for Christmas Eve. Even Bella forgot her misgivings as she spoke to her grandparents.

"Auntie Blair says if we come to her farm over Christmas holidays, we can ride her horses."

"How exciting," Russ Doyle said. "Do you like horses, Bella?"

"Yes. I want to be a veterinarian like Jamie so I can look after horses."

Jamie's throat closed with emotion. Would she still be in Bella's life when she was a young woman graduating from veterinary college and starting a new career? The idea of being forced to leave the girls, to not see them grow up, was a dagger to her heart. When Ben discovered she was going against his wishes, parting with the children would be a distinct possibility.

She couldn't think about it now. "We have to say goodbye, girls. We need to get ready for Auntie Blair's party tonight."

The girls waved goodbye and Russ and Elizabeth blew kisses. "Thanks, Jamie. We appreciate your help."

Jamie simply nodded. "Goodbye."

"Goodbye. I hope we can talk to you again real soon."

Jamie didn't make any promises. When the opportunity presented itself, she'd set up a call. Perhaps if Ben took the job with the Sioux reservation it would keep him out of town more often.

She felt guilty for even thinking it.

She put the tablet back in her purse. "Girls, maybe it's best if we don't tell your daddy about talking to Grandma and Grandpa. Okay?"

"But you said he wouldn't be mad." Bella bit her lip, her eyes full of worry.

"I promise he won't be mad at either of you. But your daddy worries about things, and I don't want him to worry about this. Can we keep our conversation with them just between us three girls?"

She didn't like having to swear them to secrecy. It wasn't healthy for their relationship with Ben. But neither was denying them access to their mother's family.

Sophie nodded solemnly. "Okay, Jamie."

"I won't say anything to Daddy," Bella said.

The trust in their eyes nearly undid her. Getting down on her knees, she pulled them in for a hug. "Thank you, girls."

"I love you, Jamie," Sophie exclaimed.

Bella hugged her neck. "I love you, too."

Their declarations took her by surprise. She held back tears as she breathed them in, loving their sweet little girl scents, a combination of shampoo and innocence. She brought them closer and kissed them.

"And I love you. Very, very much."

****

When Ben arrived home on Christmas Eve, the house was filled with the enticing scents of sugar, cinnamon, and nutmeg. He followed his nose to the kitchen where he found the girls standing on two chairs at the counter with Jamie between them. Dozens of cookies decorated in a rainbow of colors were laid out on the kitchen table. The sight of his daughters' decorating efforts made him smile.

"More cookies? I thought you guys made a bunch of cookies already."

"Merry Christmas, Daddy!" Sophie scrambled off her chair and ran to him. He picked her up and hugged her, inhaling the cinnamon clinging to her. "We had to make more cookies for Santa."

Jamie turned to him with a sheepish smile. "And we want to take some to Garrett and Blair's tonight. Turns out we ate all the cookies we made in the last couple of weeks."

"Well, they *were* delicious." Ben kissed Sophie and set her on her feet. He went to Bella, who was pushing out the edges of what looked like pie dough with a rolling pin. "What are you making, sweetheart?"

"We're making a pecan pie for Christmas dessert tomorrow."

"Really? Pecan's my favorite."

Bella nodded solemnly, her eyes still on her task. "We know. Jamie got the recipe from Auntie Blair."

Ben turned to Jamie, who shrugged. "Blair and I got to talking about favorite Christmas foods, and she told me how your grandparents would have a Christmas in July celebration when you visited them every summer. She said your grandmother's pecan pie had always been your favorite. I asked her for the recipe."

Ben stared at the bowl of pie filling, with pecans swimming in a sweet concoction of brown sugar and butter. Since they were never allowed to spend Christmas with Everett and Anna, his grandparents had always made sure to create a celebration in the summer, complete with gifts and Christmas foods. It was one of his happiest childhood memories.

"This is my Grandma Anna's recipe?"

"It is." Jamie frowned. "I hope I do it justice. I've never made pecan pie before. Or a pie crust. You may need a chain saw to cut it."

He didn't care if the pie was totally inedible. He was touched by her efforts to make his favorite dessert.

He pulled her close and kissed her forehead. "Thank you."

She looked up at him, her blue eyes wide with surprise and pleasure. "You're welcome."

Ben brushed her cheek with gentle fingers. "You've got some flour there."

She didn't take her gaze from his. "I guess I'm a messy baker."

"I can fix it."

He kissed her cheek, tasting the remnants of flour and sugar clinging to her skin. A tremor ran through her that he felt rushing through him as well. He trailed his lips across her face, then nibbled at the corner of her mouth. Her palm flattened against his chest, and for a moment he thought she meant to push him away. Instead, her fingers curled around the fabric of his shirt, as if she were trying to bring him closer. She sighed in pleasure.

It was all the invitation he needed.

Ben kissed her. He'd kissed her before, but somehow this was different. He was more aware of her, of the way she tasted on his tongue, and how she fit perfectly against him. She opened eagerly for him, her tongue tangling with his. Her arms slid around his neck and her breasts flattened against his chest, driving him wild with need.

The sound of giggling brought him back to his senses. When he lifted his head, Bella and Sophie danced in front of them.

"Daddy and Jamie are kissing," Sophie declared.

Ben groaned and rested his forehead against Jamie's. Her laughter rippled through him, making him smile. He could always depend on her good humor.

"You're a terrible person for laughing at me," he said.

Amusement danced in her eyes. "You started it."

He grinned back at her. It was good to laugh again. And it was good to hold a beautiful woman in his arms.

His laughter soon abated. Jamie deserved a partner who could make her happy, one who could give her his whole heart. Someone who could make her understand how beautiful she was, inside and out.

Someone who deserved her.

He was afraid he wasn't that guy.

Chapter Sixteen

Once Christmas and New Year's celebrations were over, Jamie didn't have any more excuses. She had to invite her parents to Masonville to meet Ben and the girls.

She reluctantly brought up the subject with Ben one evening after the girls were in bed.

"My mother has been texting me. She and Dad want to meet you and the kids." She bit her lip in worry. "I can't put them off any longer. I'm sorry."

Ben set the tea he'd made for her on the living room coffee table and sat next to her on the sofa. "It's all right, Jamie. Really. I'm sure they just want to make sure you haven't married an unemployed deadbeat."

She groaned at Ben's attempt at humor, not because it was funny but because it was true. Her mother's texts were increasingly filled with equal notes of worry and alarm. She wanted to know what Jamie was trying to hide from them.

Jamie wasn't sure she knew herself. Maybe she wanted to avoid the criticism she was sure she'd be subjected to as soon as her parents arrived in Masonville.

And she was concerned about Ben's reaction to them. He was a man who didn't deal well with parental figures, not his own and not his former wife's. She couldn't imagine he'd get along any better with her parents.

Ben read her mind. "I promise I'll be on my best behavior, if it's what you're worried about. Your parents' opinion matters to me."

She released a relieved breath. "I appreciate it."

"Are they staying here in the house with us?"

"No, absolutely not. I'll book a hotel room in Bismarck for them." The last thing Jamie wanted was for her parents to know Ben occupied a bedroom in the basement. It would be too humiliating to confess her new husband didn't want to sleep with her.

"What's going on?" Ben asked.

Jamie looked up sharply. "What do you mean?"

"That's quite the face you just made. What are you thinking?"

Her face heated with her blush. They hadn't talked about sex, or the lack thereof, and she wasn't going to bring it up now. One problem at a time.

"I was thinking I should fill you in on the Garven family dynamic so you're not blindsided when it smacks you in the face," she lied.

"All right." Ben leaned back against the sofa cushions. "I've told you about my parents. Yours couldn't possibly be worse."

"Not worse. But still challenging." She swallowed, her throat suddenly dry. "I haven't told you about my sister."

His eyes widened. "I thought you were an only child."

"No. Lisa is two years older than me." It was her fault he didn't know. Talking about her relationship with her sister was difficult for her. But she wanted Ben to understand.

"She's beautiful." Jamie hung her head, unable to look at Ben. "I've been jealous of her since I was a teenager. It's not something I'm proud of."

"We can't always help what we feel."

"No, I guess not." His understanding helped her to continue her story. "Lisa always had boyfriends and I never did. Carson was the first real boyfriend I ever had. I know my parents tried hard not to show it, but they favored her. And I resented her.

"When she was about fifteen, Lisa started having mysterious symptoms that would come and go. Her joints would swell and ache. She'd get angry red rashes on her skin and occasionally her hair would fall out. She said the worst was the overwhelming fatigue. Some days she couldn't get out of bed. It took a couple of years of testing, but she was finally diagnosed with Lupus."

Jamie paused to reach for her teacup and drink. The warm tea soothed her dry throat.

"Was she able to get treatment?" Ben asked.

"Yes, and her health stabilized, mostly. But all I saw was my parents fussing over Lisa and totally ignoring me. I know it really wasn't that way, but at the time it's how I felt."

"You were a kid. It's understandable."

"You haven't heard the whole story."

He tightened his hold on her hand. "Tell me."

The empathy on Ben's face gave her courage. "Despite her illness, Lisa finished college and became a teacher. She married Zach and she supported them while he went to veterinary college. When he graduated, they moved back to Lewiston. Zach went into partnership with my dad in the vet clinic, and Lisa got a job teaching at the elementary school.

"Meanwhile, I met Carson at university. Our first Christmas together I was excited to bring him home to meet my family. Lisa took me aside and told me she didn't like him, and she didn't like the way he treated me. I was devastated, and angry. Her criticism made me more determined than ever to marry him."

"Not the result Lisa was hoping for, I imagine."

"Hardly. We got married a few months later." Jamie sipped her tea again, her hand shaking. "Lisa had two children in quick succession. By then Carson and I were struggling with infertility and our marriage was in trouble. I didn't understand. How could Lisa, with all her health problems, conceive and give birth so easily while I went month after month, wishing and hoping and trying, and nothing happened? I stopped going home to Lewiston because I couldn't bear to see Lisa's children or watch my parents gush over them. I rarely phoned Lisa or my mother because I didn't want to hear about how wonderful my niece and nephew were."

"Did your family know about the trouble you were having with infertility?"

"Not at first. But then my mother called me. She asked why I didn't call anymore. Was Carson giving me trouble? I lost it. I told her that since she and Dad had never approved of my marriage, they'd be very happy to know it was on the rocks because I couldn't conceive. I was defective, so they shouldn't expect any grandchildren from me."

Jamie closed her eyes and let the shame wash over her. She'd heaped all her bottled-up anger and resentment on her mother's head. Then she'd hung up the phone and didn't get in touch with her parents again until after her divorce and subsequent move to Masonville.

Jamie knew the estrangement with her family was mostly her fault. Her actions shamed her, but she couldn't get past the hurt. And now her parents wanted to visit her and her new family. She wondered if they had an ulterior motive. She wouldn't stand for any criticism of Ben or of the choices she'd made.

Ben squeezed her hand once more. "Everything will be fine. Bella and Sophie will keep your parents so busy they won't have time to be critical of you and me."

Jamie chuckled. "I hope you're right."

"Despite the problems you've had with your parents, it sounds like they want to be in your life. They want to meet your new family. It doesn't sound like they're totally indifferent, like my parents."

Jamie mulled over his observation, trying to decide how she felt about it. Even though she was wary, a tiny spark of hope flickered inside her. Perhaps her parents would finally see her for who she was instead of being blinded by Lisa's bright light.

****

Jamie's parents, Helen and Jack Garven, arrived in Masonville on a bone-chillingly cold Friday evening in mid January. Ben wasn't sure what he'd expected, but he found them to be friendly and upbeat. After removing his winter coat and boots at the front door, Dr. Garven extended his hand.

"It's good to meet you. Jamie has told us good things." He turned to Bella, who was partially tucked behind Ben. "And she told us wonderful things about you girls. I'm guessing you're Bella, since you look like the older sister. It's nice to meet you."

Bella offered a shy smile. "Are you really Jamie's dad?"

"I am. And did you know I'm an animal doctor like Jamie?"

She nodded solemnly. "Yes, Jamie told me. I want to be a veterinarian when I grow up, too."

Dr. Garven smiled. "That's wonderful. You must like animals."

Bella nodded again. "I love animals, especially Hector and Sammy and Rex."

"Are you going to be our new Grandma and Grandpa?" In typical Sophie fashion, she got straight to the point.

Mrs. Garven bent to Sophie's level. "We'd like to be. Would it be okay with you?"

Sophie thought about it for a minute. "We already have a Grandma and Grandpa. They live in Wisconsin."

"Well, I always say you can never have too many Grandmas and Grandpas. Or grandchildren."

Sophie tilted her head, pursing her lips as she gazed back at Helen Garven. Ben could practically hear her five-year-old brain thinking through this statement. Finally, she spoke.

"Okay. You can be our Grandma and Grandpa, too."

Helen grinned at her daughter, and though Jamie returned the smile, it appeared strained to Ben. Jamie had been twitchy the entire week leading up to this visit. She'd fussed over the appearance of the house, the food she planned to serve, what the girls should wear for this first meeting. She'd said her parents were disappointed in her, but it wasn't what he saw. He saw two parents working hard to reconnect with their daughter.

Ben's thoughts veered toward his own parents. They'd never attempted to reconnect, and Ben wasn't sure what he'd do if they did.

Still, it would have been nice to know they cared enough to at least try. But they didn't. It was a bitter pill to swallow. Ben pushed thoughts of Victoria and Peter Greyson away and concentrated on Jamie's parents instead.

"Please, come into the living room and sit down," he said.

Jamie made tea, and the girls helped bring cookies and spoons and napkins to the living room. Ben did his best to keep a conversation going while Jamie was occupied, talking mostly about the frigid weather that had descended on North Dakota. Finally, she sat beside him on the sofa while Sophie offered cookies to her parents and Bella carried the sugar bowl.

"I remember when you and Lisa acted as our little servers when we had company," Helen Garven said as she helped herself to a chocolate chip cookie. "Those are good memories."

Beside him, he felt Jamie stiffen. "Lisa was always better at playing hostess than I was." She cleared her throat. "How are Lisa and Zach and the kids?"

"They're well. Busy," Helen replied. Ben could tell from her smile they were delving into her favorite subject. "Todd and Shannon are both playing hockey this winter."

"Really?" Jamie said, disbelief in her voice. "I guess I still think of them as toddlers. How old are they now?"

"Seven and six," Jack answered. "You should visit them sometime. I know Lisa would like to see you."

Ben noted the slight tremor in her hands as Jamie set her teacup on the coffee table. "Yes, I guess I should."

Her father's comment hadn't sounded like a rebuke to him, but Jamie appeared to take it as one. He laced his fingers with hers. Jamie jerked her head around to look at him, clearly not expecting his support. He wondered if he should be hurt by her reaction but decided not to be. Jamie simply wasn't used to someone having her back.

Then she tightened her hold on his hand and smiled, as if trying to comfort *him*. He should have expected it. In the short time they'd been together, he'd learned caring for others was part of her DNA. It's what made her special.

I want that.

He wanted someone who cared about what happened to him, the big things, as well as the small triumphs and tribulations of everyday life. He wanted to *mean* something to someone.

Not someone. *Jamie.*

Chapter Seventeen

Jamie's parents spent the night at a hotel in Bismarck and returned on Saturday for lunch. Jamie's nerves were stretched tight. She'd been afraid of her parents' reaction to her new family and what they'd say about the speed with which she'd married. She'd also been afraid they'd realize she and Ben didn't love each other. But so far they'd been open and accepting. It was a stark contrast to the first time she'd introduced Carson to her parents. After initially greeting him warmly, they'd turned cold. The divide had never healed.

Was it possible the rift between her and her parents could begin to heal now? Jamie found herself fervently wishing for it.

After a lunch of homemade lentil soup and tuna sandwiches, Bella and Sophie helped clear the table while Ben made coffee. As Bella put the last plate in the dishwasher, Jamie touched her shoulder. "Do you want to help me put whipped cream on the pudding?"

Bella's eyes lit up. "Sure!"

She was always eager to help. Jamie didn't know if it was the age she was or if helping was simply in her nature. She could hardly wait to see the person she would grow up to be.

Would she be around long enough to see her grow up?

Jamie brought the parfait glasses along with a bowl

of whipped cream out of the fridge. Bella slid her chair to the counter and carefully put a large dollop of cream on top of each one. Jamie passed one of the glasses to Sophie.

"Set this carefully on the table, sweetheart."

"We made chocolate pudding on the stove," Sophie announced as she stepped slowly to the table. "Jamie let me stir it."

"Homemade chocolate pudding is my favorite," Helen said.

"I remember," Jamie said with a smile. "I'm using your recipe."

Helen smiled warmly. "I'm looking forward to it, Jamie."

The brief moment of connection with her mother calmed her. Maybe everything would be all right.

Once all the parfait glasses were on the table, Ben poured coffee for the adults and milk for the girls and they dug in. Jack ate a spoonful and smacked his lips.

"Delicious! And you girls made this?"

Both girls beamed. The matching chocolate rings around their mouths made Jamie smile.

"We're good cooks," Sophie said.

"You certainly are," Helen exclaimed. "What else can you cook?"

"We bake cookies with Jamie, and Daddy lets us put the vegetables in the soup pot," Bella said. "Jamie said she's going to teach us how to make fudge."

Jack winked at her. "Jamie always did have a sweet tooth."

She nodded at her father's empty parfait glass. "I think I inherited it from you."

He chuckled and Jamie joined him. It was good to

laugh with her parents. It had been a long time since they'd had anything to laugh about together.

After lunch Jamie and Ben dressed the girls in their snowsuits and sent them outside to play with the dogs and blow off some pent-up energy. When they returned to the table, Ben poured more coffee.

"Your girls are wonderful, Ben," Helen said. "They're funny and bright and just a joy to be around."

Ben looked pleased. "Thank you, but I can't take all the credit. Their mother was a wonderful person."

"Jamie told us about the girls' biological parents. Such a tragedy for the girls, especially at such a young age. They're lucky to have you."

"Actually, I think I'm the lucky one. Bella and Sophie are the best things that ever happened to me."

Jamie knew he was completely sincere, and she could tell from the way her parents nodded in agreement they realized it, too.

Ben's gaze connected with hers. "I have one more person to add to that list. Jamie is a wonderful woman and the best mother my children could ask for. I'm not a particularly religious person, but I thank God every day for bringing her into our lives."

Jamie stared at him, stunned by his words. She was touched he would say such things about her to her parents. But did he mean them?

Her mother's eyes grew misty. "We're glad you found each other. Jamie deserves some happiness."

Ben kissed Jamie's forehead as he got up to leave. "I need to work on tonight's supper."

"Do you want some help?" she asked.

"Thanks, but I've got it covered. Visit with your parents while I put the roast in the oven."

Jamie wasn't sure what to talk about with her parents. Luckily, they were happy to fill her in on the goings on in her hometown. They made her laugh with stories about people she'd known for years but hadn't seen in a long time. She and her dad traded medical stories about the animals they'd treated. To her amazement, Jamie found herself relaxing and enjoying the conversation.

A short time later, the girls came back into the house with the dogs, their little faces pink with the cold. Jamie wiped the dogs' paws while Ben helped the girls out of their snowsuits. Sophie ran to Jamie's mother as soon as she was free. "Can you play Snakes and Ladders with us?"

"Sure." Helen turned to Jack. "Grandpa, do you want to play, too?"

"You bet. Let's go."

Jamie set up the board for them in the living room, then headed to the kitchen. She pulled a knife from the drawer and started to peel the potatoes Ben had washed and left in the sink.

"You don't have to help," he said. "I can handle dinner if you'd like to spend some time with your parents."

"It's okay. I think they're busy at the moment anyway."

They went back to their work, silently standing side by side at the double sink. The sound of giggles and laughter coming from the living room made Jamie smile.

"I like your parents," Ben said quietly.

Jamie lifted her head. Ben's head was down, his gaze still focused on his work. She marvelled at the perfection of his profile, the straight nose, chiseled cheeks, beautifully sculpted lips. But he was much more than his looks.

"Thanks for what you said earlier. I'm grateful you told my parents I'm a good mother. It means a lot to me."

He turned to her. "I wasn't saying it for their benefit. I mean it."

Her breath caught in her throat as they stared at each other. Had he meant the rest too, that he thanked God for bringing her into their lives? Was he grateful she was in *his* life?

"Thank you," she whispered.

He smiled. "Whatever problems you had in the past with them, they love you. As someone who knows a thing or two about parents who don't give a crap, trust me on that."

Jamie's gaze drifted toward sounds of laughter coming from the living room. Could she have a normal, loving relationship with her parents? This weekend visit had been an improvement, but was it enough to change the experiences of a lifetime?

She turned her attention back to Ben and found he was still looking at her. What was she to make of the things he'd said? Even if he meant them, could he forgive her when he found out she and the girls were in regular contact with the Doyles? She couldn't hide the truth from him forever.

She made herself smile at him, though her throat was tight. Maybe he would understand she was doing this for him. Or maybe he wouldn't.

All she could do was enjoy this time with Ben for as long as it lasted. And hope if he left it didn't destroy her.

****

At Bella's and Sophie's request, Jamie's parents helped tuck them into bed. Jack smoothed Sophie's blankets.

"We're going back to Lewiston tomorrow morning, so we won't see you until the next time we visit," he said.

"Can I come to your house sometime?" Sophie asked.

Jack winked at Jamie. "Sure. Anytime."

Jamie smiled back at her dad, though her heart was heavy. Would Sophie have the opportunity to visit them in Lewiston? She had no idea how long she'd be living with Ben and the girls.

Jamie kissed Sophie's forehead, lingering there to drink in her sweet little girl scent. She loved Sophie and Bella and always would. No matter what happened.

After they said goodnight to Bella, Ben shut the bedroom door, and the four of them returned to the living room.

"Would anyone like tea?" Ben asked.

"I'd love some," Jack answered. "And if you add a shot of rum, even better. Dark rum, if you've got it."

Jamie answered quickly. "We don't have any rum, Dad. Sorry."

"It's okay, Jamie," Ben said. He turned to face her father. "We don't have rum, or any other alcohol in the house, because I'm a recovering alcoholic."

A shocked silence fell over the room. Finally, her father cleared his throat.

"How long have you been sober?"

"Close to six years. It was either get sober or die. I

chose to live." Ben's expression was stoic as he calmly stated the facts.

The room went quiet again as her parents absorbed the information. Anger boiled inside Jamie at the looks of shock on her parents' faces. If it came to a choice between her parents and her husband, she knew exactly where she belonged.

Jamie stood at Ben's side. "Don't you dare judge Ben. He's an amazing father, brother, and friend. He's worked hard for the life he has now, and he deserves your praise, not your condemnation."

"No one's condemning him," Jack said quietly.

Ben put his arm around her and pulled her close. "It's okay, Jamie."

It wasn't all right, not even close. Jamie held back tears. She hated having her vulnerability on full display, but she refused to look away from her parents. Only the strength in Ben's arm kept her from falling to her knees.

"I'm glad you two found each other." Helen's voice quavered, and it was obvious she was holding back tears, too. "I can see how happy you are. And I can see the respect and love between you. You never had that from Carson, Jamie. He was never good enough for you."

Jamie was shocked by her mother's words. "Mom—"

"He never treated you right. We knew it from the first time we met him. You deserved better. I admit it's a shock to hear Ben say he's a recovering alcoholic, and I won't say it doesn't concern me, but we can see you belong together. We only want you to be happy, Jamie. It's all we've ever wanted."

Her last words were said on a sob. Jamie's father put his arm around her to comfort her.

"I thought you were angry at me because I failed. I failed at being a wife and I failed at being a mother. But I especially failed at being a daughter."

Helen rose to her feet. "No, Jamie, never. We were never angry with you. And you're not a failure. You're the best daughter anyone could want."

"Oh, Mom."

Jamie stepped into her mother's open arms. She felt her father's arms close around both of them and for the first time in a very long time, she felt she belonged there.

****

The Sunday Jamie's parents left for home was brilliantly sunny and excruciatingly cold, too cold to spend much time outdoors. In the afternoon, the four of them took the dogs outside for some exercise. Even Sammy and Rex needed doggie boots to protect their feet from the cold. They spent more time getting dressed than they spent outside in the back yard.

The rest of the day passed watching TV and playing board games with the girls. Bella talked with excitement about her upcoming sleepover at a new friend's house, her first friend sleepover since moving to Masonville. Sophie argued she should be allowed to have a sleepover as well, but Ben reminded her that while Bella was away, she'd have his and Jamie's undivided attention. She immediately started planning activities for the three of them.

Jamie had been mostly silent since her parents' departure, and Ben hadn't wanted to push by hovering over her. But as the day wore on, he grew more and more concerned. Jamie smiled for his daughters, but several times he caught her staring off into space, lost in her own thoughts.

And those thoughts appeared to be hurting her. It confused and worried him, because he'd believed he'd witnessed a reconciliation between Jamie and her parents the previous evening. He'd assumed a burden would be lifted from her shoulders, but just the opposite was happening.

After the girls were asleep, Ben put on the kettle and made Jamie's favorite camomile tea. He took a tray into the living room where Jamie was reading a magazine, though he noticed she hadn't turned the page since he'd left the room. He set a cup in front of her.

"Tell me what's wrong."

Her startled gaze connected with his before she looked away. "I'm fine."

"No, you're not. Talk to me."

She shook her head. "I'm sorry."

"You don't have anything to apologize for." He sat next to her on the sofa. "Come on. You'll feel better if you talk about it."

She was silent for a long time. But then her chin began to tremble. "Why was I so stupid? I spent so much time being angry because I believed my parents loved my sister more than me. I hurt them. And I hurt myself, too. How much did I miss out on because I was so resentful?"

"Don't beat yourself up." Ben tucked a honey-colored curl behind her ear. "You couldn't help how you felt. There probably was some unintentional favoritism for your sister because of her illness, and you picked up on it."

"Maybe. How messed up am I that I was jealous of my sister for being sick?"

"It's crazy the things we can be jealous of. There was a time I was jealous of my brother and sister because my parents virtually ignored them. Having attention focused strongly on you can be a burden, too."

"I suppose you're right." She sighed again and folded her feet beneath her. "At least you've been able to maintain a strong relationship with your siblings. Lisa and I have barely spoken in five years. I doubt I'll ever be able to make things up with her."

Ben pulled her against him and held her close. A desire to protect her, to make all the bad things go away, assailed him.

It was becoming harder and harder to imagine leaving her.

Chapter Eighteen

A few days later, Ben met again with the leaders of the reservation. From a legal point of view, he found their case intriguing and interesting, and he knew he could help them reach an equitable agreement with the oil company. But he still hadn't decided whether to take their case.

Neither he nor Morley had heard anything from Olivia's parents since their Christmas visit. Ben didn't know what to make of their silence since the visit hadn't ended on the happiest of terms. Maybe they realized the girls were far too energetic for them to care for on a full-time basis. At least he hoped that was the case. Until he knew what they planned to do, he was in limbo, his heart torn in two directions. He couldn't stay in Masonville if it meant losing his girls. But the thought of leaving Jamie hurt more than he'd ever thought possible.

The following Saturday night he and Jamie and the girls drove to the farm for dinner. Blair and Garrett's friends, Alison and Chris Redwick, had volunteered to cook since Alison had a couple of days off from her job as a nurse at the hospital in Bismarck. With the busy schedules they all kept, Ben didn't get a chance to see his brother and sister as frequently as he'd like. He looked forward to the evening.

Garrett greeted them at the door. "Hey, it's great to

see you guys!"

Ben ushered Jamie and the girls inside and closed the door against the cold. "Thanks for inviting us."

"Ben!" Blair came forward and hugged his neck. "It's good to see you."

Ben held his sister at arm's length and looked into her face. She looked...happy. Happy and contented and at peace. Being madly in love with her fiancé obviously agreed with her.

He slid a glance in Jamie's direction and found her grinning back at him as if she'd had exactly the same thought. He turned his attention back to Blair and kissed her cheek.

"Good to see you, too, sis."

Jamie and Ben took their places at the old wooden table that had been a fixture in this kitchen since Ben was a child. Damon, who was living on the farm until his place could be renovated, sat next to Jamie. Garrett's sister Charlotte arrived a few minutes later and took the seat next to Damon. Garrett's parents, Robert and Grace Saunders, sat at the far end of the table. Bella and Sophie ran off to play with Alison and Chris's girls.

"I stopped in at Lauren and Cole's house, but they said they couldn't come. Piper's come down with a cold and they want to keep her home," Charlotte said.

"It's nothing serious, is it?" Grace asked. Ben knew Lauren's child, Piper, was Grace and Robert's only grandchild. As a doting grandmother, Grace was naturally concerned.

"I don't think so, Mom," Charlotte replied. "When I was there, she was playing with her toys in the living room. But she's stuffed up, and Lauren's being cautious."

Ben glanced at his brother and remembered that when Damon was about five, he'd had a cough so severe it had scared him. He'd even covered his ears. But it hadn't stopped his parents from leaving the three of them with a babysitter and going to a political fundraiser. Sometime during the evening, Damon's temperature spiked, and the frightened teenage babysitter called her mother, who in turn called an ambulance. It turned out Damon had a serious case of pneumonia. Ben came close to losing his brother that night because of his parents' indifference. The memory still enraged him.

Jamie laid her hand over his fist. Ben blinked up at her and read the unspoken question in her eyes. *You okay?*

He gave a slight nod and attempted a smile. She smiled back. No one had been able to read him like Jamie. And no one had ever offered him as much support.

As much love?

Chris and Alison called the kids, and once the four girls were settled into their places, they set the food on the table. Conversation swirled around Ben, some of it about the cold, relentless weather, but much about Blair and Garrett and Damon's new project. They planned to turn their grandparents' farm into a place of rescue and haven—for horses as well as for veterans like Chris Redwick who suffered with PTSD.

"I've been meaning to ask you about your house, Ben," Chris said.

"My house?"

"Yeah, the house you inherited from your

grandfather. Since you and your family are living at Jamie's place now, would you consider selling the one next door? Alison and I are ready for a place of our own again."

"Your house would be great," Alison said as she buttered a piece of bread for her daughter. "We'd have a place of our own, but we'd still be close to friends."

"I can't sell it right now, since Granddad's Will hasn't passed probate yet. I was only able to live there because, as executors, Morley and Garrett allowed me to."

Ben hadn't thought of selling the house. It was the last tangible connection he had to his grandparents, and the thought of letting it go was…unthinkable. It was like letting his grandparents go.

"Would you consider renting it?" Chris asked.

"You can't just leave it empty," Damon added.

Ben knew he was right. He wanted to honor his grandfather's memory, but he wasn't sure if selling or renting the house was the way to do it.

"Let me think about it," he said.

"Good. We look forward to hearing from you." Chris grinned at his wife before turning back to Ben. "But we want to let you know we'd be perfect neighbors. No wild parties, no overgrown lawns, and you'd always be able to find a babysitter within easy access."

Ben laughed. "Duly noted."

He smiled at Jamie, intending to share the joke with her. Instead of laughing as he'd expected, her expression was somber, her face pale. She quickly covered it with a smile. Ben wondered what had caused the look of distress on her face.

The rest of the evening was spent catching up on each other's news. Once the dinner dishes were cleared away, Chris and Alison served coffee and a delicious dessert of homemade chocolate cheesecake.

"Mmmm." Blair closed her eyes in bliss as she ate a forkful of cheesecake. "Are you sure you want to move, Chris? We're in no hurry to have you guys leave."

"Thanks, Blair. I know that's just the cheesecake talking, but we appreciate it anyway." Chris's grin disappeared. "My recovery wouldn't be as far along as it is without you and Garrett. Even if we move, we'll stay close by. Damon has plans for me in his project, and I want to be a part of it."

Discussion returned to the veterans' retreat. Plans had been drawn up for the building Damon had inherited from their grandfather in downtown Masonville. The upper floors would be converted to living quarters for the vets and an apartment for Damon, as well as common areas for recreation and meetings. The street level would remain commercial property, enabling the building to pay for itself with rental income. Damon already had interest in some of the spaces.

After they finished their coffee, Ben and Jamie bundled up the girls and headed home. Jamie was quiet as they drove the short distance back to Masonville. Ben told himself it was because she was listening to Bella's and Sophie's stories about their evening with their friends Chloe and Hannah. But he couldn't get her earlier look of hurt out of his mind. Had he done or said something to make her unhappy? He wanted to ask but couldn't say anything in front of the girls.

After brushing their teeth, the girls scurried off to their rooms and jumped into bed. Ben and Jamie tucked Sophie in first, kissing her goodnight and pulling the covers up to her chin. As usual, she was asleep by the time they closed her bedroom door.

Ben followed Jamie into Bella's room. She was sitting up in bed, leaning against the headboard with a worried expression on her face. Ben knew from experience it could mean anything from worry over a wrong answer on a math test to serious anxiety about fitting in at school. Ben sat on one side of her bed and Jamie sat across from him.

"What's wrong, Bella?" she asked.

"How come you and Daddy don't sleep in the same bedroom like Chloe and Hannah's mom and dad? And when I stayed at Julie's house, she said her mommy and daddy sleep in the room across the hall from her. Why does Daddy sleep in the basement?"

Ben was stunned into silence. How did he answer her? The bargain he'd made with Jamie was far too complex for an eight-year-old to understand.

He wasn't sure he understood himself.

Jamie smoothed the blankets. "All families are different, sweetheart. It doesn't matter where we sleep. Your dad and I love you and Sophie, and that's the only thing that matters."

Bella bit her lip. "But mommies and daddies sleep in the same room. My first mommy and daddy did, even when Daddy was sick. Why don't you?"

"Bella, just because your dad and I sleep in separate rooms, it doesn't mean we don't care about each other." She looked up at Ben. "We care about each other very much."

He stared into Jamie's beautiful blue eyes and suddenly knew the truth. He loved her. His feelings for her were unexpected, as if they'd risen out of the ether without warning.

Yet something about Jamie made him feel he'd been waiting for her all his life.

"Yes, Bella. Jamie and I care for each other very much. Aside from you and Sophie, there's no one I care about more."

****

Jamie was relieved Ben's words reassured Bella, but they raised a world of questions for her. Ben's conversation with Chris played again in her head. Was he hesitant to sell his house because he planned to move back there when their marriage inevitably ended?

Bella snuggled into her blankets, and Ben kissed her forehead.

"It's going to be all right. I promise. Go to sleep now."

"Goodnight, Daddy." Bella's eyes were already closed.

Jamie's heart tapped a nervous beat as they walked out of the bedroom. Ben closed the door behind him, and they stared at each other in the dim light of the hallway.

"What you said..." She swallowed, her throat so dry she could barely form words. "Did you mean what you said? About caring...for me? Or did you just say it for Bella's benefit?"

He stepped closer and cupped her cheek. "I mean it."

She looked up into his face, the air whooshing out of her chest. He surrounded her, overwhelmed her.

"Jamie, I want to be a real husband to you. I want to make love with you. Do you want that, too?"

Jamie leaned her cheek into his palm. Whatever doubts she had about their future, she no longer had the strength, or the desire, to resist him. She wanted him, even if their time together was short. No matter how things ended between them, she would have no regrets. She didn't want to waste another precious minute.

"Yes," she whispered. Her gaze connected with his. "I want to make love with you, too."

"I don't have any condoms. Are you sure?"

"I'm very sure." If she hadn't become pregnant in more than three years of trying, it wasn't likely to happen now. She'd resigned herself to the fact, to the loss, a long time ago.

Ben nodded, his expression solemn. He led her into her bedroom, closing the door behind them. When he turned to look at her, his brows were drawn together.

"I suddenly feel nervous. I don't want to let you down."

"You couldn't possibly." She inhaled, her breath ragged. "I'm nervous, too. It's been a while."

The truth was, during the last few months of their marriage, Carson hadn't touched her. She'd felt worthless. Like trash to be discarded. She wanted to be wanted again.

"Ben, would you touch me?"

His face softened, the corner of his mouth turning up the way she liked. He drew her close.

"It would be my pleasure."

His mouth descended on hers with sweet urgency. She wound her arms around his neck, giving herself over to the sensations rushing through her. He touched her body with gentle strokes as if trying to commit her shape to memory. Jamie reveled in the feel of his hands on her. It felt so good, but it wasn't enough. She wanted, needed, skin on skin.

She broke their kiss to begin unbuttoning his shirt, desire making her fingers fumble. Ben kissed her forehead.

"Slow down. We've got all night."

She looked up into his hazel eyes, and his smiling face. She wanted forever with Ben. *Please let me be with him forever.* She pulled her sweater over her head, then stretched up to wrap her arms around his neck once more.

Ben kissed her again, his tongue dancing with hers. He unhooked her bra, slid the straps down her arms, and tossed it to the floor. Then his hands were on her breasts, kneading gently, rolling the nipples between his thumb and forefingers. She gasped at the pleasure. And when he bent to take one nipple into his mouth, a shock of electricity traveled straight to her core, setting her body on fire. She gave herself over to the sensation as Ben lavished her breasts with licks and sucks and gentle nips.

"Ben, it feels so good."

He lifted his head and kissed her deeply once more. "I love touching you," he whispered. He traced kisses along her jawline. "Your skin is soft, like silk. Even softer than I imagined it would be."

She blinked up at him. "You've thought of touching me?"

He grinned as he ran his fingers through her hair. "I'd have to turn in my man card if I didn't think about making love to the beautiful woman I'm married to."

"But I'm not—"

"Don't." Ben placed a finger over her lips, stopping her protest. "Don't say you're not beautiful. I wish you could see yourself through my eyes, Jamie. Then maybe you'd understand what I see."

Tears stung her eyes, but she made herself smile. "I'll have to take your word for it."

"Yeah, you will." He cupped her face. "Will you let me make love to you?"

Even now, as she stood half-naked in front of him, he wasn't sure she wanted him. She had to leave him no doubt. This time as she unbuttoned his shirt, her hands were steady.

"Yes. I want to touch you, too, to feel your skin, to see you. I want you inside me. I *need* you inside me."

Ben's eyes glittered with passion. Without another word, they undressed each other. Ben pulled back the blankets on the bed, then surprised Jamie by lifting her in his arms as if she weighed nothing. He placed her carefully on the bed and lay beside her, bringing the blankets over them.

"What do you like, Jamie?" His voice was a honeyed whisper in the darkened room. He fondled her nipple. "I already know you like this. What else do you like?"

A tremor pulsed through her. "Anything, anywhere you want to touch me."

He trailed his hand down her abdomen, then lower to the apex of her thighs. She spread her legs to give him better access, her breath releasing in little pants.

He touched and teased the moist folds of her sex. "Do you like me touching you here?"

"Yes!" She lifted her hips, wanting him closer,

wanting more.

He inserted a finger inside her, making her gasp. "Is this what you want?"

"Yes!" She stood on the edge of her climax, shaking with need and anticipation. Almost there…

Then he curled a finger inside her, touching a knot of nerves that set off an avalanche of pleasure. Wave after wave washed over her, carrying her on a high she'd never experienced before. Ben stayed with her, his clever fingers wringing every last drop of pleasure from her body, his whispered voice both arousing and assuring. Jamie rode the waves, letting herself enjoy the ride.

Gradually, she floated back down to earth, her body boneless and completely satiated. Ben grinned down at her.

"Enjoyed that, did you?"

She couldn't muster the energy to do much more than smile. "Mmmm."

He kissed her forehead and in one quick move rolled on top of her, his erection poised at the opening to her body. He held most of his weight on his forearms.

"I hope I can last more than one stroke."

Tremors raced through his body, and for the first time Jamie realized what it cost him to hold on and wait for her to climax first. He was a generous, caring lover.

Now it was her turn to be generous.

She wrapped her legs around his waist. "We can always start over again. We've got all night, remember?"

"Yeah, I remember."

With one thrust, he slipped easily inside. He rested

his forehead against hers, holding himself steady. "God, you feel good."

"So do you." *Only you.*

Slowly, he began to move, gradually building the tempo until it rose to an intricate dance of thrusts and counterstrokes between them. The pleasure was exquisite, and Jamie found herself again on the edge of release. But she hung on to the last thread of her control, determined Ben's orgasm would happen first this time.

And when his orgasm exploded out of him with a shout, she let herself follow him.

Ben held her tightly while their heart rates slowed. Jamie clung to him and prayed their time together would be more than temporary.

Chapter Nineteen

Jamie slowly blinked her eyes open. As the fuzziness of sleep cleared, she focused on Ben lying next to her. A smile slowly spread across his face, and her heart soared in response.

"Good morning, beautiful," he said. "Did you sleep well?"

She reached for him, enjoying the contrast of hard muscles beneath the warm, smooth skin of his shoulder. "I did, very well. At least until something woke me in the middle of the night. I can't imagine what it was."

Ben rolled on top of her in one smooth move. "Was it something like this?"

His hard length aroused her. Jamie's breath hitched as she writhed beneath him.

"Exactly like this."

He kissed her, and she opened for him, loving the taste of him and the intimacy of his tongue against hers. She'd lost count of the number of times they'd made love during the night, but it didn't matter. She wanted him again.

And the miracle was he wanted her, too.

An impatient knock sounded at the door. "Jamie, I want breakfast and I can't find Daddy."

They both stilled. Ben rested his forehead against hers and groaned.

"Perfect timing."

She suppressed a laugh, then called, "I'll be out in a minute, Sophie. Go wait in the kitchen."

"Okay."

Ben buried his face against her neck and groaned again. This time Jamie couldn't stop her laughter. Happiness bubbled through her in glorious, delicious waves. She was naked, in her bed, with her husband, the most beautiful man she'd ever known.

"You think this is funny?" he said.

"No." A giggle she couldn't control shook her. "Yes. I'm sorry. I guess this is what happens when you have kids."

Ben lifted his head and looked down at her with a smile. "Yeah, it is. But I wouldn't trade it for anything."

"I know you wouldn't." Jamie tightened her arms around him. "That's why I—"

She stopped herself, realizing at the last second she was about to say, "That's why I love you." She hadn't let herself even think it, but looking back she had to acknowledge it had been there from the start.

She was in love with Ben.

"That's why you what?" he asked.

She put a light note in her voice. "That's why I'm going to get up with the girls and let you stay in bed a few minutes longer."

Ben kept his arms around her, pinning her to the bed. All traces of laughter disappeared from his face. "Tonight, after the girls are in bed, can I come here to your room again? Will you make love with me?"

Jamie raked her knuckles gently over his cheek. How could he not know how much she wanted him, how much she wanted a life with him? "Yes. I'd like that, very much."

He kissed her one last time, a long and lingering kiss that almost made her forget her stepdaughters were in the other room. Then, with a sigh, Ben slid off her. Jamie sat up reluctantly and left the bed. As she walked naked across the room to grab her robe from a hook on the back of the door, she was aware Ben watched her. She quickly slipped on the robe and tied the belt at her waist. Lifting her hand to her hair, she discovered it was as big a rat's nest as she imagined. She tried to smooth it, regretting she'd left her brush in the bathroom.

"Don't."

Jamie turned to face him, not understanding. "What?"

Ben watched her from the bed, his head propped by one arm. With the sheet partially covering the lower half of his body, he looked like a painting created by an old master. *Lover in Repose.*

"Don't try to tame your hair. You look wild and elemental, like a woman who has just been made love to, very thoroughly. You're beautiful, Jamie."

It was on the tip of her tongue to laugh off his remark, to take it as a joke because he couldn't possibly mean it. But something in his eyes stopped her. He wasn't joking or saying something he thought she wanted to hear. He actually believed it.

Jamie dropped her arms, ignoring the wildness of her hair. She wanted to tell him how much she loved him, how precious he was to her, how she cherished their first night together.

Instead, she made herself smile. "I'll put on some coffee."

He grinned the lopsided smile she loved so much. "You're my hero."

Jamie left the room, her heart beating wildly and a voice in her head singing, *I love you, I love you, I love you.*

****

Ben yawned and tried to concentrate on the Will he was writing for a client, but his thoughts were back at home, in the bedroom he'd been sharing with Jamie for the last two weeks. He'd made love to her every night, and occasionally in the mornings if they weren't interrupted by the girls. He found himself thinking about Jamie during the day, about the silkiness of her skin, her soft sighs, the way she looked at him and said his name when he entered her body. The sounds she made as she climaxed.

Every day he fell more and more in love with her.

He wanted to tell her, but the words stuck in his throat, frozen in fear. At first, he wasn't even sure what he was afraid of, what was stopping him from saying the words out loud. Then one morning at breakfast, as he watched Jamie kiss the girls good morning, it hit him. She was in the marriage for the children, not him.

She'd never made a secret of it. The only reason she'd married him was because she wanted children and couldn't have any of her own. Their marriage gave her the opportunity to be a mother, and she was amazing at it.

He wasn't blameless. He'd made her believe the sole reason he'd married her was to retain custody.

Was history repeating itself? Olivia had married him because she needed help with the children. She cared about him, but he always knew she didn't love him the way he loved her.

Ben told himself he was wrong. Jamie wouldn't

respond to his lovemaking the way she did if she didn't feel something for him that went beyond gratitude or friendship. But the insecure boy inside him, the one who had never been loved for himself, couldn't believe it.

The outer door opened and Morley entered, a gust of cold wind following him into the office.

"She's a nasty one out there." He removed his hat and coat and hung them on the hall tree near the door. Since it was Carmen's day off, the outer office was empty. "Aren't you driving to the Indian reservation today?"

"No, we decided to postpone our meeting for a day or two because of the weather."

Morley stepped into Ben's office and lowered himself into a chair. "You have to give them an answer soon. If you're not going to take their case, you need to let them look for other representation."

"I know."

"As your lawyer, I urge you to take the case. Establishing yourself here in Masonville as a member of the community will undermine any argument the Doyles might make about your instability. As your friend, I'm telling you the same thing. Forget about running. Make a life here with your children and your wife. Get to know her better and work on your marriage. It's the best thing you can do for your family and your case. And for yourself."

Ben nodded. He wanted nothing more than to make a life with Jamie. Did she want a life with him, too? At night, when they were making love, he could believe it, but in the cold light of day, he wasn't sure.

"Have you heard anything from the Doyles lately?"

Ben asked.

"No, nothing. Perhaps their silence means they were satisfied by their visit at Christmas."

Ben doubted it. They hadn't left on the happiest of terms. But the fact they hadn't moved forward in their quest for custody said something. Maybe they were impressed enough by Jamie to give them a chance to be a family.

Morley was right. The best thing for his family was to put down roots in Masonville and strengthen the bond he was building with Jamie.

"I'll take the case."

Morley smiled in satisfaction. "You've made the right decision."

Ben hoped so. The survival of his family depended on it.

****

Jamie flipped a page on her calendar as February slid into March. The changing date reminded her it had been some time since her last period. It wasn't unusual for her periods to be late or nonexistent. But for a brief moment she allowed herself to believe she could be pregnant. She pushed the hope aside. She'd been down that road before, and it only brought pain.

But she couldn't explain the nausea she'd been experiencing the last few mornings. Could it be morning sickness?

Again, she made herself tamp down the hope. She'd been crushed by disappointment too many times. She couldn't go through it again.

Her thoughts flew to Ben, as they often did. For the last five weeks, he'd kept her warm at night in their bed. He was in her thoughts all through the day, no matter what she was doing. She'd hear a piece of news and couldn't wait to tell Ben. If she had a difficult case at work, he was the person she wanted to talk to about it.

And she couldn't wait for the evenings. After they put the girls to bed, they went to her room and made love. Jamie had never felt so insatiable before, but with Ben she couldn't seem to get enough.

She was happy. She had a wonderful man in her life, a man she loved deeply and completely, a man she wanted to spend the rest of her life with. And she had two stepdaughters she couldn't love more if she'd given birth to them herself.

But there were dark shadows looming on the edges of her sunny happiness. She continued to bring the girls to her office to contact the Doyles online. Her scheme had been successful to this point. The girls' grandparents seemed happy with the arrangement and had not taken their custody suit any further. At the beginning, she believed if Ben found out what she was doing, she'd willingly suffer the consequences if it meant he and the girls remained together. But now that they'd been intimate, now that she knew what being in love with Ben was like, she was afraid of losing him. Jamie thought about coming clean and telling him the truth. But the fear of losing him kept her silent. After growing up the way he had, Ben valued honesty and truth and wouldn't accept anything less.

The other thing she hadn't been honest about was her feeling for him. She loved Ben so much she ached with it, but she was afraid to be the first to say the words. What if he didn't feel the same way? The way Ben made love to her, she knew he had to feel something for her, but was it love? The idea of laying bare her heart only to have it ripped to pieces the way it had in her first marriage prevented her from saying, "I love you."

So did the fact that Ben hadn't done anything with the house he owned next door. He could have easily rented it to Chris and Alison, but he hadn't. Was he hanging on to it for insurance, to have some place to go when he eventually left her?

The questions made her dizzy with doubt.

After work, Jamie stopped at the grocery store before going home. Ben planned to pick up the girls after school, since it was her day to work late at the clinic. As she entered the back door of the house, she called a greeting.

"Hi, I'm home."

"Jamie! Jamie!" Sophie ran toward her, her eyes wide with excitement. "Bella says Daddy doesn't sleep in the basement anymore. He sleeps in your room. Is it true?"

Jamie stared mutely at the child, unsure how to respond. Luckily, Ben was one step behind her. "Sophie, can you let Jamie take off her coat and boots before you interrogate her?"

Bella stood behind Ben, the look on her face hopeful, yet fearful, as if she was afraid the thing she most wished for would be yanked from her grasp. Bella had had the rug pulled out from under her world too many times, and Jamie wanted to reassure her this time everything would be fine.

Jamie met Ben's eyes. At least she hoped everything would be fine.

She took off her boots and hung up her coat in the

closet before walking to the kitchen. As she passed her bag of groceries to Ben, he leaned in for a hungry, lingering kiss, surprising her. When they finally broke the kiss, Jamie swayed, lightheaded.

"I think I need a cup of tea."

Ben gave her a wry grin as he filled the kettle, his voice full of amusement. "Why don't you sit at the table with the girls? They're almost finished with their homework."

"Homework" for Sophie consisted of coloring a picture while Bella worked on multiplication tables.

"What are you drawing, Sophie?" she asked.

"I'm drawing our family. See?" Sophie set the picture in front of her and pointed to the figures she'd drawn. "The tall one is Daddy and this is you."

She pointed to the stick figure with the wildly curly hair and the huge smile standing next to Ben's avatar. She noticed the figures were holding hands, and with their wide smiles they certainly looked happy. Jamie hoped it was how Sophie saw the family they'd created—happy.

"And this is Bella, and this is me," she said pointing to two yellow-haired figures wearing flower-print dresses. "Sammy and Rex are beside us, and Hector is flying around the ceiling, and the fish are in the tank right there."

"This is beautiful, Sophie." Jamie leaned over to kiss her.

As she finished quizzing Bella on her multiplication tables, Ben placed the tea on the table in front of Jamie. He took the seat across from her and the girls.

"Dinner is ready, but I thought we'd take a few

minutes to talk first."

Jamie nodded, her stomach making a nervous flip. Sophie had obviously already decided the four of them were a family, and she seemed happy about it. But Bella was a different story. She noticed things, felt things deeply. When she'd questioned why they hadn't been sharing a room before, Jamie thought it was what she wanted. But she hadn't said a word since she arrived home, making her wonder if she'd misinterpreted Bella's wishes.

"When Jamie and I married and the three of us moved into this house, she and I hadn't known each other for very long. But the more time we spent together, the more we liked each other. Eventually we decided we wanted to share a bedroom, like other moms and dads do."

Bella turned serious blue eyes to Ben. "Like Chloe and Hannah's mom and dad?"

"Yes."

"Daddy, does it mean we're staying here with Jamie?"

Jamie held her breath. From the somber expression on Bella's face, she couldn't tell if it was what she wanted.

Ben's voice was kind. "Yes, that's what it means. Are you okay with that?"

"Yes, Daddy." Bella turned to Jamie, her eyes full of relief. "I want us to stay with Jamie. I want her to be our mom."

Jamie gathered her in her arms and held her tightly. "I want to be your mom too, Bella."

Sophie wiggled her way onto to her lap and Jamie laughed as she juggled the two girls, her joy and gratitude mixing with her tears. She sent a prayer heavenward.

Please, please, please let me be a mother to these children. Please let Ben love me the way I love him.

And please let him forgive me.

Chapter Twenty

Jamie finished examining a parrot and walked with her client to the reception area. Lauren came around her desk and handed her a piece of paper.

"The school just called. They want you to call back right away. The school secretary said it was urgent. The number's on the paper."

"Urgent?"

"Yeah. The secretary wouldn't tell me what they wanted to talk to you about, but she sounded concerned."

Jamie quickly said goodbye to her client and went back to the examining room to make the call.

"Hi, this is Jamie Greyson. I'm Sophie and Bella Carruther's stepmother. I understand the school called for me."

"Yes, we did. Bella became suddenly sick to her stomach this afternoon, and I believe she's running a fever. She's complaining of a headache and muscle pain, and seems disoriented, too. Can you come for her?"

That was a long list of symptoms. And a worrying one. "I'll be right there."

She grabbed her purse and jacket from the staff break room and ran to the reception desk to talk to Lauren.

"Bella is sick. I have to pick her up from the

school." She tried to stick her arms into her jacket but kept missing the sleeves. "Damn it. What is the matter with this stupid thing?"

Lauren held her jacket and gently guided her into it. "It's okay, Jamie. Kids get sick all the time. It's probably a bad cold and she'll feel better after a couple of days of chicken soup and pampering."

"Yeah." Jamie hoped that was the case, but the secretary's comment about Bella being disoriented didn't sound like an ordinary cold. "I don't think I'll be back this afternoon. Can you reschedule my appointments?"

"For sure. I'll see if Dr. Waverly can come in to see patients this afternoon. You go take care of your kid."

With a nod, Jamie ran out the front door of the clinic to her car and was at the school in minutes. Thank God Masonville was such a small town.

She went directly to the school secretary's office, which was next door to the principal's office. They were both there when she arrived.

"Thank you for coming right away." The older woman nodded at Jamie in greeting. "I'm Principal Hardy. We tried to call your husband, as he's the only one on our contact list, but we couldn't reach him. Luckily some of our staff knew you recently married Mr. Greyson and that you work at the vet clinic."

"My husband is out of town today." Ben had left early in the morning for a meeting at the reservation. Neither of them had remembered to make her an emergency contact for the school, but Masonville being what it was, everyone knew they were together now. For the first time, she was grateful for the small town grapevine. "Where is Bella?"

"She's lying down in the sick room." The principal indicated the open door of an adjoining room. "We turned off the lights because she said the brightness hurt her eyes."

Jamie entered the room and found Bella lying on a cot, the only illumination a lamp in the corner. Bella thrashed her head from side to side, and when Jamie went down on her knees beside the cot and touched her little girl's head, it burned with fever.

"Mommy, I want Mommy," Bella cried. Her eyes were unfocused, and Jamie wasn't sure if she recognized her.

"I'm right here, baby. Daddy and I are going to look after you, and you'll feel better soon. I promise."

"Mommy, Mommy." Was Bella calling for her or for Olivia?

It didn't matter. Only her daughter's health mattered right now.

Jamie helped Bella to a sitting position, and the principal slipped on her coat. Jamie scooped her into her arms, and Principal Hardy walked beside her as they hurried to the door.

"I urge you to take Bella to the hospital in Bismarck right away. I've seen these symptoms before, and if it's what I think it is, she needs immediate medical attention."

Jamie nodded, her whole body going cold. "I will."

"Please let us know what they find out as soon as possible. We may have to take measures here at the school."

"Yes, all right." This was definitely not a common cold.

The principal helped Jamie buckle Bella into a seatbelt in the back seat of her car. Then she tore away from the curb and headed toward the highway and the nearest hospital.

****

Someone knocked on the door of the conference room and stuck her head inside.

"I'm sorry to interrupt, but there's a call on the main line from Mr. Greyson's wife, and she says it's very important."

Ben got to his feet. The cell reception on the reservation was spotty at best, making him unreachable for much of the day. If Jamie had gone through the trouble of contacting the reservation's office, something must be seriously wrong.

"I've got to take this," he told the members of the council. "Please excuse me."

They nodded, and Ben hurried out of the room, following the assistant to a phone in the outer office.

"Your wife's on line one," the assistant said, and then stepped away to give him privacy.

Ben pushed the blinking button. "Jamie? What's going on?"

"It's Bella. She's sick. I'm at the hospital in Bismarck with her."

"At the hospital? What's wrong?"

"The doctors say she has a form of bacterial meningitis. They suspected meningitis as soon as we got here, because of her symptoms, and they confirmed it with blood tests and a spinal tap."

"Dear God." He dropped into a nearby chair and clutched the phone.

"They asked me if Bella was ever vaccinated

against meningitis, and I couldn't tell them. They said they don't see this strain of meningitis in children much anymore because most kids get the vaccine when they're small. Did she get it?"

Ben hung his head. This was an area where he and Olivia had disagreed. "No, never. Olivia didn't believe in vaccinations. Neither of the girls have ever been vaccinated for any childhood diseases."

"Neither of them? For anything?" Jamie sounded incredulous. He heard her take a deep breath. "Okay, I'll let the doctors know. And the school. You and I and Sophie may need to take antibiotics as a precaution."

Ben checked his watch. It was nearly three-thirty. "Where is Sophie now?"

"I asked Blair to pick her up from school and bring her here to the hospital. They should arrive soon. If she tests positive for the meningitis bacteria, I want to make sure she's treated right away."

Ben rubbed his forehead. *Dear God, Sophie too?*

"Jamie." He cleared his dry throat and tried again. "Jamie, is Bella going to be okay?"

"We got to the hospital quickly. They've already started her on intravenous antibiotics."

It wasn't exactly the positive answer he'd been looking for, and it told him how serious the situation was. "I'll leave here right away, but it's going to take me a couple of hours to get to Bismarck."

"I know." For the first time her voice broke. "Hurry, okay?"

"I will, baby."

Ben told the council what was going on as he grabbed his laptop and papers from the conference room. They wished his family well as he was leaving and said they'd pray to the Creator for his daughter's safety.

He sincerely hoped the Creator heard their prayers.

****

Jamie sat at Bella's bedside, wearing a mask and gloves and a gown. Bella looked small and vulnerable in her hospital bed, but at least she appeared to be resting more comfortably. Her doctors had prescribed corticosteroids to prevent swelling of the brain and to ease the pain of her headache. She'd remember her stepdaughter's cries of pain as long as she lived.

"How long till we see some improvement?" she asked the nurse.

"Her temperature has gone down, so there's already a big improvement. Right now, she needs rest and fluids. It will take a few days of intravenous antibiotics to totally get rid of the meningitis bacteria."

Another nurse entered the room. "Mrs. Greyson? Your sister-in-law is here with your stepdaughter. They're asking for you."

"Yes. Thank you." Dear God, would they have to perform a lumbar puncture on Sophie to determine whether she had the disease as well? She was probably already scared being brought here to the hospital and told her sister was sick. Being poked and prodded by strangers would be terrifying for her. But they had to do what they could to keep her safe.

"I'll be back soon, sweetheart." Jamie knew Bella couldn't hear her right now, but she hoped she somehow recognized she wasn't alone. With a tired sigh, Jamie left the room. She deposited her gown and mask and gloves in the receptacles outside the isolation room and went in search of Blair and Sophie.

She found them in a waiting room on the other side of the isolation ward's locked doors. Sophie ran to her as soon as she saw her.

"Jamie!" Her cheeks were streaked with tears. "Is Bella going to die?"

Jamie scooped her into her arms and held her tight. "No, Sophie. Bella is very sick, but the doctors and nurses are looking after her, and she's going to get better soon."

"My first mommy and daddy died."

"I know, but it won't happen this time." She prayed she was telling the truth.

She sat next to Blair with Sophie on her lap. Her daughter's face was tucked into the crook of her neck.

"Sophie, you and I have to take a test to make sure we don't have what Bella has. The doctors will take some blood from our arms for the test. There will be a little poke, and it might hurt for a minute, but then it will be over. Do you think you can be brave for that long?"

Sophie nodded her head against her neck as Jamie rubbed her back.

"Good girl. The doctors will also want to give us vaccinations. That's medicine they'll give us in a needle so we don't get the nasty bug. They'll give us the needle in our arms, up here." She touched Sophie's upper arm. "It might hurt too, but it will be over quickly."

"I've had this needle, and I promise it only hurts for a minute," Blair said.

"You've been vaccinated for meningitis?" Jamie asked.

Blair nodded. "Someone I worked with in

Rochester came down with it. Everyone in the clinic was vaccinated as a precaution."

"Did anyone else in the clinic get sick?"

Blair touched her arm. "No, everyone was fine. You and Sophie and Ben will be fine, too."

Jamie nodded and hugged Sophie tighter.

Soon, a lab technician came for her and Sophie. Setting her stepdaughter on her feet, Jamie hugged Blair.

"Thank you for picking up Sophie."

Blair whispered in her ear. "It's going to be okay, Jamie. Your kids will be okay."

They have to be. Jamie squeezed her eyes shut and held Blair tighter. *They just have to be.*

Finally, she let her sister-in-law go. She took Sophie's hand and followed the technician.

They walked down a long hallway to a lab. The technician, who told Sophie her name was Gail, led them into a small cubicle and kindly explained what she was going to do. Sophie sat on Jamie's knee as Gail drew blood, and then gave her a needle. Though Sophie's chin wobbled, she didn't cry.

"Is it over now?" she asked.

Gail put a Dora-the-Explorer Band-Aid over the site of the injection on Sophie's arm.

"All done. You were a very brave girl. Now it's your mommy's turn."

Sophie put her arm around Jamie's neck. "It's okay, Jamie. It'll be over quick."

Jamie couldn't help but smile. "Good to know."

She set Sophie on her feet, and she ran off to check out the toys in a corner of the waiting room.

She rolled up her sleeve, and Gail tied a latex

tourniquet just above her elbow. After examining her veins, she inserted a needle and drew a vial of blood. Gail removed the needle and labeled the vial before turning back to Jamie.

"We administer three separate vaccines to adults. Have you ever been vaccinated for meningitis with any vaccine before?"

"No, never."

"Two of the three vaccines are perfectly safe for pregnant and lactating mothers, but we're concerned about the third, mostly because it hasn't been tested on pregnant women. So I have to ask if there's any chance you may be pregnant."

Jamie opened her mouth to say no, and then stopped, remembering the missing periods and the morning nausea. A spark of hope shone through the worry and fear.

She glanced toward Sophie and saw she was engrossed with the toys and not listening to their conversation. She turned to Gail. "I don't know. I guess it's a possibility, but definitely a longshot."

Gail smiled kindly. "Then let's find out for sure."

She tied the stretchy rubber band to her arm once more and drew another vial of blood. "This will tell us definitively in a couple of hours. I'll let you know as soon as I have the results. In the meantime, I'll give you the vaccines I know are safe."

When Gail was finished with her, Jamie sat in the waiting room and watched Sophie play. Her mind whirled. Pregnant? How?

She shook her head at herself. Of course she knew *how*. She and Ben made love nearly every night. It was the most wonderful experience of her life, and she loved Ben more each time they were together. To have his child would be a dream come true.

Looking after Sophie and Bella kept them both busy. To have a third child…

She was getting ahead of herself. She'd been disappointed in the past, many times, positive she'd been pregnant when it turned out to be nothing.

Her cell phone rang and she saw Ben was calling. "Hi. Where are you?"

"I just got to Bismarck. I should be at the hospital soon. How do I get to Bella's room?"

Jamie gave him directions and told him they'd meet him in the waiting room outside the isolation ward. "Sophie and I just got our vaccinations."

"How's Sophie doing?"

"She's a champ. Not a single tear."

"That's my girl." For a moment he was silent. She heard him draw in a breath. "And Bella?"

"Her temperature is down, so that's a good sign."

"Okay, good."

Jamie hoped he hadn't had time to search the Internet for complications of meningitis in children, the way she had. She read of hearing loss, brain damage, and learning disabilities. She hoped Bella didn't sustain any permanent damage, but if she did, they'd deal with it when the time came. Right now, she only wanted Bella to survive.

"It's going to be okay, Ben. Bella is going to be fine."

"Yeah."

Jamie heard the emotion in his one-word response, and knew he was scared.

"Ben—"

It was on the tip of her tongue to tell him her news, of the possibility of new life inside her. New life they'd created together. But she didn't know if the pregnancy was real, or how he'd react to it if it was. After all, she'd told him there was no possibility of pregnancy. She didn't want to give him anything more to worry about right now.

"Jamie?"

"I'm glad you're home."

"Me too. I'll see you soon."

Jamie ended the call and put the phone in her pocket. *I love you, Ben.*

She wished she could tell him that, too.

Chapter Twenty-One

Ben ran up the stairs two at a time, too keyed up to wait for the elevator to take him to the isolation ward on the second floor of the hospital. After a couple of hours cooped up in his car, he was relieved to finally be at Bella's side, but afraid of what he'd find when he saw her. The thought of his sweet little girl so ill, potentially on the verge of death, nearly brought him to his knees.

He pushed the fear away. He had to be strong—for Bella, and for Sophie, and especially for Jamie. For the last few hours, she'd dealt with Bella's illness on her own. She'd reacted quickly and calmly, getting her medical attention immediately. She'd relayed the information to him in a quiet, efficient manner, slipping into a crisis mindset she probably used in her job in an emergency. But he knew Jamie well enough to know she'd be terrified for Bella.

Following Jamie's directions, he made his way to the ward, forcing himself not to run down the long hallway. When he opened the door to the waiting room and Sophie saw him, she exploded out of her chair.

"Daddy! Daddy!" She ran to him and Ben picked her up and held her close. "Bella is sick."

"I know, baby. But the doctors and nurses here at the hospital will help her get better."

"Okay." She rested her head against his shoulder

and stuck her thumb into her mouth, something she hadn't done since she was three.

Ben kissed the top of her head, his eyes on Jamie. She slowly rose from her chair. From the strained smile she gave him, it was clear she was barely holding herself together. He shifted Sophie to one arm and reached his free hand out to her. Jamie grabbed it, then pressed her face against his shoulder. He held her close.

"It's going to be okay, Jamie. Everything will be okay."

She looked up at him with tear-filled eyes and a trembling smile.

"Yeah. Everything will be okay."

****

When Ben was admitted into the isolation ward, Jamie went home with Sophie. She would have liked to stay close to Bella, but Sophie needed her, too. She needed some normalcy, though nothing would be normal until Bella was home and well.

And Jamie had to admit she was dead on her feet. Until today, she'd put her recent tiredness down to the hectic pace of her life, or perhaps a touch of the flu. But now...

She put a palm over her still flat abdomen and wondered if a miracle had occurred, and she'd been too busy to notice.

"Is your tummy sick, Jamie?"

Sophie watched her with worried eyes. She was normally such an exuberant, happy child that it shocked Jamie to see her this anxious, even though she had every reason to be scared.

"No, I'm fine. What would you like for dinner?"

She shrugged. "I don't know."

"I'm not real hungry either, but you know what I'd like? Breakfast for dinner."

"What's that?"

"We'll have eggs and toast. You can help me scramble the eggs."

Sophie helped break eggs into a bowl, chattering as she did. Even though she had to fish some eggshell from the bowl, Jamie was happy to have Sophie exhibiting a facsimile of her usual spunky personality.

After buttering the toast, Jamie and Sophie took their food to the table. Jamie poured milk for them both and set her phone next to her plate, wanting it close by in case the hospital or Ben called. The phone rang just as they began eating, and when Jamie saw who was calling, she groaned out loud. In all the chaos of the day she'd forgotten the video chat she'd scheduled with the Doyles for after school.

"Hello, Mrs. Doyle."

"Hi, Jamie. We were waiting for your call. We had a chat set up for today, didn't we?"

"Yes, we did. I'm sorry." There was no easy way to tell them. "Bella got sick today. She's in the hospital. They're treating her for bacterial meningitis."

Mrs. Doyle inhaled sharply. "Oh, my God!"

"She's responding well to the treatment, and her temperature has gone down, but she'll need some time to recover. Ben's with her right now." She told her everything the doctors had told her about Bella's condition.

"We'll drive to Masonville tomorrow. If we leave early, we can get there by late afternoon."

"No, please." Bella's grandparents should be here, had every right to be at their granddaughter's side. But their presence would upset Ben, and Bella would feel the tension. Aside from that, Jamie wasn't ready for him to find out she'd been going behind his back and letting the girls talk to their grandparents. "She can't manage a lot of visitors right now. I'll keep you posted, I promise. Please."

"You're afraid of what Ben will say, aren't you?" Anger dripped off Mrs. Doyle's words.

Jamie glanced at Sophie, who'd stopped eating and was watching her intently, her brow furrowed with worry. "Sophie is here with me. Perhaps we can talk about it another day."

Mrs. Doyle sighed. "Okay, fine. I don't want to upset Sophie either. We'll stay put for now, but we are going to come at some point."

"I know. Sophie wants to talk to you."

As soon as Jamie clicked the speaker phone button, Sophie started to talk. "Grandma, Bella's in the hospital and I got a needle."

"A needle?"

Jamie broke in. "A vaccination against meningitis."

"My daughter was worried about vaccinations. She thought they did more harm than good. But perhaps if Bella had been vaccinated, she wouldn't be sick now."

"When Bella is well again, I'm going to see about getting them caught up on all their vaccinations."

"I think it's good idea."

"Does it mean I have to get more needles?" Sophie asked.

"Probably, but it will keep you from getting sick."

"Like Bella?"

"Yeah. Like Bella."

Sophie chatted with her grandmother until her

slumped posture and half-closed eyes told Jamie her little girl was exhausted. "I think we're going to have to say goodnight. Sophie needs to get ready for bed."

"Good night, girls. You'll call tomorrow, Jamie?"

"I will. I promise."

She ended the call. "Come on, sweetie. Let's clear the dishes and then run your bath."

"Can I have some bubbles tonight?"

With a grin, Jamie leaned over and kissed her. "Sure."

"You won't get sick, will you, Jamie?"

"I got the vaccine like you did. Right now, the vaccine soldiers are fighting off the bad guys inside us who are trying to make us sick."

"Will Daddy get the vaccine, too?"

"Yes, he will." Jamie would make sure of it.

"I don't want Daddy to die."

Jamie held back a sob. Sophie had experienced too much death for someone her age. "Your Daddy is very strong, sweetheart. He's not going to die."

After a quick bubble bath, Jamie dried Sophie off and tucked her into bed. Though she was tired, she took a long time to settle. Jamie read the book *Love You Forever* three times before she finally succumbed to sleep. With a tired sigh, Jamie softly closed the bedroom door and walked into the living room.

It was nearly nine p.m., too early to go to bed. She wanted to wait up for Ben and hear if there was any change in Bella's condition. But she was too tired to keep her eyes open. Maybe she could rest until he got home.

Covering herself with an afghan, she stretched out on the couch and closed her eyes.

Ringing startled her awake. Disoriented, Jamie sat up and blindly groped for her phone on the coffee table.

"Hello?"

"Mrs. Greyson? Hi, it's Gail at the hospital lab. I met you earlier today when you and your daughter were vaccinated. I drew your blood."

Jamie came instantly awake. "Yes, of course. Hello, Gail."

"I know it's late, but I thought you'd like to know. Your blood work came back positive. You're pregnant, Mrs. Greyson."

****

Ben unlocked the back door and removed his winter coat and boots, fatigue making his movements slow. The house was quiet, but lights shone from the living room. He hoped Jamie was still awake, even though it was past eleven. He wanted to talk to her, to hold her. He wanted her to tell him their kids were going to be fine.

He hesitated, trying to make sense of his feelings. It scared him how much he needed her, depended on her. He'd never wanted to be dependent on anyone ever again. He'd once needed Olivia, but she'd never needed him, at least not in the same way. But Jamie was different. She was honest and true. If she said something, she meant it.

Ben mounted the two steps leading from the landing to the kitchen and headed into the living room. The TV flickered in a corner of the room, the sound off. Jamie lay curled on her side on the couch, asleep, her hair a riot of curls spilling across the cushion.

He knelt beside her and looked into her face. The dark circles under her eyes told him he wasn't the only one who was exhausted. She'd dealt with everything while he was away, and he knew it couldn't have been easy for her. Tenderness for his wife overwhelmed him.

His wife. Though they'd begun their marriage as a sort of business transaction, each seeking a benefit from the other, it had become much more. At least for him.

He loved Jamie. He loved her kindness, her determination, even her foibles. He loved her sense of fun and spontaneity. Until Jamie, his life had been gray, though he hadn't recognized it until he saw the difference color could make. Now it bloomed with life. His body hummed with energy. He felt alive, maybe for the first time.

Ben couldn't resist one touch. He ran his finger down the petal-soft skin of her cheek. Her eyelids fluttered, then opened, and her mouth curved into a smile as her eyes focused on him.

"Ben." She breathed out his name on a sigh. Her eyes closed again. "What time is it?"

"It's late, and you're tired. Let's get you to bed."

She snuggled beneath her blanket, bringing it up to her chin. "But it's so comfy here."

Ben chuckled softly. "I know. But you'll be more comfortable in bed."

Jamie pushed herself to a seated position. Ben helped her to her feet, then pulled her into his arms. She melted into him, her cheek pressed against his chest and her arms tight around his waist.

"You should have gone to bed," he said.

"I was waiting for you, for news about Bella."

"I would have called you if something happened tonight." He tightened his hold on her, hoping to reassure her. "She's doing okay. She was awake, and a little scared, so I stayed until she fell asleep again. Don't worry, okay? We'll get through this."

Jamie's body stiffened, as if she were trying to hold her emotions inside to keep them in check. For several long moments she said nothing. Ben rubbed her back in what he hoped was a soothing pattern. She'd been a tower of strength for him today. Now it was his turn.

"If you want to cry, I'm right here, holding on to you."

Her body softened against him once more. She leaned back to look into his face, cupping his cheek with one hand. Ben squirmed under her gaze, knowing she understood his every insecurity and fear in a way no one ever had before. It was frightening to be known so well.

"Maybe we can cry together."

He rested his forehead against hers. Then, unexpectedly, the tears and anguish and fear he'd been holding inside burst out of him in a torrent of emotion he couldn't control. Jamie held him tightly.

"We'll get through this, Ben, I promise."

****

Ben left for the hospital early the next morning, while Jamie was still in bed. She dimly heard him leave their room but was too tired to say goodbye. After he left and the house was quiet again, she drifted back to sleep. In her dreams, she was running, though she didn't know what she was running to, or from. She only knew she was afraid. Then Bella appeared, reaching for her and begging for help. But before Jamie could reach her, Bella was dragged away by an unseen force. Jamie screamed and tried to run toward her, but her feet were stuck in mud that sucked her down and down until it covered her mouth and she could no longer scream.

Jamie woke suddenly, her heart racing and her breathing heavy, the terror of losing Bella fresh in her mind. She told herself it was only a dream, a product of her fears. Gradually, her heart rate slowed, and she became aware she wasn't alone. When she opened her eyes, Sophie sat next to her, watching her closely with anxious eyes.

"Did you have a bad dream, Jamie?" she asked.

She pulled Sophie close, bringing the blankets over her. "I did, but it's gone now. I don't remember it anymore."

Sophie snuggled next to her, one thumb in her mouth and her other hand tangled in Jamie's hair. "Where's Daddy?"

"He went to the hospital to be with Bella."

"Will I get sick, too?"

Jamie hesitated. She didn't want to scare Sophie, but she didn't want to lie to her either. "I don't think so. We got vaccinations, remember?"

She felt Sophie's head nod against her chest. "When will Bella come home?"

"I don't know for sure. Not till she's all better. We have to be patient and wait."

Sophie seemed satisfied with her answer. They lay cuddled quietly for several minutes until Sophie started to squirm.

"Can we have breakfast now?"

"Sure."

Sophie scrambled off the bed. Jamie sat up slowly, twisting her body to sit on the edge of the bed. A wave of nausea struck and she thought she was going to be sick, but then it passed as quickly as it arrived. Jamie cautiously stood and stepped toward the door. Her stomach was unhappy, but at least she no longer felt like throwing up.

In the kitchen she poured Sophie's favorite cereal into a bowl and added milk before letting out the dogs and feeding them. She removed the cloth cover from Hector's cage and let him fly around for some exercise. She thought about making coffee and then rejected the idea. Instead, she put bread in the toaster and had two slices of toast with butter and a glass of water.

As they ate, Jamie's thoughts wandered, even though Sophie chattered beside her. She thought of her sister Lisa. They'd been close as children but had drifted apart through their teen and adult years, mostly because of Jamie's jealousy.

She clearly remembered one conversation with her sister. Lisa had just found out she was pregnant with her first child, and she told her she kept the nausea of the first few weeks under control by eating a plain saltine cracker before even lifting her head from the pillow. *Funny the things you remember.* She'd have to put some in her night table.

Her cell phone rang, pulling her out of her reverie. She saw her parents' phone number flash on the screen.

"Hello?"

"Hello, Jamie." Her mother's voice sounded cheery. "How are you, dear?"

"Hi, Mom. I'm—" She tried to say she was fine, but the words stuck in her throat.

"Jamie? What's wrong?"

She breathed in deeply and tried again. "Bella is sick."

She told her mother the whole story, being careful not to break down in tears or express her worry too openly with Sophie listening to every word. "Ben's at the hospital with her right now."

"Okay. Your dad's here with me, and he's been listening. We're leaving for Masonville as soon as we can. We should get there later this afternoon."

"Mom, you don't have to come. What about the clinic?"

Her father answered. "Zach can look after things for a few days. Unless you don't want us to come?"

All three of them went momentarily silent. Jamie glanced at Sophie, who'd stopped eating to listen, her eyes wide and her thumb in her mouth once more. Maybe they all needed some support. "I want you to come. Please."

She longed to tell them of her pregnancy, knowing they'd be pleased for her. She wanted to confide in someone. But now wasn't the time.

"Good." Her father sounded relieved. "We should get there before dinner."

"But don't worry about cooking," her mother added. "Dad and I will pick up some food and bring it to your house. We can stay at the same hotel in Bismarck we stayed in last time. I'll see if I can get a reservation."

"No, I'd like you to stay here with us. We've got an extra room."

"Are you sure?" her mother asked.

She suddenly realized how much she missed them. How much she needed them. "Yes, I'm sure."

"Okay, then that's what we'll do."

Jamie smiled at the no-nonsense tone of her

mother's voice. It was one she remembered from childhood. "Okay."

"We'll see you this afternoon. It'll be okay, honey. Hang on."

"I will. Bye, Mom."

She disconnected the call. Sophie climbed into her lap and snuggled close once more.

"It'll be okay, honey."

Her mother's words somehow made her feel better.

Chapter Twenty-Two

While Bella slept, Ben took the opportunity to remove his disposable mask and gloves. Peeling off his hospital gown, he tossed it into a large laundry basket. He breathed a sigh of relief to get rid of the uncomfortable, hot mask and the rest of the protective clothing.

Retrieving his phone from the nurses' station, he checked his messages and found that Jamie had sent him a text.

—*My mom and dad driving to Masonville this afternoon. When I told them about Bella they wanted to come. Okay with u?*—

If her parents' presence made Jamie feel better, he was all for it.

—*I'm totally okay. Are u?*—

Her reply came a few moments later.

—*Yeah. I really want to see them. They can help look after Sophie while she's home from school.*—

—*Yeah, for sure,*— he replied.

—*I asked them to stay here at the house. Okay?*—

If Jamie had asked them to stay at the house, she must be feeling vulnerable. And scared. She was trying so hard to be strong for him. It only made him love her more.

—*Of course.*—
—*Thank you.*—

He wanted Jamie to have no doubt her parents were welcome in their home. Given his history with his own parents, it felt strange to think that way, but he had to remember all parents weren't like his.

Some of them actually gave a damn.

He texted Jamie with the latest on Bella's condition and told her he'd be home in time for dinner. He was about to sign off when another message arrived.

—I miss you.—

Ben's heart ached. He longed to tell her how much he loved her. But a text message wasn't the way he wanted to tell her.

—I miss you too. I'll be home soon, baby.—

When Bella recovered, he'd throw caution to the wind and tell Jamie how he felt. Even if she couldn't feel the same way about him, he needed to say the words.

****

Jamie pulled her Honda into the driveway and turned off the ignition. For a moment she closed her eyes and clutched the steering wheel, barely having enough energy to pull herself out of the car. Today was Bella's fifth day in the hospital, and it was beginning to take a toll, both emotionally and physically. She'd spent her morning at work looking after clients, and then after lunch switched places with Ben so he could go to work while she sat with Bella. She and Ben passed each other in hallways on their way someplace else. At night, she was usually asleep by the time he came home. She missed him desperately.

It had been a chaotic, and frightening, five days. They'd both been scared for Bella and terrified the illness might affect Sophie as well. Thankfully, she'd shown no signs of meningitis, but they kept her home from kindergarten and the babysitter in case she was a carrier and could pass the disease to other children.

Her parents' arrival in Masonville eased much of the workload. They shopped for food, prepared meals, and even looked after her animals. With her mom and dad there to help entertain and look after Sophie, Jamie was able to go to work, at least for a few hours at a time. Dr. Waverly took over many of her appointments, but he wasn't equipped to treat some of her more exotic feathered and scaled patients. For a few hours, Jamie could immerse herself in work and try to forget Bella was fighting for her life.

On the fourth day, they finally got some good news. Sophie's blood test revealed she didn't have the bacteria and was not contagious to other children. And, much to their relief, Bella was moved to a regular ward. The doctors felt she was no longer contagious, but they couldn't give them any idea when she might be released from the hospital. Meningitis was tricky, they told them. Though Bella had improved, she was still a very sick little girl. Until the bacteria totally left her body, she'd remain in the hospital undergoing treatment. No one could give them a timeline for her release.

At least they could visit without having to suit up in masks and gowns and gloves. The protective gear was hot and uncomfortable, and Jamie was glad she no longer needed to wear it. Mostly she was glad because it meant her baby would no longer be exposed to the illness.

She still hadn't told Ben she was pregnant. She'd wanted to, the first night Bella was in the hospital. But when Ben came home, he'd been worn out and worried, and she didn't want to add any more to his already overwhelmed plate.

And if she was honest with herself, she was afraid to tell him, afraid of his reaction. She'd assured Ben pregnancy was not a possibility. She'd even told him they didn't need to use birth control. He might think she'd been lying to him all along about not being able to get pregnant.

She couldn't keep the news from him much longer. Her body was already beginning to change. Her breasts were fuller and more tender, and when she looked in the mirror, she was sure she detected a tiny baby bump. She was already keeping too many secrets from Ben. She'd been keeping the Doyles appraised of Bella's condition on a daily basis. It was the only thing keeping them from coming to Masonville themselves.

She had to find a way to tell Ben that, against his wishes, she and the girls had been in touch with the Doyles. Surely, if she explained how their regular video calls had kept them from pursuing custody, he'd see she'd done the right thing.

Wouldn't he?

One problem at a time. First, she needed to tell Ben about the baby. Jamie wanted to celebrate her pregnancy, wanted to shout the news from the rooftops. Her pregnancy was a true miracle. She only hoped Ben would want to celebrate with her.

With a sigh, Jamie opened her car door and got out. As she walked to the front door, Ben pulled his car into the driveway next to hers. Seeing him made her heart lift. They hadn't had a meal together all week.

"Hi." Jamie smiled as Ben got out of the car and walked toward her. "I didn't expect to see you."

"Hi yourself." He reached for her hand. "I needed to see you. It's been a while."

He pulled her into his arms and kissed her. Jamie sighed against his lips. She missed this. She missed *them.*

How she loved this man.

When the kiss ended, Ben looped his arms loosely around her shoulders and smiled down into her face. "How was your day?"

"Busy. I treated Pedro the parrot for a bad cold and gave a boa constrictor an antibiotic injection. Bella and I played some board games this afternoon, until she got too tired. She's starting to ask when she can come home."

"What did you tell her?"

"The same thing the doctors told us. When all the nasty meningitis bacteria vacate the premises."

"I can hardly wait."

"It'll be nice to have our family all together again."

Ben rested his forehead against hers. "I've missed you."

"I've missed you, too." Maybe now, while they had a quiet moment, she could tell him about the pregnancy. "Ben—"

"Daddy! Jamie! Come in the house. Grandma says dinner is ready." Sophie stood in the open door, waving furiously.

Ben chuckled. "So much for time with my wife."

Her announcement would have to wait. "Come on, let's go inside. I'm starved."

They entered the house, and Ben lifted an excited Sophie into his arms with a laugh and hugged her close. As he kissed her and set her back on her feet, Jamie told herself Ben would surely welcome another child. He was such a kind, loving father.

Another thought struck. This would be Ben's first biological child. Her heart filled with gratitude to know she'd be able to give him this gift.

"Hey, you two," Jack said. "We didn't expect both of you home at the same time."

"Neither did I, Dad." She smiled into Ben's eyes. "But it's a nice surprise."

His return smile warmed her. "After dinner, I'll go back to the hospital for a while and read to Bella until she falls asleep."

Jamie nodded. Their time together would be short this evening, but she was determined to enjoy every moment of it.

Helen set a hot casserole dish onto a trivet. "Come and get it."

"I appreciate everything you and Jack have done for us, Helen, especially all the cooking. It's great to come home to a delicious, hot meal."

"You're more than welcome. It's what families do. They look after each other in tough times." Helen stuck a large spoon into the casserole and set a tossed salad on the table. "Enjoy."

"This is wonderful, Mom," she said. "I'm glad you came."

Helen smiled. "So are we. We're happy to help."

If any good had come from Bella's terrible illness, it was finding her way back to her parents.

****

By the time Ben got home at ten-thirty, the house was dark, the only light on the one over the front door. He slipped quietly into the house and closed the door behind him. As he walked into the kitchen to get a drink of water, he heard the low hum of the television that told him one or both of Jamie's parents was still awake downstairs. He finished his water and made his way in the dark to Sophie's room. As he opened the door, her night light illuminated her small, sweet face. Thank God Sophie hadn't contracted meningitis. He didn't think he could cope with both kids being sick at the same time. The possibility of losing them both—

Ben forced the thought from his head before it could take root.

He tucked the blankets securely around Sophie and left the room. The door to the bedroom he shared with Jamie was closed. Ben hesitated. She'd looked tired this evening, totally worn out. The stress of work, keeping Sophie occupied, and sitting with Bella at the hospital was taking a toll on her. If her folks weren't occupying the downstairs bedroom, he'd sleep there tonight and let Jamie have her rest, but it wasn't possible.

Ben quietly turned the knob and went inside. If he was careful, perhaps he wouldn't wake her.

He stripped off his clothes and slid into the bed beside her, being careful not to touch her or jostle the mattress too much. To his dismay, she sighed and rolled over to face him.

"Ben?" she asked sleepily. She set one hand on his chest, over his heart.

"Were you expecting someone else?"

He heard her throaty chuckle. "Don't want anyone else, smart guy. Just you."

Ben's heart expanded at her words. He'd never been the only one to any woman. Olivia married him, had even slept with him, but her heart belonged to Rob, even in death.

"I'm sorry I woke you. Go back to sleep." His voice was thick with the emotion racing through his veins.

"But you're here now, and we haven't made love in days." Her hand slid down his chest and past his waist. His body immediately came to life.

As much as he wanted her, she needed sleep. "Baby, you're tired."

"I'll sleep better after we make love." In one deft move she rolled on top of him, her soft breasts pressing against his chest. "Please?"

Ben stroked the silky fabric of her nightshirt, felt the warmth of her soft flesh beneath the garment, and knew he was lost. He couldn't deny her anything. Especially when he wanted it just as much.

"You're the only one I want too, Jamie."

He pulled her nightshirt over her head and tossed it to the floor, then touched her creamy skin. She was soft and beautiful. He loved her so much he ached with it. And he needed her more than he'd ever believed he could need anyone.

"I need to be inside you, Jamie."

Her uneven breathing told him she was as aroused as he was. "Yes, I need that too."

She positioned herself over him, and he slid easily inside her. She was wet and warm and welcoming.

She was his home.

Without another word they moved together, reaching higher and higher until he teetered on the edge of his climax. But he waited for Jamie to fall first. He loved watching the emotions flit across her face as he made love to her—pleasure, ecstasy, happiness. He wanted to be the man who made her feel those emotions for the rest of her life.

Jamie's body stiffened, and she gasped as her climax gripped her. She tightly closed her eyes.

"Baby, look at me."

He watched her blink open her eyes and focus on him. He imagined he saw joy and love reflected in her eyes. Love for him.

Ben let himself fall over the edge, and hoped she could see love in his eyes, too.

****

By the time Ben woke the next morning, Jamie had already left their bed. She must have been very quiet. Ben wasn't the deepest of sleepers, and any noise or movement usually woke him. The stress of the last week must have affected him more than he realized.

Making love with Jamie last night had been amazing. What he wouldn't give to drag her back to bed and feel her warmth surround him again. But muted voices coming from the kitchen, along with the smell of frying bacon, told him Sophie and Jamie's parents were already up. With a sigh, he pulled back the blankets and got out of bed.

After a quick shower, Ben dressed and joined the rest of the family in the kitchen. Sophie spotted him first, pointing at him with her fork, a piece of bacon impaled on it.

"Hi, Daddy!"

"Good morning, Sophie."

"Daddy, Grandpa says since it's Saturday, we're going to go to a movie this afternoon in Bismarck. It's my favorite movie ever." She named a popular animated kids' movie.

"It sounds like fun, but you've already seen that movie."

She pointed her fork at him again. "Yeah, but Grandma and Grandpa haven't. They want to see it."

"We'd meant to talk to you about it first, but Little Miss Excited here couldn't hold it in," Jack said with a grin. "I hope it's okay with you."

"Of course." To his shock, Ben discovered he trusted Jamie's parents. They'd come to Masonville out of concern, to help in any way they could. They didn't have an ulterior motive, unless it was to prove to Jamie they loved her. And the way they treated Sophie and Bella and accepted them as their grandchildren further endeared them to Ben.

Seeing Sophie with the Garvens made Ben think of her other grandparents. Jamie was convinced the Doyles only launched their custody suit in order to maintain contact with the girls. Maybe she was right. Maybe they only wanted to be grandparents, like the Garvens. His daughters deserved to know them the way he and his brother and sister had known their grandparents.

He'd talk to Morley soon and see if they could work something out with the Doyles.

He turned to Jamie, and as his gaze connected with hers, a zing of electricity sang through his veins. Her warm smile told him last night had been special to her, too.

She'd be pleased with his decision about the Doyles. It was the only thing they'd disagreed about. He didn't want anything coming between them any longer.

He looped his arms around her and gave her a

brief, but fervent kiss, aware of their audience.

"Did you sleep well?"

"Very well. I feel much better today."

He kissed her again and tucked a strand of hair behind her ear. "Glad to hear it. What are your plans for today?"

"I'm going into the clinic this morning. Dr. Waverly has a c-section scheduled on a cocker spaniel, and he asked me to assist."

"I'd say good luck, but I know you'll do great."

"Thanks."

For a moment they simply gazed at each other, smiling. He felt completely in tune with Jamie, as if they could read each other's minds, feel what the other was feeling. He'd never experienced such a sense of *oneness* before.

He'd never loved anyone as much as he loved Jamie. The remarkable, totally incredible thing was that he was sure she felt the same way, even though she hadn't said the words.

"Here you go, Ben." Jamie's mom set a plate of scrambled eggs, bacon, and toast before him. "There's a fruit salad on the table if you're interested. Enjoy."

"Thanks, Helen." With one last smile at Jamie, Ben took a seat beside Sophie.

With a start, he realized Sophie and Jamie's parents would be away for the afternoon, leaving the house empty. He and Jamie could have some time together alone. He looked up sharply and caught Jamie's knowing grin.

What took you so long to figure it out, Bennington?

Today. He'd tell her he loved her today. No matter what.

Chapter Twenty-Three

"Daddy, look! I get to go up the ladder."

Bella chortled with glee as she moved her playing piece up a long ladder, in what had to be their tenth game of Snakes and Ladders. Ben feigned gruffness.

"Sure, you're going up now, but there are plenty of snakes for you to ride to the basement."

"I'm going to beat you." Bella's cheeks wore a pink glow instead of the sickly pallor of the last week. Perhaps it was due to the excitement of their spirited game, but Ben wanted to believe it was because she was growing stronger.

He couldn't wait to bring his baby home.

He shook the die and cautiously moved his piece, landing on a safe spot. Bella grabbed the die, but instead of shaking it she dropped it suddenly and looked up with a wide smile.

"Grandma! Grandpa!"

Ben turned, assuming Jamie's parents were making a surprise visit. Instead, the Doyles stood in the doorway. Everything inside him turned cold.

"Bella, sweetheart." As Mrs. Doyle came forward to give Bella a hug, Ben stepped away from the bed. Mr. Doyle walked slowly into the room, his eyes narrowing as they met Ben's.

"I'm glad to see you, Grandma. I missed you."

"I missed you too, darling."

What were they doing here? How would they know Bella was sick unless...

Ben forced his voice to remain calm. "How did you know Bella was in the hospital?"

Mr. Doyle faced him, his chin lifted at a defiant angle. "Jamie told us. She thought we should know."

"We talk to Grandma and Grandpa all the time from Jamie's clinic. We do video chats with them." Bella was too happy at seeing her grandparents to be aware of the sudden tension in the room. "I've missed seeing you since I've been here."

Ben staggered back a step as a loud buzzing sounded in his ears. "How...how long have you been communicating with Jamie and the girls?"

"Since Christmas. We felt it was important to stay in touch with our granddaughters, our only family. And Jamie agreed," Mrs. Doyle said.

The words drove a stake through his chest and he couldn't breathe. Jamie lied to him. She'd gone behind his back for four months, nearly the whole time they'd been married, knowing how he felt about the Doyles. Knowing they'd threatened to take his children away from him.

Just this morning he'd thought of coming to a visitation agreement with the Doyles, but it was totally off the table now. He obviously couldn't trust them to keep their word.

And Jamie. Oh, God. *Jamie.*

The pain was overwhelming, the betrayal beyond comprehension. It hurt so much he could barely stand. How could she do this him? What else had she lied to him about?

The buzzing in his ears grew louder, making him

dizzy. He had to get out of this room before he splintered into a thousand pieces.

He carefully placed the game board on the bedside table. "We'll play again later, Bella. I have to go now."

Bella's happy smile disappeared, and Ben realized she was beginning to pick up on his distress. "Daddy?"

He had to leave before he said something in front of his daughter he'd regret. He leaned over to kiss her forehead. "I'll see you later, sweetheart."

"Bye, Daddy."

Ben hurried from the room. He concentrated on each step, carefully putting one foot in front of the other until he made it out of the hospital. By the time he reached the parking lot, shock gave way to anger. He broke into a run.

How could she do this to me? How could she blatantly lie, go behind my back?

I can never trust her again.

****

Jamie kicked off her shoes at the door, then hurried to the bedroom and stripped out of the clothes she'd worn to work. She'd jump in the shower before Ben got home. For their afternoon together, she wanted to smell of soap and sweet perfume instead of antiseptic and dog kennel.

Standing naked in front of the mirror, Jamie touched the soft swell of her belly. She'd tell Ben about the baby today. Jamie closed her eyes, imagining his reaction. He'd be surprised, of course, and perhaps concerned about raising a third child. But she *knew* Ben, knew in the end he'd be excited and thrilled and grateful to bring a new life into the world. A life they'd created together with their love.

As she slipped on her robe, she heard the front door open and close. She smiled to herself, her heart racing in anticipation. *Ben.* He was early, and as eager to meet in their bedroom as she was. Her only regret was not having her shower. Perhaps they could shower later, together. The possibility made Jamie tingle with excitement.

"Ben, I'm in the bedroom," she called.

A moment later the door flew open, but instead of anticipation in Ben's eyes she saw anger. And disgust. She took an involuntary step back.

"Guess who showed up in Bella's hospital room this morning?" She could hear the barely restrained anger in his voice.

She had a good idea. "Who?"

"The Doyles. Imagine my surprise to discover my wife and children have been communicating with them for months behind my back. Did you tell Bella and Sophie to lie to me about it?"

She tightened the tie of her robe. "I asked them not to say anything to you. They already understood you had an unreasonable dislike of their grandparents, and they didn't want to upset you."

"Unreasonable?" He gave a disbelieving laugh. "How am I being unreasonable? They threatened to take my children away!"

"Because you wouldn't let the girls talk to them. The Doyles haven't pursued their custody suit in the last few months because we've been keeping in touch. It's all they wanted. To talk to their granddaughters and to know they were happy and safe."

"I told them the girls were happy. It should have been enough for them."

Jamie shook her head. They'd been through this before, and he still didn't get it. "But it wasn't, was it? Your stubbornness is the whole reason they launched their custody suit. I tried to tell you, but you didn't want to listen. So I did what I thought was best for the girls, and for you."

"What was best for me? How is losing my children what's best for me? They're everything to me!"

She grasped his arm. "I know."

"You had no right to interfere in our lives." He shrugged her off as if he couldn't stand her touch. "You have no idea what my children mean to me. Aside from my brother and sister, they're the only family I have. They're the only people I love. I thought I loved you, too, but you've destroyed those feelings."

Jamie's breath caught. "Ben, don't say that."

"You lied to me." It was obvious nothing she said would penetrate his anger. He glanced at the bed. "What else have you lied about, Jamie? Did you pretend when we were in bed together?"

"No! Never!"

Ben shook his head. "I can't trust you. I can never trust you again. When your parents return with Sophie, she and I will move back to my house. As soon as Bella is released from the hospital, the three of us will move back to Chicago."

Shock exploded through Jamie's body. "Ben, no. Don't say that."

"I'll have someone come over to pack our things. Until we move, I don't want you to see the girls."

"Ben!"

"I can't trust you. I thought I could, but I was wrong."

His voice was hard and final. This was a different Ben from the one she'd known and loved these past months. This Ben was inflexible and uncompromising and unwilling to listen. Where the Doyles were concerned, he wore blinders that didn't allow him to see anything but danger. Jamie made one last attempt to get through to him.

"If you leave now, you'll lose everything. You're trying to hold so tight to the girls you can't see them slipping out of your grasp. Bella and Sophie won't understand you taking them away from their grandparents, or away from me. And I know you don't care right now, but you'll lose me, too."

Something flashed in his eyes, a recognition he'd heard her. But in an instant it was gone. He turned on his heel and headed for the door.

"Tell your parents to pack Sophie's things and bring her to my house as soon as they get home."

Then he was gone. She stood in the middle of the bedroom, unmoving, the slamming of the front door echoing in her ears. Jamie sank to her knees. As the grief and pain washed over her and the tears came, she vowed to protect her unborn child, no matter what.

****

After a long, exhausting evening, Sophie finally fell asleep. She'd cried for hours, kicking and screaming in anger and pain after Ben told her they would no longer be living with Jamie.

"I want Jamie," she cried. "I want my mommy!"

Hearing his baby girl say those words nearly killed him. He hadn't realized how deep the connection between Jamie and Sophie had become.

But he should have.

Had he been so blind, so starved for affection he hadn't seen she'd turned his children against him?

Ben shook his head in misery. That wasn't fair. Jamie believed she was doing the right thing for his daughters. However wrong and misguided she might have been, she cared for the girls.

God, he missed her.

Ben rose to his feet and began to pace the living room. The shock and anger was beginning to wear off, leaving only the pain. He made himself remember her betrayal, her lies of omission. He made himself remember he could never trust her again.

Knowing the trust between them was gone hurt the most of all. He'd opened up to Jamie. He'd trusted her with his children, and now he was paying for it.

He had to get out of Masonville. Moving here was a mistake. He'd thought living in a small, safe little town would appease the Doyles, but it hadn't. They wouldn't be happy until they destroyed his family. As soon as Bella was released from the hospital, they'd go back to Chicago.

Ben groaned. No matter where he went, he wouldn't outrun his memories of Jamie. Of the way she laughed. Or the way she kissed him, held him. The sounds she made when he entered her body.

Stop!

He couldn't stand it. He was going to lose his mind. He'd already lost his heart, and he was never getting it back.

His cell phone rang. When he pulled it from his back pocket and checked the screen, he groaned. The last person he wanted to talk to was his mother. Neither of his parents had contacted him since the day after his grandfather's funeral last summer, when Morley read Everett Branson's last will and testament. His mother, Victoria, Everett's only child, received a cash bequest but nothing more. He'd left the bulk of his estate, including the house Ben was currently living in, to him and his brother and sister. Victoria had been furious she hadn't inherited the entire estate.

He hit the off button to end the call. But his mother was nothing if not persistent. A few moments later his phone rang again. If Ben didn't talk to her now, she'd continue phoning until he picked up. Victoria wasn't one to take no for an answer.

His day couldn't get much worse.

He hit the talk button. "Hello, Mother."

"Hello, darling. How are you? It's been too long since we talked."

Ben wasn't in the mood for small talk, especially with her. "What do you want, Victoria?"

She signed dramatically. "Can't a mother have a nice conversation with her son, see how he's doing?"

"A normal mother, sure. Not you. What do you want?"

"All right, fine." Victoria's voice changed, losing its faux-friendly tone. "Daddy and I find ourselves short on cash. We need money. Five hundred thousand dollars."

Ben was taken aback. "Five hundred thousand! Why do you need that much money?"

"We have a few debts to settle." She sounded both defensive and disdainful. "And we need something to tide us over until my father's Will is probated. Though I should have inherited the entire estate."

Ben was grateful for his granddad's foresight. His

parents would surely have liquidated all the assets, like the farm Blair loved and the building in downtown Masonville Damon planned to turn into a retreat for veterans. Victoria and Peter's lifestyle required a steady stream of income, preferably one they didn't have to work for themselves.

"So, go ask Grandfather Greyson. He's the one with all the cash."

Victoria sniffed. "Peter's father has cut him off. The selfish old goat."

It was probably long overdue. For years his wealthy grandfather, Bennington Greyson, enabled his father's drinking by giving him money and covering up any embarrassing displays of public drunkenness. Ben knew he'd come perilously close to going down the same path as his father.

"Even if I had that much money, I wouldn't give it to you." Ben rubbed a tired hand over his face. "You and Dad need help, Mother. Go to an addictions councillor, or an AA meeting. It's all I can offer you."

"Then you leave me with no choice." Victoria's voice turned hard. "I'll contest the Will. The farm and the building in Masonville must have some value."

"Granddad's Will is ironclad. You have no basis on which to contest it."

"Your father believes we do. And you remember what a brilliant lawyer he is."

"When he's not drunk. Does he even have a license to practice law anymore?"

She ignored his jab. "Peter says we can argue that Morley Walker exerted undue influence on my father and convinced him to give me only a tiny portion of his assets. And even if we don't succeed in recovering my rightful inheritance, we can keep the Will tied up in the courts for years. No renovations can be made to the properties until ownership is determined. It would be a shame if Damon and Blair couldn't open the retreat for veterans they're so anxious to build."

Ben swore under his breath. His mother knew all his weak spots, and she went straight for them. She knew he couldn't allow any harm to come to his brother or sister.

But how did she know about their plans for the retreat? He was sure they wouldn't have told her.

"You'll have to give me time to put some cash together." Maybe he could stall long enough to come up with another option. His mind raced. What would he do if he was forced to come up with the cash? Since Granddad's Will was still in probate, he didn't own the house in Masonville yet, and couldn't sell it. He had some money put aside from the sale of his loft in Chicago, earmarked for his children's futures. But Victoria didn't give a damn. She'd never considered Bella and Sophie her grandchildren.

"Fine, but don't take too long." Her voice turned sweet once more. "You are a dear boy. I wish you'd move to St. Paul to be closer to us. We miss you, darling."

The thought of spending time with his parents sickened Ben. They only cared about him when they thought they could get something from him. When he was no longer of any use to them, they tossed him aside without a qualm.

"I'll be in touch."

Ben quickly punched the off button and threw down the phone. He swore again, barely resisting the urge to punch his fist through a wall.

He didn't think this day could get any worse, but he'd been wrong.

For the first time in over five years, the desire for a drink consumed him, calling his name with its sweet siren song. Bourbon, scotch, vodka, it didn't matter. Anything to take away the pain.

He was after all, his father's son.

Chapter Twenty-Four

Jamie dragged herself out of bed the next morning and made her way to the kitchen, though the thought of food held no appeal. But she needed to eat something for the baby's sake.

Her head pounded. Sleep had eluded her. She kept replaying yesterday over and over in her mind until she felt sick. Thank God it was her day off. She couldn't see people right now. She couldn't smile and do her job and pretend everything was all right, because it wasn't.

Yesterday had been the worst day of her life. Ben's cold dismissal, and his anger, had been awful. He'd ended their relationship without a second thought, without trying to understand her side. It hurt to know she meant so little to him.

She'd understood the risk. She'd known he'd be upset when he learned she'd been in contact with the Doyles. But she'd hoped she could make him see reason. They'd become so close, or at least she thought they had.

Jamie sat at the kitchen table and stared out the window. Sophie's cries still echoed in her ears.

"I want to stay with Jamie! I'll be good. I promise I'll be good. Please let me stay with Jamie. Mommy, Mommy, help me!"

Ben's leaving broke her heart, but Sophie's loss broke her spirit. Would Bella wonder where she was and why she didn't visit her in the hospital? Would she think she didn't love her anymore? Jamie hoped Ben didn't tell the girls lies about her. At one time she wouldn't have believed it, but now she wasn't sure.

If she didn't have the baby to consider, Jamie didn't think she could go on. The baby was the only bright spot in her life right now, the only thing keeping her sane. She'd wanted to share the news with Ben; she'd planned to tell him yesterday—before her world imploded. Ben had the right to know he was going to be a father.

Would he try to take the baby away from her?

Her whole body went cold at the thought. She rejected the idea. Ben wasn't a monster. He wouldn't take a baby away from her mother. Her pregnancy hormones must have run amok for her to even think such a thing.

Jamie took a deep breath to calm herself. Being stressed wasn't good for the baby. For the next few months she needed to focus on her child's well-being. She prayed things went well with the pregnancy. If not...

She couldn't go there or the black depression would claim her, the way it had after Carson left.

She gave a bitter laugh. By now she should be used to a man leaving her.

Jamie pushed herself to her feet. She'd keep busy. If her mind was occupied, maybe she could make it through today...and all the long, lonely days to come.

She heard footsteps coming up the stairs, and a moment later her mother entered the kitchen.

"Hi, sweetheart. Were you able to sleep at all last night?" she asked.

"A little." Having her parents witness the ugly dissolution of her marriage was humiliating. Once again, she was the screw-up, the daughter who couldn't do anything right. At least when Carson left her, she didn't have an audience.

"I'm sorry. I know how much you must be hurting."

Jamie turned away, her motions stiff. After getting bread from the fridge, she stuffed a piece into the toaster and pushed down hard on the lever.

"I could make you some eggs," her mother offered. "Or pancakes. You love pancakes."

"No, thanks, Mom. Toast is fine."

The toaster popped, and Jamie buttered the bread but left it untouched on her plate. She began to pace the small kitchen, unable to be still. She didn't know what to do with her feelings, her hurt. Her anger.

She needed something to do. A counter in the corner of the kitchen was a catchall for newspapers and other miscellaneous junk they'd been too busy to deal with since Bella's illness. Jamie sifted through newspapers, setting them in a pile to go to recycling. She found a misplaced telephone bill, as well as a newsletter from the girls' school. Jamie made herself put it on the pile with the recycling. She couldn't dwell on the what-ifs.

Her dad padded up the kitchen steps and entered the kitchen. He put his arm around her shoulders.

"Good morning. I'm going to make some coffee. Would you like some?"

Her stomach rebelled at the thought. "No, thanks."

So much junk. She found a set of keys she'd been looking for. Take-out menus, grocery lists, cards from last Christmas. Why had she kept those?

"At least drink some orange juice, Jamie." Her mother poured a glass and set it next to her on the counter. Jamie sipped some juice, then put down the glass, too engrossed in her project to stop.

From beneath the last newspaper in the pile, she pulled out a child's drawing, a naïve depiction of four stick people, wide smiles on their round faces. A gray parrot flew perilously close to the beaming sun, and two dogs, their tongues lolling happily, stood guard beside the littlest stick figure. Even the fish in the tank wore smiles.

Sophie's depiction of their family. Their happy family.

It had all been an illusion. Make-believe.

She couldn't stand it anymore. It was all gone. The beautiful, happy children. Gone. The man she'd loved, the man she still loved, God help her.

Gone.

Jamie didn't realize the low, keening sound that filled the kitchen was coming from her until her mother put her arms around her.

"I'm sorry, Jamie. I'm so sorry," she whispered.

Jamie was suddenly angry, angrier than she'd ever been in her life. She pushed away from her mother.

"Go ahead, Mom. Say it. I know you're dying to."

Helen shook her head. "Say what? What are you talking about?"

"Tell me how badly I messed up—again. Tell me how no one in our family has ever been divorced *twice*. Go ahead." She turned to face her mother, making a show of lifting her chin, even though it trembled. Her dignity hung by a fragile thread. "You want to tell me I shouldn't have rushed into marriage with Ben. I barely knew him and I only got what I deserved. I know I'm a disappointment to you. I always have been."

"That's not true. None of it is true."

"I know Lisa has always been your favorite. Lisa was the perfect child. She always did everything right. She married the right man and gave birth to two perfect children. She's beautiful, inside and out, the perfect wife and mother. All the things I'm not."

Her dad grasped her arm. "Jamie, stop."

She pushed him away. "You wish it was me who was sick instead of Lisa. You wouldn't give a damn if I died."

Her parents stared at her in stunned disbelief. Then her mother began to cry.

"How can you say that? How you can believe something so awful about us?"

Helen swayed as she made her way to the table, gripping the countertop to steady herself as she passed. She slowly lowered into a chair, and Jack sat next to her. He kept his eyes on his wife as he spoke.

"If you truly believe those things, Jamie, I guess we should leave."

Something broke inside her. If she lost her parents, she was truly alone. Completely and utterly alone. Fear and self-loathing burst inside her. Jamie ran to her mother and got down on her knees in front of her. She grasped her hands.

"I'm sorry, Mom. I'm sorry. Please forgive me."

Her mother smiled sadly through her tears. "Of course, I forgive you. I'm your mother."

Jamie laid her head in her mother's lap and wept.

****

Morley waved an envelope at Ben as he entered the office. "The Doyles have relaunched their custody suit."

He'd expected as much. The Doyles' hostility toward him at the hospital had been palpable. He didn't care what they thought of him, but their anger distressed Bella and affected her recovery.

And they'd convinced Jamie to betray him.

A voice in his head asked what exactly was so wrong about Jamie's actions. She'd only let the girls speak to Olivia's parents. He pushed aside the excuses. Jamie was his wife. She was supposed to be on his side. She was supposed to support him.

He'd lost his wife. The woman he loved.

If you really loved her, you'd forgive her. You'd build a life with her.

How could he do that when he couldn't trust her?

"What are you going to do?" Morley asked.

"I'll fight them. I won't let them take my girls away."

Morley sighed and leaned back in his chair. "I talked to Mr. Doyle. He told me they'd let their suit drop because Jamie was good about keeping them in touch with their grandchildren. They saw how fond she was of them and how much Bella and Sophie adored her. But now that she's no longer in the picture..." He gave an eloquent shrug. "They don't trust you."

"The feeling is mutual."

"Ben, for God's sake, can't you bend a little? This fight could get ugly. They'll bring up your alcoholism, dig up every drunken incident they can find and splash it all over the court. You'll be humiliated. And do you really want to expose your children to a battle like this?

They're the ones who'll get hurt."

If they hadn't all conspired against him, maybe he'd be willing to talk. But not anymore. "I can't let them take them away. They *belong* with me."

Morley shook his head. "Do you hear yourself? It's all about you and what you want. When are you going to think about what's best for the children?"

Ben stiffened. "Maybe I should think about getting a new lawyer."

"Do what you have to do, Ben." Morley removed his glasses and wiped the lens. "Until then, I'll represent you to the best of my abilities. My advice is to come to some sort of settlement with the Doyles. And for God's sake, don't run. If you do, you'll lose everything."

Ben closed his eyes. Morley's words closely echoed Jamie's. *"If you leave now, you'll lose everything... And I know you don't care right now, but you'll lose me, too."*

The office walls closed in on him. He had to get out. He needed to breathe.

He needed a drink.

Ben had never been more scared in his life.

****

Jamie gripped the warm mug of tea her father put in front of her and stared into the amber brew, shame making her unable to look at her parents.

Her mother sipped some tea and set down her cup. "There are some things we should say to you, things we probably should have said a long time ago."

Jamie braced herself for a lecture. "Go ahead."

"We're sorry."

"What?"

"We're sorry we didn't give you the attention you needed and deserved when you were growing up." Her mother's eyes glistened with tears. "Lisa was always a delicate child. She seemed to get every cold and flu going around and was always sicker than anyone else. From the time she was young we watched her closely to make sure she was eating properly and getting enough sleep. As a teenager, she hated the restrictions we put on her.

"But you were always robust, even as an infant. It was such a relief not to have to worry about you. Frankly, I couldn't bear the thought of having two children to constantly worry about, so I told myself you were okay. You were the strong one.

"When Lisa was diagnosed with Lupus, it put us over the edge. We were hypervigilant and constantly worried. You were self-sufficient and focused on your goal of being a veterinarian. We thought you were fine. But obviously we weren't paying enough attention to you, and I'm sorry for that."

Jamie sighed and bowed her head. After being a stepmother to Bella and Sophie these past few months, she was able to better understand what her parents faced. Bella's illness consumed so much of her attention and energy that she had feared she might short-change Sophie. But she truly loved the girls equally.

Would she ever see them again?

"I'm sorry, too, Mom. What I said was stupid and hurtful."

"You've had a terrible twenty-four hours. We understand."

The tears started again. "I'm sorry."

"It's all over now, Jamie," she said soothingly. "We've both made mistakes. Let's try to learn from them and move on."

Jamie wiped her eyes with the sleeve of her robe and nodded. "Yes. It's what I want, too."

Her father handed her a tissue. "Good."

As Jamie blew her nose, she made a decision. "In the spirit of building a new relationship, there's something you should know. I'm pregnant."

Her parents both stared at her, shock rendering them silent. Finally, her mother spoke.

"You're sure?"

"Yes." She told them about having the pregnancy test at the hospital when Bella was admitted. "I didn't think it was possible, so we didn't use birth control."

"Does Ben know?" Jack asked.

"No. I was going to tell him yesterday, when we were supposed to have some time alone together, but then everything fell apart." Jamie sucked in a shaky breath. "So, what do you think?"

"What do we think?" Her mother beamed. "We think it's wonderful, honey. Such a blessing. We're going to have another grandchild, Jack!"

They hugged and laughed and cried together. Jamie was grateful for her parents' support, and their love. She vowed to make this new relationship between them work. Her child would need support from Helen and Jack. Almost as much as she would.

Chapter Twenty-Five

Ben unlocked the door to his house and tossed the keys into a bowl near the door. Damon turned off the TV with the remote and rose from the couch.

"How was your meeting?" he asked.

"Fine." It helped to go to an AA meeting, to talk to people who understood the craving, and the constant struggle to stay sober. For the first time, he'd spoken in front of this new group and shared some of what he was going through—the illness of his child, the custody threat, and the dissolution of his marriage.

Acknowledging his marriage was over hurt so much he could barely breathe.

"How was Sophie?"

"She was subdued tonight and couldn't sleep. I stayed in her room with her and read a bunch of books until she finally dropped off. I think she was afraid I'd leave her as soon as she fell asleep."

Ben dropped onto the sofa. Last night Sophie had kept asking why Jamie didn't love her anymore. It broke his heart. He'd tried to explain it had nothing to do with her, that it was him and Jamie who couldn't get along, but all Sophie understood was that Jamie was gone.

Damon sat in the chair across from him. "Ben, what the hell is going on? Why have you moved back to this house?"

When he'd asked Damon to stay with Sophie, he hadn't told him the reason. "It's over. Jamie and I didn't work out." Ben rubbed his eyes. "We shouldn't have rushed into marriage."

"I'm sorry." Damon leaned forward, his elbows braced on his knees. "Tell me what happened."

"Not much to tell. She lied to me."

"What did she lie about?"

"She allowed the girls to connect with Olivia's parents through video calls. Apparently, they'd been doing it since Christmas, even though I specifically forbade her and the girls from having contact with the Doyles. She knew exactly how I felt, and she went behind my back anyway."

"Do you hear yourself?" Damon said. "You *forbade* Jamie? You don't want the girls to have contact with their grandparents? It sounds like Jamie disagreed with you and the only way she could connect the girls with their grandparents was to go behind your back because you're being totally unreasonable."

Ben exploded from his seat. "What the hell do you know? Have you ever been a parent? Do you have any idea how terrified I am about losing the girls? Jamie was my wife. She was supposed to be on my side, but she turned against me. She betrayed me, and I can never trust her again!"

"Keep your voice down. You don't want to wake Sophie. She'll be frightened if she sees you this upset."

Ben groaned and threw back his head. Sophie was already confused. He sat on the couch once more.

"I'm sorry you and the girls are going through such a terrible time right now, but maybe there's an answer. Maybe you and Jamie can talk and come to an agreement about the Doyles that satisfies both of you."

"There's nothing to talk about. As soon as Bella is out of the hospital, we're going back to Chicago." He'd decided Morley was right about one thing. Disappearing with the girls would strip them of their identities, and he couldn't do that to them. He'd have to gamble he could win a custody battle with the Doyles.

Damon sat up straighter. "You're leaving? Aren't you even going to try to work things out with Jamie?"

"No. There's no point."

"Because you don't love her?"

"Because she lied to me!" Why couldn't Damon understand?

"But do you love her?"

Ben looked away from his brother's intense gaze. But he found he couldn't lie to him. "I have…feelings for her, but I can't trust her. I have to leave."

"Ben, if you love her, don't walk away. We'll find a marriage counselor who can help you and Jamie stay together. There are mediators who can work out a custody solution between you and the Doyles. Leaving Masonville isn't your only option."

"No. The girls and I have to leave. As soon as Granddad's Will passes probate, I'm going to sell this house."

"Sell the house? Why? Maybe you'll want to come back to Masonville some day."

Ben shook his head. He could never come back to Masonville, not when Jamie lived right next door. It would be too painful.

And besides, he'd likely need the money from the sale of the house to get his mother off his back. But he couldn't tell Damon about that. He didn't want anything to interfere with Damon and Blair's plans for the farm, and he didn't want either of them to worry. Blair was finally happy and building a life with Garrett. And Damon had had enough worry to last a lifetime. He wasn't going to add to it.

"Look, Damon, I'm tired. I can't talk about this anymore."

Damon blew out a breath and got to his feet. "Fair enough, but this conversation isn't over."

"It is as far as I'm concerned."

"Why are you being so stubborn? No wonder Jamie felt she had to go behind your back."

His brother's words twisted the knife deeper into his chest. "Thanks for sitting with Sophie tonight."

Damon pulled his jacket from the closet. "Let me know when you want to go to a meeting again. I'll stay with Sophie any time."

He left the house with a quiet click of the door. Ben expelled a relieved breath. His brother drove him crazy, but he was going to miss him when he left. Blair, too.

Doubt crept into his thoughts. When they moved back to Chicago, they wouldn't have extended family close by. Or people he trusted with his girls, like Chris and Alison.

Or Jamie. Was leaving really the best decision?

Yes. Leaving was the only solution.

****

Jamie steeled herself before opening the clinic door. She'd been off work a couple of days, and she wasn't sure if her colleagues knew Ben had moved out. She hoped not. She couldn't bear the stunned looks, or the condolences.

Or in Blair's case, the recriminations. She and Blair were friends, but she was Ben's sister and bound to take his side.

Jamie let out her breath. She didn't have any choice but to suck it up and do her work.

Lauren greeted her with a smile as she looked up from the reception desk. "Hi, Jamie. Did you have a nice couple of days off?"

Aside from my world falling apart, yeah, it was great. "It was fine, thanks."

"How's Bella?"

"Getting better." She hoped it was the truth.

Jamie hurried away before Lauren could ask any more questions. She hung up her jacket in the staff room and pulled on a lab coat. With any luck she'd be too busy to talk to anyone or think about Ben and the kids.

After taking a calming breath, she headed back to the reception desk to begin her day.

Lauren gave her a file folder containing medical records. "Mrs. Lawrence is in examining room three with Potsy."

"Potsy?"

"Her new guinea pig."

She could do this. She could do the work she'd trained for and keep it together. One patient at a time. One hour at a time.

Here goes nothing.

Nodding at Lauren, Jamie opened the examining room door.

Nine hours later, she was ready to call it a day. Her wish had come true. The clinic had been hectic with scheduled appointments and urgent drop-ins, leaving no time to chat with her co-workers. There'd been no time to dwell on the turn her life had taken, either. Jamie knew this was only a short reprieve. Soon the whole staff would know the truth. She couldn't avoid it forever.

But one more day without having to publicly acknowledge her marriage was over was a blessing. Maybe tomorrow she'd be stronger.

She was about to leave when Blair entered through the front door. Since she'd been out on farm calls with Cole most of the day, it had been easy to avoid her. She gave Jamie a bright smile.

"Hi, I've been wanting to talk to you, but our paths haven't crossed all day. How's Bella? I haven't visited her today."

Jamie gave her standard response. "She's getting better."

Blair tilted her head and gazed at her with concern in her gray-green eyes. "You okay?"

Jamie forced a smile. "I'm fine."

"Is it Bella? Has something happened? Is Sophie sick now, too?"

"No, they're fine." At least Jamie hoped they were. Surely Ben would have told her if something had happened to the girls in the last two days.

"Then what's wrong?"

Jamie closed her eyes. With a sigh she grabbed Blair's arm. "Let's talk outside."

She led Blair out into the parking lot, to a spot where they wouldn't be overheard. Jamie sighed before squaring her shoulders and facing Blair.

"Ben and I have split. He's moved back into his house with Sophie."

Blair's eyes widened in shock. "What? No! You two were so good together. What happened?"

"I did something Ben couldn't forgive. It's over."

"What do you mean? What did you do?"

Jamie swallowed. "I set up online chats between the girls and Olivia's parents, against Ben's wishes. He didn't want Bella and Sophie to have anything to do with them."

Blair stared at her. "That's the terrible thing you did? He told Damon and me they were threatening to sue for custody, but do you mean Ben doesn't want his kids to know their grandparents at all?"

"Yes. The Doyles decided to go the legal route because Ben wouldn't allow them any access to the girls."

"That idiot." Blair shook her head. "Why is he doing this?"

"Don't be angry with him. Please." Ben was going to need his family now more than ever. "He's scared."

Blair sighed. "Yeah, I guess he is. Has he told you anything about our parents, and how we grew up?"

"Some. I know he didn't have an easy childhood. Your parents, especially your mother, put a lot of pressure on him. It contributed to his alcoholism."

"I'm glad he told you." She shook her head. "But not allowing his kids to know their own grandparents doesn't make sense. Especially since our relationship with our grandparents was so precious to us. He should realize how precious it is to Bella and Sophie, too."

"He's afraid of losing them." Jamie's voice cracked. "But I'm worried the more he fights, the more likely it is to happen."

Blair pulled her into a hug. "Oh, honey, I'm sorry."

Jamie clung to her, trying not to cry. In a way, it was good to talk. Holding her horrible secret inside was eating her up. Finally, she pulled away.

"I should get home. My folks are still at my house, and they'll be wondering where I am."

Blair nodded and wiped a tear from the corner of her eye. "Yeah. I should get home, too. I'm sorry, Jamie."

With one last wave, Blair walked to her truck and drove away. Jamie got into her car and slowly drove home.

In a few minutes, she pulled into her driveway. As she got out of her car, Ben drove up to his house. She tried to hurry inside, not wanting to talk to him. But Ben wasn't alone. Sophie shot out of the car and ran toward her.

"Jamie! Jamie!"

Sophie wrapped her arms around Jamie's leg. Jamie wanted to lift her in her arms and hold her tight, but she knew Ben wouldn't like it if she did. In this moment she hated him for his stubbornness, his inflexibility.

She gently peeled the little girl's fingers from her leg. "Sophie, honey, you have to go with your daddy."

"No, I want to stay with you!" Sophie began to sob. "I'm sorry I was bad. I promise I'll be good if I can live with you again."

Jamie couldn't stop the tears. She bent over Sophie, holding her as close as she dared. "You did nothing wrong. You're the best little girl in the world. Don't ever forget it. But your daddy and I aren't living in the same house anymore so we can't be together. I'm sorry, Sophie."

Through her tears Jamie was aware of her parents standing beside her. Ben was also there, his face expressionless. He reached for Sophie.

"Come on, Sophie. We need to go to our house."

She hit him with her small fists. "No! I want to go with Jamie. I want my Mommy!"

The pain nearly brought Jamie to her knees. She was never going to be Sophie's mommy again.

Her eyes met Ben's for a split second.

"I'm sorry," he whispered.

He lifted Sophie in his arms and despite her flailing limbs and anguished cries, he carried her away. A moment later he unlocked the door to his house and went inside. The sudden silence was deafening.

Jamie stood frozen. *Oh, Sophie. My poor baby.*

Her father put his arm around her shoulders. "Come on, Jamie. Let's go inside."

Helen opened the door while Jack led her inside. Jamie was numb with grief and shock and pain. This was all her fault. She'd thought she could have it all—a loving husband, children. She should have known better.

Her mother helped her remove her coat and boots. "I'll make some tea."

"Let's sit on the couch," Jack said.

Jamie let herself be guided to the couch. She sat and stared straight ahead. Funny how when you were really hurting you were too numb to feel anything.

Jack sat beside her and held her hand. "Your mom and I have been thinking about something, and we want to run it by you."

Her mother arrived with a tray of tea and set it on the coffee table. Jamie turned to look at her dad but said nothing.

"Why don't you come home with us for a while? At least until things settle down."

Jamie shook her head. "I can't. My job, my pets."

"Talk to the people at work and ask for leave. I'm sure they'll be understanding. We can take the dogs and Hector with us. The fish tank will have to stay, but with the automatic feeder they'll be fine. I can run back here in a few days to clean the tank and check on the house."

"I don't know."

"With Ben and the girls next door, you're bound to run into them again," Helen said. "We can't have a repeat of the heartache we just witnessed."

"No. I don't want Sophie to be upset again."

"Or you. You have the baby to think of."

"Yes." She had to keep her baby safe.

"If you like," her father said, "I can talk to the people at your clinic for you."

"Thanks, Dad, but no. They deserve to hear it from me."

Her parents were right. She couldn't stay here and expose Sophie to potential trauma on a daily basis. She rose to her feet. "I'll call Cole and Lauren."

Jamie trembled as she scrolled through her contacts to find Cole's cell phone number. He answered after a couple of rings.

"Hey, Jamie. What's up?"

Her throat went dry. She swallowed before she could speak. "I have something I need to tell you. Something important."

"Okay." Cole's voice turned serious. "What's going on?"

"Ben and I have split, and I need to leave town for

a while. I'll be staying with my parents. But I don't know for how long."

"Listen, Lauren is right here. Do you mind if I tell her what's going on?"

"No, go ahead."

Cole put the call on speaker phone and repeated what Jamie had said. Lauren inhaled sharply. "Oh, Jamie, I'm sorry. Are you all right?"

No, I'm not all right at all. The man I love doesn't want me. "I'm fine. I'm sorry to put you in a predicament like this. If you want me to resign so you can hire someone new right away, I will."

"No, we don't want you to do that," Lauren said.

"Absolutely not." Cole's voice was firm. "Take whatever time you need. We'll hire a locum vet to fill in for a while, and when you're ready to come back, your job will be waiting for you."

Jamie held back tears, her voice quivering. "Thank you. I appreciate your understanding."

"Take care of yourself, Jamie," Lauren said. "Keep in touch, okay?"

Jamie disconnected the call and released a ragged breath before turning to face her parents.

"How soon do you think we can go?"

"If you pack your things tonight, there's no reason we can't leave first thing in the morning," her father said.

Jamie nodded. The sooner she got out of Masonville, the better.

Chapter Twenty-Six

At noon, Damon and Blair arrived unannounced at Ben's law office just as Morley and Carmen were about to go for lunch.

"We need to talk to you," Blair said. Ben rarely saw his sister as angry as she now appeared. He closed his eyes in misery. It probably meant Jamie had told her he'd moved out. He wondered what else she'd told her about him. Likely, that he was the scum of the earth.

And she wouldn't be wrong.

Damon turned to Morley and Carmen. "Would you mind giving us a few moments?"

"Not at all. Maybe you can talk some sense into him. I certainly haven't been able to." Morley slipped on his jacket. "Come on, Carmen. I'll buy lunch."

As soon as they left the office, Blair lit into him. "What is wrong with you?"

"It's nice to see you, too, Blair." He was too tired to play games. "Say what you want to say and get it over with."

"Jamie's left town. And it's your fault."

The news caught him off guard. "What do you mean, she's left?"

"She called Cole and Lauren last night and asked for a leave. They said she sounded upset."

Last night. After Sophie's meltdown. Sophie cried herself to sleep again last night. She didn't understand why she couldn't be with Jamie anymore. He hadn't told Bella about the breakup. He was afraid the news would affect her recovery, but she was already asking why Jamie didn't come to see her. He couldn't put off telling her much longer.

"There was an…an incident yesterday afternoon." He told them about arriving home at the same time as Jamie and how Sophie reacted.

"It sounds like Jamie is trying to get out of your way to avoid upsetting Sophie again," Damon remarked.

He couldn't deny she cared for his daughters. "Did she say where she was going?"

"She's staying with her parents for a while." Blair shook her head. "I don't get it. She told me you left her because she let the girls talk to Olivia's parents. She only did it to keep them from seeking custody. Why are you being so hard on her?"

"She knew how I felt and she let the girls talk to them anyway. She should have respected my wishes."

"Jamie understood keeping them apart wasn't right." Damon shook his head. "You're fighting to control the situation, but you can't control the love between your daughters and their grandparents. You shouldn't even try."

Anger swelled in Ben's gut at the look of disappointment in his brother's eyes. "I can't believe you're taking her side. You're my family!"

"Jamie told me not to be angry with you." Blair's eyes were shiny with tears. "But I'm having a hard time with that right now."

His sister's words hit hard. Jamie could have spoken harshly about him, but instead she'd defended him.

Doubt crept into his thoughts. Had he done the right thing by leaving her?

He sat up taller. How could he live with someone he didn't trust? He pushed to his feet.

"I have to go. I want to visit Bella over the lunch hour." The Doyles were still in town and likely would stay as long as Bella was in the hospital. By silent mutual agreement they were usually gone over the noon hour, allowing Ben to visit Bella without having to see them.

"We'll go with you," Damon said. "We can have lunch together after."

The thought of lunch held no appeal. He hadn't been able to eat much in the last couple of days. "I can't go to lunch. I have an errand to run, after the hospital."

"We'll come with you," Blair said. "We can help you pick up groceries, or whatever you need."

"No." His voice came out sharper than he'd intended. He was meeting Chris and Alison Redwick to show them his house. Chris had sounded excited when he talked to him on the phone about renting it to them. "I appreciate the offer, but I'm fine."

"You're not alone, you know," Damon said. "We're here for you."

Ben nodded. He appreciated their support, but he didn't want to upset them with the knowledge that their mother was threatening their plans for the retreat. And he didn't want them to know how much Jamie's betrayal had destroyed him. There was nothing they could do to help him. He was on his own.

****

Alison Redwick turned slowly in a circle as she

examined Ben's kitchen. "I like it. It's not a huge house, but it's got all the room the four of us will need. I think we should take Ben up on his offer and rent this house, Chris."

Chris put an arm around his wife's shoulders. "I think so too."

They shared a grin and a moment of perfect harmony. Ben turned away. He'd had that once with Jamie. Or at least he'd thought so. But now it was gone. He rubbed at a sudden ache in his chest and cleared his throat.

"I'll need some time to clear out the house. If it's okay with you, I can draw up a rental agreement with a rent-to-own clause."

"Sounds good," Chris agreed.

"I'm excited," Alison said. "I've loved living on the farm, but it's going to be nice to have our own place again."

"The great thing is our friends will still be close by."

"And we'll be neighbors to Ben and Jamie." Alison turned to Ben with excitement in her eyes. "Our girls are going to be thrilled when we tell them we're moving next door to Sophie and Bella."

Ben cleared his throat again. "I'm sorry. I thought you knew."

"Knew what?"

"Jamie and I have split. The girls and I will be moving back to Chicago." It didn't get any easier to talk about. If only Jamie had respected his wishes, they could have been happy together.

"Oh, Ben, I'm sorry."

"Sophie and I have been living here for the last

couple of days. Once Bella is released from the hospital, we'll start packing up. We'll be out within thirty days."

"If you need more time, it's no problem. I know your sister won't mind if we stay at the farm a few days longer," Chris said.

"Thanks, but we should be fine."

Ben's online search for rental accommodations in Chicago hadn't yet found something suitable. He'd searched for a new job as well and had sent out a couple of resumes.

Is it fair to Sophie and Bella to tear them away from family, from friends like Alison and Chris and their girls?

He had to stop that line of thinking. It was better for all of them, including Jamie, if they moved.

"So, we have a deal?" he asked.

Alison and Chris looked at one another again. "Yes, absolutely."

"All right. I'll get the paperwork together."

After Chris and Alison left, Ben wandered around the house. Though he hadn't lived in the house long, memories screamed at him from every corner. The house reminded him of his grandparents and the love they'd lavished on him. Without his grandparents, what would his childhood have been like?

He knew the answer. It would have been miserable. Loveless. Unhappy.

Then why are you trying to separate your children from their grandparents? Don't they deserve to have a special relationship with their grandparents like you had with yours?

Ben walked into his bedroom and opened the top

drawer of his dresser. He pulled out the small box he'd stashed there. Flipping open the lid, he stared at the wedding ring Jamie had given him. God, he missed her. Regrets and memories and if-onlys swirled in his brain until he was dizzy.

His grandfather had always treated Grandma Anna like something precious. He never would have left her, no matter what she'd done. Their lives weren't always easy, and Ben knew they sometimes disagreed, especially about his mother, but neither of them walked away.

The way he had.

How long until he didn't miss Jamie anymore? How long until he could tell himself he no longer loved her?

He didn't have an answer.

****

Jamie listened to the breath sounds in the chest of a Pomeranian. The heartrate of the tiny bundle of fur accelerated as she continued her examination, but it was only to be expected. A visit to the vet's office wasn't a high point in any dog's day.

She removed the stethoscope from her ears. "Bitsy's chest sounds fine, Mrs. Thompson. We'll take some blood and check for heartworm. Once we get her set up with her annual flea-and-tick medication, you'll be all set to go."

"Thanks, Jamie." The older woman grinned. "I suppose I should call you Dr. Garven, but it seems strange to call someone I've known since infancy 'doctor.' "

" 'Jamie' is just fine."

"Your parents used to bring you in here when you

were a baby. That was at least four dogs ago, and your father and then your brother-in-law have looked after each one. And now it's your turn."

"My stay is temporary, Mrs. Thompson, but I'm happy to treat Bitsy while I'm here."

Jamie needed to keep busy while she was in Lewiston, and since the clinic was down a vet there was plenty of work.

Mrs. Thompson scooped the Pomeranian from the examining table. "It was lovely to see you again. How long are you planning to stay in Lewiston?"

Jamie knew speculation about her in her hometown was rampant. They wanted to know why she'd suddenly shown up. She'd even heard a rumor she'd come home to marry a widowed farmer in the area, a man she'd never met. What the small-town grapevine couldn't verify it made up.

"I'm helping out through flea-and-tick season." The season usually lasted into June.

"Well, it's lovely to have you here, Jamie. I hope to see you around town."

Jamie only smiled. Aside from helping out at the clinic and walking her dogs, she'd stuck close to her parents' home in the last week. Outside of the confines of the clinic, she didn't want to talk to people, didn't want to have to answer their curious questions.

She'd have to leave before she started to show, or the gossip mill would work overtime.

After delivering Bitsy to the techs in the lab, Jamie took a quick break to use the washroom. She'd been doing that a lot, but she was okay with it since it was one of the side effects of a normal pregnancy. On her arrival in Lewiston, she'd visited a doctor, and was assured her pregnancy was proceeding as it should. However, the doctor told her she needed to be monitored closely. Her history with Polycystic Ovarian Syndrome meant she could have complications.

As she looked at herself in the mirror, she pulled the chain she wore around her neck from beneath her T-shirt. The evening before she left Masonville, she'd attached her wedding ring to the gold chain. She'd worn it close to her heart every day since. Though the ring reminded her of what she'd lost, she couldn't make herself put it away.

The four diamonds that had been such a happy symbol of their family mocked her now. Jamie sighed and tucked the chain and the ring under her clothes again.

When she left the washroom and rounded a corner, she ran into her brother-in-law, Zach.

"Oh, I'm sorry."

Zach grinned. "No problem. I should watch where I'm going."

Jamie attempted to go around him, but Zach touched her arm. "Can we talk?"

"Sure. Do you have an exotic you want a consult on?"

"Let's take a break and walk outside."

She glanced toward the waiting room. "I've got clients waiting."

"So do I, but I promise we won't be long."

The clinic was located on the outskirts of Lewiston, away from the residential area of town. They walked a short distance down the gravel road that passed the clinic, to an area where they couldn't be seen from the building.

"Lisa would like to see you. She wonders why you haven't called or visited since you've been in Lewiston."

"I've been busy."

Zach raised an eyebrow but didn't say anything. She *had* been busy since she got to Lewiston, but they both knew it wasn't the reason she hadn't gone to see her sister. Jamie sighed.

"Okay, fine. I've been avoiding Lisa."

"Why?"

For the same reasons she'd avoided her sister for years. Embarrassment, jealousy, shame. She could now add guilt to the list.

Despite her illness, Lisa accomplished so much. She had a strong marriage, two beautiful kids, and a successful career as a teacher. Her mother told her Lisa volunteered with a support group for people with Lupus. She never let her illness stop her from doing anything. Jamie felt totally inadequate next to her.

Jamie stared at her shoes, noting the dust from the gravel road settling on them. "Because once again my life is in the toilet and I don't need to be reminded that Lisa's life is perfect."

"Trust me, Lisa's life isn't perfect," Zach said. "Lupus is hardly a piece of cake."

"I know."

"Are you sure about that? Did your mom and dad tell you how sick Lisa was before Christmas? We nearly lost her."

"What?" Jamie lifted her head to stare at Zach. "What happened?"

"She developed a particularly virulent pneumonia that wouldn't respond to treatment and was in the hospital for nearly three weeks, part of it in intensive care. She only went back to school in the last couple of weeks, and that was against her doctor's orders. They wanted her to stay home and rest for the remainder of the school year. The best I could do was to convince her two days a week was enough right now."

"Why didn't Mom and Dad tell me?" Lisa could have died and she wouldn't have even said goodbye.

"Lisa didn't want them to. She didn't want to bother you with her problems, especially after she heard you got married again."

"She didn't want to bother me?"

He blew out a breath. "Yeah. She's probably going to kill me for telling you now."

Jamie's heart ached. Was this what their relationship had come to? Her sister was on the verge of death and she didn't want to bother her? Did Lisa think she didn't care?

This was her fault. She'd let her jealousies blind her for too long.

She inhaled an unsteady breath. "I'll go see her."

"Good. Don't tell her I spilled the beans, or I'll never hear the end of it."

"I'm pretty sure she'll figure it out." Jamie touched his arm. "You're a good husband, Zach."

"I hope so. Come on, we'd better get back to work."

They walked back toward the clinic. They were almost at the door when Zach spoke again. "I never got a chance to tell you how sorry I am things didn't work out between you and your husband."

She'd given her parents the okay to share the reasons for her stay in Lewiston with Zach. Jamie assumed he'd told Lisa.

"I appreciate your concern."

"On the up side, you'll soon have a baby in your life. That's wonderful news."

"Yeah, it is. Thanks."

But she'd never have Ben in her life again.

Jamie had done a lot of thinking since she left Masonville. She'd probably always love Ben. In so many ways he was a wonderful, caring man. But he had a fatal flaw. He couldn't see that only by giving love away could he hold it close. She knew now she deserved someone who could love her without reservation.

She and Ben had likely been doomed from the start. But for one bright, shining moment, she'd felt beautiful in his arms.

Chapter Twenty-Seven

Ben groaned out loud when his phone rang and he saw his mother's name on the screen. She was the last person he wanted to talk to, but he knew Victoria wouldn't leave him alone until she got what she wanted.

"Hello, Mother."

"Hello, Ben. Do you have my money?"

Nice to talk to you, too. "Not yet. I can't get access to the funds for at least thirty days." He'd cashed in investments he'd made from the sale of his loft in Chicago. The rest he was in the process of trying to borrow, but since the house in Masonville was still in probate, lenders were leery about using it as collateral.

"Thirty days is unacceptable. We need the money now. You owe us!"

"I owe you? How do you figure that?"

Victoria sniffed. "Simply by virtue of being your parents. Show some respect."

The ridiculousness of her words made him laugh despite his looming headache and the anger roiling in his gut. "I have absolutely zero respect for either one of you."

"What a terrible thing to say to your mother. You owe me your life, and you owe me your loyalty. My parents turned you and your brother and sister against me. I never should have permitted the three of you to

267

stay with them all those summers."

She was truly self-deluded. As Ben remembered it, she couldn't wait for school to be out so she could ship them off to the farm. But he didn't have the mental energy to argue with her about the past, so he let it go.

"Why do you need this much money anyway? Five hundred thousand is a lot of cash."

"We have our reasons. I'm only asking for what should have been mine in the first place. I deserve the money."

Ben reached the end of his patience. "So do my kids. That money is meant for their futures. And for the present. Bella has been sick and the medical bills are piling up. If you give up all claim to Blair's and Damon's inheritance, in writing, I'll give you what I can. But it ends there. You have to swear in writing never to ask any of us for money again. It's a fair offer. Take it or leave it."

"Those precious children of yours you're so fond of? I understand your late first wife's parents are quite fond of them, too."

Ben went cold inside. "What do you know about Olivia's parents?"

Her voice purred with confidence. "I know they've filed for custody. Think how strong their case would be if your own mother and father testified you are an unfit parent. We tried to help you with your alcoholism, but you wouldn't accept our assistance. And sadly, since you didn't accept our help, your drinking is still out of control."

Ben couldn't speak. He'd always known his mother was ruthless, but this was a whole new depth of depravity, even for her.

He wiped the back of his hand across his mouth. "What do you want?"

"Our original agreement. Five hundred thousand dollars, but in two weeks, not thirty days. If you don't comply, we'll go straight to the Doyles."

"That's blackmail."

"It's nothing personal, darling. Simply business."

She sounded well pleased with herself, knowing she had him under her thumb.

A picture clearly emerged for Ben. She'd never leave him alone. Ever. Since Grandfather Greyson had cut them off, Victoria needed a new source of money. She'd extort cash from Ben until every last cent was gone, until he and the girls were destitute, because she knew he'd go to any length to keep his children.

Despair overwhelmed him. He had no choice but to pack up his kids and disappear.

Now.

"I'll let you know when the money is ready." With that, he hung up on her. He hurried to his bedroom and rummaged in a suitcase stored in his closet until he found the bag of cash he'd hidden there along with the prepaid phone he'd purchased shortly before he married Jamie. He'd hoped he would never have to use it.

He hesitated. If he used this phone, he'd set events in motion he couldn't stop. There'd be no going back.

But if he did nothing, his children would pay the price of his mother's greed. He couldn't let them suffer.

He plugged the phone into its charger and when it charged sufficiently, he dialed a number he'd committed to memory. A man answered on the first ring.

"Yeah?"

Ben identified himself. "We spoke a few months ago about new identifications for me and my two daughters. I need to pull the trigger. Now."

"It'll cost you." The man named a price. Ben cringed at the number.

"Fine. How long will it take?"

"Two days."

"How do I get the money to you and receive the identifications?"

He listened carefully, memorizing the instructions.

As if his life depended on it.

****

As per his instructions, Ben transferred the money to the forger in the evening. Early the following morning, the forger sent a text to the burner phone with the address he'd need to go to in Chicago to pick up the IDs in two days. Time to put his plan in motion.

After taking Sophie to school, Ben drove to his bank and withdrew more cash, being careful not to withdraw an amount large enough to raise alarm bells. He'd withdraw the rest once he got to Chicago and use it to buy a used vehicle in the name on his new fake ID.

When he finished at the bank, he drove to the hospital in Bismarck and went straight to Bella's doctor's office. Luckily, he was there.

Ben knocked on the open door. "Dr. Kenney, can I speak to you for a minute?"

"A minute's about all I've got. I'm on my way to do rounds."

"This won't take long. I'd like you to release Bella. You said she's no longer infectious and a danger to others, including her sister. She's bored out of her mind here, and I'm afraid the anxiety will be a real detriment to her recovery."

"We don't want to keep Bella any longer than we have to. But she was a very sick little girl. She needs time for rest and recovery."

"She can finish her recovery at home. I'm self-employed, so I can take time off to stay with her and make sure she gets the rest she needs."

Dr. Kenney tapped his fingers on the desk. "I'm leaving now to do my rounds. How about I check on Bella, and if I'm satisfied her recovery can continue at home, I'll release her. But only if I'm convinced she's ready."

Ben breathed a sigh of relief. "That's fair. Thank you."

"I'll see you in Bella's room shortly."

Ben left the doctor's office, stopping in the hallway to catch his breath, one palm braced against the wall and his head bowed. He'd taken only a tentative step onto this murky path and already he was drained. Lying didn't come easily for him, but if he was going to keep his children safe, he'd need to become a master liar.

He pushed himself away from the wall and with renewed determination made his way to Bella's room. The Doyles would likely be there. To avoid a confrontation in front of Bella, he sat in a small nearby waiting room where he could see people coming and going from her room. As soon as he saw Dr. Kenney enter her room with a nurse, he jumped up and followed them.

"How are you feeling today, Bella?" Ben heard the doctor ask.

"Good."

Ben walked inside and Bella's face broke into a

smile as soon as she saw him, lifting his spirits.

"Hi, Daddy!"

She raised her arms, and Ben hugged her close. Over her shoulder, his gaze connected with the Doyles, who wore identical expressions of surprise and suspicion.

Ben let her go and the nurse took her temperature and other vital signs. The doctor used his stethoscope to listen to her chest. When he was done, he removed the stethoscope from his ears and turned to his nurse.

"Any temperature?"

"It's a perfectly normal ninety-eight point six. All vitals are normal as well."

"Her chest sounds good, too." Dr. Kenney turned to Ben. "I see no reason to keep her in the hospital any longer. I'll sign Bella's discharge papers, and she can go home this morning."

Ben let out a relieved breath. "Thank you, Doctor."

"Bella's going home?" Mrs. Doyle asked. "Right now?"

"Yes, she can finish her recovery at home. I'm sure she'll be much more comfortable there." Dr. Kenney turned to Ben. "I'll leave some instructions about her care. She should get plenty of rest. Make an appointment to see me in two weeks."

"I will." Another lie. He'd make the appointment, but in two weeks' time he and the girls would be far, far away.

"You've been a very good patient, but it's time to say goodbye, Bella." The doctor held out his hand, and Bella solemnly shook it.

"Bye."

As soon as Dr. Kenney and his nurse left the room,

Ben began gathering Bella's things, mostly toys and games he'd brought from home to keep her occupied. He stuffed them into a large shopping bag, trying to slow himself down. He didn't want to appear to be rushing or panicking.

He found Bella's clothes in a closet and gave them to her, making himself smile with what he hoped looked like reassurance. "Why don't you go change in the bathroom?"

"Okay, Daddy." She slipped off the bed and headed to the bathroom. As soon as the door closed, Mr. Doyle turned on him, his voice low.

"So you're getting her out of here. Now you'll whisk her home where we can't visit her. This round may go to you, but I can assure you the fight isn't over. We'll be pushing our custody suit forward."

"What does Jamie think of all this? We haven't seen her in a while. Bella's been asking about her," Mrs. Doyle said.

"Jamie's gone to stay with her parents for a while." Simply saying the words hurt. He'd loved her and she betrayed him.

"She left, just like that? I can't believe she would simply leave the girls."

"We're no longer together," Ben said quietly. "I haven't told Bella yet."

"Jamie was the only reason we suspended our custody suit. We were in contact with her and the girls, and we knew they were happy." Mr. Doyle shook his head in disgust. "Whatever you did to make her leave, you made a big mistake."

Bella emerged from the bathroom. Her gaze darted between Ben and her grandparents. She obviously sensed the tension in the room.

"Daddy?"

"Say goodbye to your grandparents, Bella. They'll be going back to Wisconsin now."

Bella hugged them. "Bye, Grandma, bye, Grandpa. I'll talk to you online soon, right?"

Mr. Doyle glanced at Ben before answering. "I hope so. We love you a lot. Remember that, okay?"

"I love you, too."

With one last hug, the Doyles left the room. Ben breathed a sigh of relief. Another hurdle crossed.

After getting Bella's discharge papers, he led her out of the hospital and out to his car. Once he'd strapped her into her car seat, Bella turned troubled blue eyes to him.

"How come Jamie hasn't visited me? Doesn't she like me anymore? Is it because I was sick?"

"No, Bella." He couldn't lie to her. "Jamie still likes you a lot. But she and I have decided we shouldn't be married anymore. We made a mistake. Jamie went back to her hometown with her parents."

Bella's chin wobbled and tears filled her eyes. "You mean she's not going to be our mommy anymore?"

Ben closed his eyes. With a sigh, he reopened his eyes and faced his daughter.

"No, she's not. I'm sorry, Bella."

Tears rolled down her cheeks. "I miss Jamie."

"I know, baby." *I miss her, too.*

****

Jamie stood on her sister's front step, her hand poised to knock. She hesitated, nerves jangling. Though Zach said Lisa wanted to see her, she wasn't sure how she'd be received. Maybe Lisa wanted to tell her off.

She didn't blame her if she did.

She closed her eyes, took a deep breath, and knocked. When her sister answered the door, her face first registered surprise, and then pleasure.

"Jamie? Hi!"

Jamie wasn't sure what to do with her hands. She clasped them tightly in front of her. "How are you, Lisa?"

"I'm good." An orange cat wound itself around Lisa's legs. "I was about to make tea. Would you like some?"

Relief made her smile. At least she wasn't being turned away. "I'd love tea."

She imagined she saw relief on her sister's face as well. "Good. Come on in."

Jamie stepped into the small bungalow. Kids' toys and sports equipment were strewn next to the front entrance. Lisa gave her an apologetic smile.

"Sorry about the mess. Apparently, I didn't nag the kids hard enough about putting away their things."

A picture of Sophie's and Bella's toys littering the floor rushed into her mind, and longing for them threatened to overwhelm her. "Don't worry about it."

Jamie followed her to the kitchen and sat at the table while Lisa put on the kettle and got a teapot ready.

"I'm glad you came, Jamie. I've been wanting to see you."

"Zach told me." She suddenly remembered she wasn't supposed to tell Lisa about her conversation with him. "Don't be mad at him. He was only trying to help. And frankly, if he hadn't spoken to me, I likely would have procrastinated even longer."

"Is it so hard to speak to me?"

"I've made it hard. I've been doing a lousy job as a sister for a long time." Jamie toyed with her teacup. "I've been jealous of you for years."

Lisa's eyes widened. "Jealous of me? Why?"

"A lot of stupid reasons. Because Mom and Dad paid more attention to you because of your illness, because you have a solid marriage and mine failed. Twice. Because you have kids and for a long time I didn't think it was possible for me."

"But now it is. I'm happy for you, Jamie."

"Thank you." She sniffed back tears, knowing she needed to be honest. "Okay, here's the stupidest reason. I've been jealous of you since we were teenagers because you're beautiful and I'm...not."

Lisa stared at her. "What?"

"You had boyfriends all through high school. I didn't have a real boyfriend until I met Carson. People would say, 'Jamie's the smart one, but Lisa got all the looks.' "

"Yeah, I heard those remarks, too. How do you think it made me feel to have people say I was stupid?"

Jamie was speechless. She'd never considered things from her sister's point of view.

"I wasn't going to let some dumb remarks stop me. I worked hard to get my teaching degree. And I'm a damn fine teacher."

"I have no doubt you are."

"Those remarks aren't even true. You're beautiful, Jamie."

Jamie stiffened. "Please, don't patronize me."

Lisa leaned back in her chair. "Wow. Carson really did a number on you."

"I was plain long before I met Carson."

"Before Carson, we didn't always get along, but at least we could talk. He was totally wrong for you."

"Yes, I remember you telling me. So, after meeting him once and deciding he was wrong for me, you felt you had the right to tell me not to marry him?" Jamie couldn't stop the note of bitterness in her voice.

Lisa blew out a breath. "I regret doing that. I ruined our relationship and made you even more determined to marry Carson. But I could see the moment I met him how self-absorbed and self-centered he was."

Jamie wished she could have recognized it as quickly. But at the time all she'd seen was that a handsome man wanted her.

Why did she keep falling into the same trap?

She slumped in her seat. "I realize now you were only trying to protect me. I certainly don't blame you for my mistakes, so you don't need to butter me up by saying I'm beautiful."

"I didn't say it to butter you up. It's the truth." The compassion in Lisa's eyes caused a lump to form in Jamie's throat. "What did Carson say to make you believe you weren't attractive?"

"Nothing." That was a lie. Jamie closed her eyes. "He said things. He liked to point out attractive women he saw on TV or in magazines. He'd say if only my hair was a different color, or if only my boobs were bigger or my nose was smaller. He talked about you. He always said it was too bad I didn't look like my sister."

"Bastard."

Jamie grinned at the vehemence in her sister's voice. "I can't argue with you there."

"He was jealous of you."

"Jealous?"

"Of course. You both wanted to be veterinarians, right? You got accepted into some of the best veterinary colleges in the country and he didn't. So he got even by breaking down your confidence. He knew your looks were a sensitive subject for you, so he picked away and picked away until he bled you dry."

Jamie wrapped her hands around her teacup and let the warmth seep into her bones. Lisa's insight let her see her marriage to Carson more clearly. She remembered numerous times when she'd needed to study for an exam, but he'd insist they go out instead. Was he trying to sabotage her career?

The answer came swiftly—*Yes. Of course.*

She and Carson were happy at first. But when he was denied entry into veterinary school and she was accepted into every school she applied to, things changed. It was subtle at first. He told her he was happy for her but made her feel guilty for her success. He began complaining about the cost of her education. He started pressuring her to have a baby before she finished vet school, and though she too wanted a family, the timing was terrible. And when she couldn't conceive, he found fresh ammunition for his criticism, and an excuse to leave.

The past was clearer now. It was crazy she'd never recognized Carson's behavior for what it was. He'd done a masterful job of eroding her self-confidence.

Something else was clear. She owed her sister an apology.

"I'm sorry. Do you think we can start over?" Jamie's voice wobbled. "I could really use a sister right now."

Lisa lifted her teacup, her eyes brimming with tears. "What a coincidence. I could really use a sister, too."

****

The next morning Jamie woke refreshed after having her first decent sleep since staying in her parents' house. Her reconciliation with her sister lightened her heart and lifted a burden.

She sniffed the air appreciatively as she walked into the kitchen. "Mmmm. Smells heavenly. Did you get up extra early to make cinnamon buns, Mom?"

Her mother wiped her hands on a towel. "I did. I know they're your favorite."

"If you keep feeding me like this, I'm going to be the size of a whale."

"Nonsense. You're a perfect weight. I'm just making sure my grandchild and my daughter are well nourished."

"Thanks, Mom." Jamie appreciated the love and care her parents were lavishing on her. She needed it desperately right now.

Jack Garven sniffed the air as he entered the kitchen. "Do I smell cinnamon buns?"

"You do, but they're for later." Helen turned to Jamie. "Why don't you sit down? Dad and I want to talk something over with you."

Jamie climbed onto a stool at the kitchen island. "What is it?"

"We'd like to make you a job offer," Jack said. "You've been an invaluable asset to the clinic in the last week. Zach and I can barely keep up most of the time, but with you seeing our small animal clients, we've been flying. We would bring you in as a full partner."

"Oh." The offer astonished her.

"You'll be good for our bottom line." Her mother poured coffee. She worked part-time at the clinic, doing the books and ordering supplies. "Your experience with exotic animals could bring a whole new clientele to the clinic."

"Besides, we want you close, especially now with the baby coming. We could help with child care. It's been good to be in your life again."

Jamie leaned her head against her dad's shoulder. "It's been good for me, too."

"So, what do you think? Is working here in Lewiston something you'd consider?"

"I have some things I need to think through, but I'll definitely consider it. Thank you."

They were making an exceedingly generous offer. Living close to her parents would give her the emotional and practical support she'd need once the baby was born. And her child deserved a family.

She also owed Ben the opportunity to know he was going to be a father. She'd accepted the fact their marriage was over. But she hadn't worked up the courage to tell him she was pregnant.

The ringing of her phone interrupted her thoughts. When she saw Elizabeth Doyle's name on her screen, her heartrate picked up. Had something happened to Bella? Did she have a relapse?

"Hello?"

"Jamie, hello. I'm glad you picked up."

"Is everything okay? How's Bella?"

"She's fine. Ben took her home yesterday. That's what I wanted to talk to you about."

It was a relief to know Bella was well enough to go

home. "What is it?"

"He told us the two of you are no longer together, and I'm truly sorry if your breakup was because of us. But now Ben has total control over the girls again. Is there any way you can intervene on our behalf, to ask him to let us call them?"

"Ben doesn't want to hear from me, Elizabeth, especially not when it comes to you and the girls. He's made it abundantly clear."

"I was afraid of that." Jamie heard the tears in Elizabeth's voice. "We were just getting to know Bella and Sophie again. I'm afraid they'll be lost to us forever now."

"I'm sorry." Jamie knew exactly how she felt. Bella and Sophie were lost to her, too.

"Ben couldn't wait to get Bella out of the hospital. He convinced the doctor she'd be better off at home, and then he whisked her away. He didn't like the idea of us visiting Bella."

An alarm went off in Jamie's head. *Couldn't wait to get Bella out of the hospital? Whisked her away?* Was Ben getting ready to run?

She struggled to keep her voice calm. "I'll do what I can. I'll talk to his sister and brother and see if they can convince him to let you speak to the girls, but don't get your hopes up."

"We appreciate it, Jamie. Stay well, dear."

"You too, Elizabeth."

As soon as she disconnected, Jamie thumbed through her phone contacts until she found Blair's number. Jack stood next to her.

"What's wrong?"

"Bella's been released from the hospital at Ben's

request. He talked about going back to Chicago when she got out, but I've got a bad feeling."

"What do you mean?"

She might as well come clean with her parents. She was tired of secrets.

"The reason Ben and I married was to keep the Doyles from gaining custody. Ben was on the verge of running away and disappearing with the girls." She told them the whole story, holding nothing back.

"That's a hell of a reason to get married," Jack said.

"I know it wasn't the greatest start, but it was working. Until Ben found out I'd let the girls video conference with their grandparents. He couldn't forgive me."

"So you didn't marry for love?" Helen asked.

It was on the tip of her tongue to agree, to say she didn't love Ben when they first married. But she knew herself well enough to realize she couldn't have married him if she wasn't in love.

"I loved Ben from the beginning. And I adored the girls."

"And you wanted to be a mother to them," her mother added.

"Yes." Her eyes welled with tears. "I still do. I miss them. But I'm afraid Ben's planning to run again."

She let out a shuddering breath. She needed to focus. Bella and Sophie needed her. She could feel it. She hit Blair's number and the phone began to ring.

"Hello? Jamie?" Blair's voice was a welcome sound.

"Blair, hi. Listen, did Ben tell you Bella was released from the hospital yesterday?"

"No, he didn't." Blair sounded surprised.

"Have you talked to him this morning?"

"No. Why? What's wrong?"

"I think he's getting ready to take the kids and run."

"You mean back to Chicago?"

"No, I mean he plans to disappear."

"What?"

"Can you go to his house right now? I know this sounds crazy, but it's important." Jamie paced around the kitchen. "Call Damon. Have him come with you."

"I…okay." Blair sounded stunned. "I'll call Damon right away."

"Call me later when you get a chance. Please?"

"I will."

Jamie disconnected the call, her heart racing. Her dad put his arm around her shoulders and led her back to the island. Her mother set a steaming bowl of oatmeal in front of her. Her appetite was gone, but she attempted to eat it anyway. Her father sat next to her.

"It's going to be all right. Blair and Damon will talk Ben out of taking the girls away."

Jamie nodded. She hoped they got to Ben in time.

Chapter Twenty-Eight

"Where are we going, Daddy?" Bella's face registered confusion along with a touch of fear.

"We're going on an adventure, sweetie. It'll be fun." He tried to sound upbeat, but he was afraid his words were falling flat.

"I like it here. Why do we have to leave?" Sophie's mouth twisted, a sure sign tears were imminent. "I want Jamie."

Ben closed his eyes. *I want Jamie, too.*

"I need you to be a big, brave girl, Sophie. Can you be brave for me?"

Her chin wobbled, but she nodded. "Okay, Daddy."

Ben sighed in relief. "Thanks, sweetie. I've packed your clothes in your suitcase. Why don't you pick out the toys you want to take with you and put them into the suitcase on your bed?"

She nodded and trudged toward her room, her shoulders slumped. Ben's heart ached. He hated to see his baby unhappy, but he was doing this was for her own good.

When he turned, Bella was lying on the couch, her eyes closed. Ben went to her and touched her forehead.

"What's wrong, sweetheart?"

"I'm tired, Daddy."

Worst case scenarios rushed through his head. What would he do if Bella relapsed? He'd have no choice but to take her to a hospital. Questions would be asked, and if the complete truth came out, his girls would be taken away from him.

Bella's forehead was cool to the touch, but she was obviously tired. She was still recovering her strength.

"I'll help you pack your toys. Is there anything in particular you want to take with you?"

She opened her eyes, her gaze connecting with his. "When we moved here, I got to bring all my toys. Why do I have to choose now?"

Bella was a smart kid, not easily fooled. Maybe she was old enough to know a small taste of the truth.

"Because right now we can only take as much stuff as we can fit in the car. We'll be going away for a while, just the three of us."

"But we can call Grandma and Grandpa Doyle on your cell phone, right? And Auntie Blair and Uncle Damon? And Jamie?"

Ben swallowed. "No, sweetheart. It'll be just us for a while."

Bella pushed herself to a sitting position and stared at him. "Why?"

Overwhelming despair gripped him. *Because I can't lose you. You're all I have.*

"Let's go pack your toys." He held out his hand to her.

Bella hesitated. Then with a sigh, she pushed herself off the couch and grasped his hand. Ben sighed in relief.

The relief was short-lived. The doorbell rang, and when he didn't immediately answer it, someone pounded at the door.

"Ben, I know you're in there. Open the door."

He recognized Damon's voice. *Damn.* He'd hoped to get away before either of his siblings realized he'd left. He bent toward Bella.

"You start packing, and I'll be with you in a little while. I have to see what Uncle Damon wants."

She nodded solemnly and headed down the hall. Ben waited until she'd disappeared into her room before opening the door. Both Damon and Blair were standing on his front step.

"What's up?" He tried to sound normal, and not like he was anxious for them to leave.

They both walked past him and entered the house without being invited.

"We wanted to see how the three of you were doing. We heard Bella was released from the hospital," Damon said.

"We're fine. We're about to have breakfast, and then Sophie is going to school." He realized too late there was no sign of breakfast in the kitchen, no smells of food cooking. He'd planned to pick up something from a drive-thru to eat on the road.

Neither of them looked convinced. Blair glanced around the living room to the cardboard boxes he'd packed with mementos and photo albums belonging to Olivia and Rob, knowing the girls would want to know their history someday.

"Chris and Alison told us they're going to rent this house," she said. "If you're not living with Jamie anymore, where are you and the girls planning to live?"

"We're going back to Chicago."

"Have you found a job there?" Damon asked. "A place to live?"

"Not yet, but I will."

Damon and Blair stood stiffly, their faces unsmiling. Blair appeared anxious.

"There's no need for you to move," she said. "You've got a support system here, family and friends who'll help you with whatever you need."

"I can't stay here." Ben lowered his voice. "I can't continue to live next door to Jamie and subject the girls to heartache every time they run into her."

That much at least was true.

"Then move to Bismarck or stay with Garrett and me on the farm until you figure out what to do. You don't have to go so far away."

Blair had no idea how far he planned to go.

"I know you're hurting, but now is not the time to leave." Blair stepped forward, her eyes imploring him. "Now is the time to be with your family, to let us help you."

Ben wished they could help, but there was nothing they could do. There was nothing anyone could do. If he didn't get away, their mother would make sure his children were penniless. Between being squeezed for money by their mother and threatened by the Doyles, there was no choice but to disappear and never come back.

Sophie skipped into the living room. "Auntie Blair! Uncle Damon!!"

She ran straight into Blair's open arms. Ben looked away from his child's obvious delight at seeing her aunt and uncle.

I'm taking her away from everything familiar, from everyone she loves.

"I'm packing my toys. Daddy says I only get one suitcase for toys, so I have to make sure they're my very favorites. You wanna see?"

Blair looked up sharply at Ben before addressing Sophie with a smile. "Why can you only have one suitcase for toys?"

Sophie shrugged. "I don't know."

"I'll have the rest of our stuff packed up and sent to us later," Ben said.

"When are you planning to leave?" Damon asked.

"Next week." Ben hated to lie to his brother but it couldn't be helped.

"But Daddy, you said we had to pack 'cause we're leaving today." Sophie's innocent blue eyes were filled with confusion. "Can we stay? I like it here."

"Sophie honey, where's Bella?" Blair asked.

"She's lying down on her bed. She said she's tired."

Blair took Sophie's hand. "Let's go say hello to her, okay?"

As soon as they were out of the room, Damon turned on him, his voice low. "What the hell is going on?"

"I told you. We're moving back to Chicago."

He folded his arms over his chest. "I don't believe you. Try again."

"I can't help what you believe."

"That's not an answer, and you know it. Where are you going?"

Blair led his daughters into the living room. "The girls say they haven't eaten breakfast and they're hungry. I'm taking them to the Homestead Restaurant."

"Sounds like a good idea." Damon got down on his haunches in front of Bella. "I'm glad you're out of the hospital. How are you feeling?"

"I'm good," she said quietly.

"I hear you're tired."

Bella nodded. "Yeah. Daddy says I can sleep in the car."

Damon shot him a look, then turned back to Bella with a smile. "Where are you going?"

She shrugged. "I don't know. Daddy says it will be just the three of us for a while. We won't be able to talk to Grandma and Grandpa over the phone. Or you and Auntie Blair."

Damon nodded, his expression giving nothing away. He smiled at Bella once more. "Have a nice breakfast with Auntie Blair. We'll see you when you get back."

He rose to his full height and leveled a hard look at Ben but said nothing. Blair helped the girls put on their jackets and shoes and ushered them out the door. As soon as the door closed, Damon turned to Ben.

"I want the truth, and I want it now."

Ben sighed and dropped into an armchair. Damon wouldn't accept any more evasions or half-truths, so he might as well come clean.

"I plan to take the girls somewhere far away."

Damon sat on the sofa. "How do you plan to do that?"

He gave a brief outline of the false identities, the untraceable phone, the minivan he planned to buy in his new name.

"Jesus." Damon shook his head. "Ben, this is crazy. You don't have to do this. I swear to you, we can work something out with the Doyles."

"No!" Ben jumped out of his seat, nearly tipping his armchair. "We *have* to go. Why can't anyone understand?"

"Jamie couldn't understand, could she?"

"She betrayed me!"

"How did she betray you, Ben? By loving your children? By loving you?"

He glared at his brother, frustration and pain eating him alive. "You don't understand! You have no idea the pressure I'm under. Victoria is—"

Ben cut off his tirade and cursed under his breath, angry at himself for uttering their mother's name and revealing more than he'd intended.

"What is Victoria pressuring you to do?" Damon's quietly asked question belied the fire in his eyes.

Ben resumed his seat, leaning forward to place his elbows on his knees and stare at his feet. "She says she'll contest Granddad's Will unless I give her money."

"Don't be ridiculous. She doesn't have a hope of overturning the Will."

"She and Peter believe they can tie up the Will in the courts for years and ruin your plans for opening the retreat." He lifted his head and met Damon's gaze. "She's threatening to testify on behalf of the Doyles in the custody suit if I don't give her five hundred thousand dollars. She'll tell the court I'm still an active alcoholic and that my drinking continues to be out of control. Now that she's got her hooks into me, she'll never let me go. She'll come after me over and over again until there's nothing left. Don't you see? I have to disappear with the girls. It's the only way I can stop her."

Damon stunned him by laughing. "For a smart man you're being incredibly stupid."

"You think this is funny?"

"I think you're letting Victoria get into your head and cloud your judgment. You're forgetting *we* have all the power in this situation, not her."

"How do you figure that?"

"If she's squeezing you for money, it must mean she and Peter are desperate."

"Grandfather Greyson has cut them off."

Damon scoffed in disdain. "It's about time. What possible grounds could she use to contest the Will? I thought Granddad and Morley made the Will airtight."

"Victoria says she'll argue Morley exerted undue influence over Granddad when he wrote his Will, forcing him to give her only a small portion of his estate. She and Peter believe it gives her grounds to contest."

"Ben, you saw Granddad's video. He was very clear about why he didn't leave Victoria the bulk of his estate, and it was obvious no one influenced him."

Ben nodded slowly. Everett Branson had made a video Will shortly before his death. The video showed a man of sound mind, whose wishes were his own. Granddad wanted his grandchildren to inherit his properties to keep them out of Victoria's hands.

The blinders he'd allowed his mother to place over his eyes began to lift.

"Have you told Morley about Victoria's attempt to blackmail you?"

"No."

"I'm sure he'd have something to say about it. My guess is he could come up with some legal remedy that involves pain for Victoria and stops the blackmail." He sat in the seat across from Ben. "Now that we've removed your need to run away because of our money-hungry parents, you can stay here in Masonville and be close to family."

"You know damn well I can't."

"Why not?"

Because Jamie is here. Because I can't see her and not want to be with her. "Because the Doyles still want to take the kids away."

"Why are you opposed to letting them have a relationship with Bella and Sophie? What are you afraid of, Ben?"

"They're trying to take them away from me!"

"The girls have the right to know their grandparents the way we did. Don't you want the same for them as we had?"

He knew Damon was right. He'd thought the same often enough. "I don't want to lose them."

"Why do you think you'd lose them?"

"For God's sake, Damon, they've filed the papers to take them away from me."

"Why do you think they want to take them away?"

Ben jumped to his feet and began pacing the living room. "How the hell should I know? Why are you asking me these stupid questions?"

"You must have some idea. Why do the Doyles want to take the girls away from you?"

Ben couldn't take anymore. "Because they hate me! And they have every right to. I'm nothing but a drunk." He shouted his answer at Damon. "I don't deserve to be Bella and Sophie's father. I'm not good enough! How could I ever be good enough?"

His knees gave way and he sank to floor. Wave after wave of pain and shame washed over him.

Damon knelt beside him, his arm around his shoulders. "It's not true. You're a strong, honorable man and the best big brother in the world. You've worked hard to overcome your addiction and be a man your children can be proud of. You deserve to be a father to Bella and Sophie. You deserve happiness and love and every good thing the world has to offer."

Damon's words opened a dam holding back a torrent of grief. The tears overwhelmed him, doubling him over in anguish. Damon held him, and Ben cried until he couldn't cry anymore, until he was totally spent.

Exhausted, Ben sat on the floor with his back against the sofa and accepted the tissue his brother gave him. Damon sat next to him and stretched out his legs. "Did you leave Jamie because you don't believe you deserve her?"

Ben stared at Damon, his heartrate picking up once more. "I needed someone I could trust, and Jamie betrayed me."

"You know denying your daughters access to their only blood relatives is wrong. So how did she betray you?"

Ben shook his head. "If she cared about me, she would have respected my wishes."

"Maybe she cared about you too much to let you make a mistake."

It hurt too much to think about Jamie. "No, you're wrong."

"You know what I think? I think you love Jamie. Maybe things didn't start out that way, but you fell in love. And it scared the crap out of you."

"You're delusional."

Damon ignored him. "It scared you because love scares you. Olivia cared about you, but she was still in love with her dead husband so she was safe. But Jamie isn't safe. She makes you feel things, want things. Maybe you don't believe you deserve someone like Jamie, just like you don't deserve other good things in life."

He couldn't bear to think about Jamie. "You don't know what you're talking about."

"When you found out Jamie had been video-calling the Doyles, you saw it as proof she didn't love you. Proof you didn't deserve love. So you left her. Before she could leave you."

"Is that your professional opinion as a therapist?" Ben packed as much sarcasm as he could muster into his voice.

"No, it's my opinion as your brother." He pulled his phone from his pocket. "I'm sending Blair a text to see if she can stay with the girls today. You and I are going to talk to Morley."

When his text was done, Damon scrambled to his feet and reached out his hand. Ben grabbed it and let his brother haul him to his feet. When he would have let go, Damon hung on.

"I'm staying with you and the girls for a few days. I won't let you disappear. Losing you would kill Blair and me."

Ben closed his eyes in shame. He'd never considered how disappearing would affect his brother and sister. If things were reversed, and one of them intentionally disappeared without a word of explanation, he'd be devastated.

"I'm sorry. I'm not going anywhere."

Damon clapped him on the back. "Good. But I'm still staying with you."

They left the house and headed to Damon's car. As he opened the passenger door, Ben looked across the roof at his brother. "How did you know we were about to leave town? What made you come to my house when you did?"

"Jamie called Blair and begged her to check on you. Blair called me." He opened his door. "So, please don't tell me Jamie doesn't love you. I'm not going to believe you."

Then he slipped into the driver's seat, leaving Ben to wonder what it all meant.

Chapter Twenty-Nine

Jamie waited anxiously for news about Ben and the girls. Finally, in the middle of an examination of a cocker spaniel, her phone rang. It was Blair.

"I'm sorry, I need to take this call," she told her client.

She went into the hallway to answer the phone. "Blair? Is everything all right? Did you talk to Ben?"

"It's okay, Jamie. Ben is fine. He's with Damon. They went to talk to Morley."

Profound relief brought tears to her eyes. It didn't take much to make her cry these days.

"Good, I'm glad. What about the girls? How is Bella?"

"I'm with them right now. Bella is taking a nap. I took them to the Homestead for breakfast, and she was tired when we got home, so I tucked her into bed. Sophie and I are playing board games, but she's in the washroom right now. Would you like to talk to her when she gets back?"

More than anything she'd like to hear Sophie's voice. But it wouldn't be good for either of them if she did.

"It's best if I don't. I don't want to upset her again. Please don't tell her you talked to me, Okay?"

She heard Blair's sigh. "Okay. I wanted to let you know everyone is present and accounted for. But it was a close thing. Ben was minutes from leaving when we got here."

"Thank you. I appreciate you letting me know." She sucked in a breath. "Is Ben truly okay? He's not going to disappear with the girls as soon as you leave?"

"No, I'm certain he won't. But to make doubly sure, Damon is staying with them."

"Good. I'm glad."

"Sophie's coming," Blair whispered. "I'll update you as soon as I can. I've got to run. Bye."

Jamie placed her now silent phone in her back pocket. Her dad emerged from the examining room across the hall.

"You okay?"

"Yeah. I just heard from Ben's sister. He and the kids are still in Masonville, and they're fine. Blair and Damon are looking out for them."

"Thank goodness."

This time she couldn't stop the tears. Her father pulled her into his arms.

"It'll be okay, honey. You're going to get through this."

"It's just…" Jamie closed her eyes.

"You want to be with them. With your family."

But they'd never be together again. She wiped her eyes with the cuff of her lab coat. "I'd better get back to work. I left Dickie halfway through his examination."

Her father gave her one last hug. "Go get 'em, Doc."

Jamie didn't know how she would have survived the dissolution of her marriage without her parents, and now her sister.

"Same to you, Doc."

****

Morley was only too happy to deal with Victoria. Ben and Damon listened as Morley contacted their parents and told them if they didn't stop harassing Ben he would go to the police and have them charged with extortion.

"Let me be clear, Victoria. I hope you *do* try to contact Ben and attempt to extort money. It would give me infinite pleasure to bring the full weight of the law down on your head. I see it as just punishment for the anguish you caused your parents and your children over the years. Your father never stopped blaming himself for your behavior, and we both know it was a burden he shouldn't have had to bear."

"Go to hell, old man."

"Nice talking to you, too, Victoria."

After a frustrated scream, Victoria hung up. Morley only chuckled.

"We'll follow up this call with a very official letter in my best legalese. It should keep her off your back for a while. I'll explain the concept of a no-contest clause in terms even Victoria can understand."

Ben understood what he meant. If a Will was contested in North Dakota, and if that challenge to the Will was subsequently lost, it meant that the person contesting the Will would lose anything they were entitled to inherit. Ben had written enough Wills in the last few months to know Victoria's case was very weak. She stood to lose the three hundred thousand dollars in cash that Granddad left her. That should give her pause.

Morley gave Ben a pointed look. "You should have come to me right away. Things wouldn't have gone as far as they did."

"I was trying to handle things on my own."

"Right. And how'd that work for you?"

Ben knew it was a rhetorical question but he answered anyway. "Not well. Even after all these years and me knowing exactly what she's about, Victoria can still push my buttons. I can't believe I fell for it."

"Don't blame yourself. She's a master manipulator," Damon said.

"I've never understood why Peter has stayed with her all these years. Or why she stays with him."

Damon shrugged. "They're dependent on each other, or at least they used to be. She's enabled him to continue drinking, and he's provided her with a steady flow of cash and a well-respected name. The name alone allowed her entry into some fancy social circles."

"What happens now that Grandfather Greyson has cut them off?"

"The dynamics of their relationship are different now. Maybe they don't need each other the way they used to. It'll be interesting to see what happens," Damon said.

Morley snorted. "It'll be interesting, all right. Like a train wreck is interesting."

Ben got to his feet, too restless to sit anymore. "I don't care what they do to each other as long as the people I love don't get hit in the crossfire."

Damon rose as well. "I've got some things to check on at my building. Will you be all right here for a while, Ben?"

"I'll be fine." Damon was actually asking whether he planned to run while his back was turned. He'd probably need to work hard to earn his brother's trust again. "I'll see you at my house after work, right?"

"Right. I'm going to give the Doyles a call later today and see if they're willing to talk."

The bottom dropped out of Ben's stomach at the thought of the Doyles, but he knew coming to some sort of accommodation with them was the only way forward.

"Okay."

Damon gave him a brisk nod. "I'll pick up some food from the Homestead and bring it home for dinner."

With a goodbye to Morley, Damon left. Ben stood and began to pace, suddenly itchy with restlessness. What did he do now? He'd been so focused on planning his escape he'd never really planned for what to do if he simply stayed and lived his life in Masonville.

Morley sensed his mood. "You ready to get back to work? The reservation's leaders have been asking about you. I've been filling them in on Bella's condition, and they wanted you to know they've been praying for your family."

Ben was deeply touched. "That was kind of them."

"Now it's time to return their kindness. They still have a deal with the oil company to negotiate."

It was important work. But he'd never let himself become fully engaged because he believed he wouldn't be around to see it through.

Things were different now. He was going to make a life for himself in Masonville, a life he prayed would include his children.

I wish it could include Jamie, too.

Damon's words about believing he didn't deserve Jamie surfaced, but he tossed them aside. Their marriage was over because he'd lost trust in Jamie. He might have been wrong about the way he'd dealt with the Doyles, but Jamie was his wife. She was supposed to be on his side, even if she didn't agree with him. How could he ever trust her again?

It was over and done with. He needed to accept it.

****

Jamie and Lisa walked her dogs through a quiet neighborhood not far from their parents' house. Though still March, the weather was warm and sunny. The exercise was good for both her and the dogs, and talking to Lisa helped her see things more clearly. She needed clarity to make good decisions for her baby.

"Tell me about Ben," Lisa said. "What's he like? Why did you fall in love with him?"

It was a good question, one she'd been asking herself a lot lately. "He's smart, he's kind, he's stubborn. And he's a patient and loving father, which is all the more remarkable considering the way he was brought up."

"What do you mean?"

"Ben and his brother and sister come from a dysfunctional family. I don't think Ben ever felt loved. It's hard for him to trust."

"Even you?"

"Especially me."

Jamie wished she'd been able to push past the walls of distrust Ben had built around his heart. She'd seen only glimpses of the real man behind those walls. Like when he was with his children. Or when they made love.

The real Ben was full of laughter and joy. He was the best man she'd ever known. It broke her heart to know what might have been.

"You didn't answer my question. Why did you fall

in love with Ben?"

"Why does anyone fall in love? Something clicked between us, I suppose. At least for me."

"You don't think Ben loved you?"

"I don't know. He never said."

"Did you tell him you loved him?"

"No." Would it have made a difference if she had? "I was afraid he couldn't say the words back."

"You wanna know what made me fall in love with Zach?"

"Was this back in high school?"

"Yeah. I got my Lupus diagnosis in our senior year. I was depressed and feeling sorry for myself."

"You were entitled."

Lisa grinned at her. "Maybe, but I took feeling sorry for myself to whole new levels. I stopped going to school. I wouldn't see my friends or even leave the house. I barely left my room."

Jamie remembered the tension in the house and her parents' worry. But she'd been too preoccupied with her own feelings of hurt to understand what Lisa was going through.

"Zach and I were friends. We'd known each other for years and hung out together, but we'd never dated. When he found out I was sick, he came over to our house and insisted on seeing me. He told me to get over myself and get back to school. He wasn't going to let me wallow in self-pity. I needed to suck it up."

"Did it work? Did you go back to school?"

"Hell, no. At least not the first day. But Zach kept coming back until I gave in just so he'd stop badgering me. He's stood beside me every moment since. I realized later I fell in love with him because he wouldn't give up on me, even when I'd given up on myself."

"Ben gave up on me at the first sign of trouble."

"Maybe he's like me and he needs someone to believe in him before he can believe in himself."

Jamie didn't reply. She didn't know if Ben cared what she believed. But she knew for certain her heart couldn't deal with another rejection.

****

Damon convinced the Doyles to speak with Ben. The next morning he and Damon were at the office with Morley when Olivia's parents called.

"Good morning," Morley said. "Thank you for agreeing to speak to us."

"We're doing this for the children." Mr. Doyle's voice was curt. "Damon tells us Ben no longer plans to move back to Chicago."

Damon hadn't told them how close he'd come to running away. Ben cleared his dry throat. "No. I realize the best place for them is here in Masonville. The girls have the safety of living in a small town, and we have the support of family and friends close by."

"What about Jamie? Is she no longer in the picture?" Mrs. Doyle asked.

"No."

"That's unfortunate. We know how much she loved the girls. Is she all right?"

Ben realized he didn't know the answer to her question. Was she all right? Knowing he'd inflicted pain on Jamie brought overwhelming guilt. "She's staying with her parents right now."

"We're talking about a situation where Ben has sole custody, much the same as after Olivia's death."

"Yes, but with some changes." It wasn't easy for him to admit to his mistakes. "I was wrong to try to exclude you from Bella's and Sophie's lives. They need you, and they have a right to know their heritage."

"Are you saying we can phone them or visit any time?" Mrs. Doyle asked cautiously.

"Yes, I am." He paused, weighing his words. "Damon and I and our sister had a close relationship with our grandparents. I let myself forget how special the bond between grandparents and grandchildren can be. I want that for my children."

The line went silent. Ben held his breath. Finally, Mr. Doyle spoke. "How do we know we can trust you? You've changed your mind before. If Jamie was still in the picture, it would be a different story, but as it stands…"

He didn't finish. He didn't have to. He couldn't blame the Doyles for not trusting him.

"If you want to write up a formal visitation agreement, I'll sign it." Ben hoped to make them understand. "I know from a legal standpoint my case for custody is not a strong one. I was only married to Olivia for a short time and I didn't get a chance to legally adopt the girls. But I've been with Bella and Sophie since before Sophie was born. They're my life. The day Bella first called me Daddy was the day I found my purpose in life. I was meant to be her father, and Sophie's, to care for them, and love them."

Ben's throat closed, preventing him from saying any more. He bowed his head, waiting for some sort of response.

"I think we would like some sort of formal agreement, at least initially." Mr. Doyle's voice took on the tone and authority of the police officer he used to be. "Our intention is not to interfere with the day-to-day raising of the children. We want to be a part of the girls' lives, a big part, but we don't want to take over Ben's parental role. We simply don't want to be shut out completely."

"We lost our only daughter. We don't want to lose her children as well," Mrs. Doyle added.

"I'm confident we can work this out," Morley said. "Everyone here wants what's best for the kids."

Damon nodded at Ben. "The girls need every part of their family."

"We couldn't agree more," Mr. Doyle said.

Morley grinned. "Let's get to work then, shall we?"

****

The ringing of his phone woke Ben from his first decent sleep in days. He reached for his cell on the bedside table, too groggy to wonder why someone was calling in the middle of the night.

"Hello?"

"How dare you? How dare you block my calls? I was forced to get another phone just so I could call you. How dare you go back on our agreement? Who the hell do you think you're dealing with?"

Ben's sleep-deprived brain shifted to full alert at the sound of the strident female voice. *Victoria.*

"What do you want, Mother?"

"What do I want? I want what's owed to me. I want what you promised me before you instructed that old fool to threaten me. You dare to threaten your own mother?"

"You won't get a dime out of me, so you might as

well give it up. Goodnight, Victoria."

"Don't you *dare* hang up on me," she hissed. "You betrayed me! The whole family betrayed me, starting with my own parents."

He stilled at her words. *Betrayed.* "What are you talking about?"

"I'm talking about your precious grandparents and how they ignored me as a child. They never cared about me. They cared more about their stupid farm and their ridiculous friends than they cared for me. My father left more money to his precious charities than he did to me, his only child!"

Ben knew for a fact his grandparents had reached out many times to his mother. Ben witnessed some of those calls during their summer visits. His grandparents repeatedly begged his mother to visit them, or to at least call. Victoria always declined, making excuses about having something better to do. He'd seen how hurtful her neglect had been to his grandparents. On more than one occasion his grandmother had cried, though she tried to hide it.

His grandmother never stopped trying to reach out to Victoria. Not until the end. Granddad confided that Grandma Anna's fatal heart attack came not long after Victoria told her she was an embarrassment to her. She bragged how she told her friends she'd been raised in Minneapolis and her parents were dead. Anna had been devastated.

"Now you've betrayed me by backing out of our agreement. You promised to give me the money I need, and now you've reneged on our agreement."

"It was an agreement made under duress. You tried to blackmail me into doing what you wanted."

"Don't be ridiculous." Ben could imagine Victoria's expression of disdain, something she'd perfected over the years. "It wasn't blackmail. I was simply attempting to obtain what was rightfully mine. What my father denied me."

"You're delusional."

"Bennington, listen to me." Her voice grew wheedling. "I'm your mother. I deserve the money. You owe me the money. Let's forget about lawyers and work out things between us, just you and me."

She was persistent, he'd give her that. But he was done dancing to Victoria's tune.

"Goodbye, Victoria. Don't call again."

"You ungrateful bastard! I will never forget this betrayal, and I will never forgive it. You think you're so high and mighty? You're a drunk like your father."

This was old news. "Good night, Victoria."

"And guess what, Bennington? You're more like me than you care to admit. When you've been wronged, you hold a grudge and you don't let it go. You don't take betrayal lightly either. You sent your wife away for her betrayal, didn't you? Disloyalty can never be forgiven."

Ben clutched his phone, his heart racing. "What do you know about my wife?"

"I know she didn't abide by your wishes, and for that she needs to be punished. You took the appropriate measures required."

"Have you been spying on me?"

"Let's simply say I have my sources. My point is we're two of a kind. People like us need to stick together. If you help me out now, I'll help you later. Now, can we dispense with this ridiculous notion of blackmail and get back to business?"

"Goodbye, Victoria."

He ended the call before she could utter another word. Then he powered down his phone and threw it on the bed. He stared at it, his rational mind telling him the device couldn't hurt him, but the ten-year-old boy inside him was afraid the phone would come to life once more and bring Victoria back into his room.

Ben began to shake. Victoria's voice shouted in his ears. *We're two of a kind... People like us...*

Dear God! Was it true? Was he like his mother? He groaned and covered his face.

Of course it was true.

He'd accused Jamie of betraying him, banishing her from their family like some sort of medieval dictator. He'd treated her like a pariah—and for what? For caring for his children? For making it possible for him to keep Bella and Sophie?

"Oh, God. Jamie." *What have I done?*

Ben scrambled out of bed and stumbled to the kitchen. Panic set in. He couldn't get enough air into his lungs. He braced his hands on the counter and bowed his head, willing himself to breathe deeply, to slow his racing heart and mind.

Eventually his breathing returned to normal. He stepped away from the counter and straightened his back. What did he do now?

Could he make things right with Jamie again? Could she forgive him? If he were in her position, he wasn't sure he could.

The light came on in the kitchen and Ben pivoted, surprised to see Damon.

"Sorry. Did I wake you?" he asked.

"Couldn't sleep." Damon's eyes were half-closed, his hair mussed. "I heard footsteps. What's going on?"

"Victoria phoned."

Damon swore softly. "What do we have to do for her to get the message? Why won't she give up?"

"Because she knows I'm exactly like her." Ben gave a self-mocking laugh. "Like mother, like son. I'm as vindictive and twisted as she is. And here I thought I was simply a drunk like dear old dad."

"It's not true."

"Isn't it? I accused Jamie of betraying me. I sent her away. I ended our marriage because she didn't do exactly what I wanted her to do. It's a move straight out of Victoria's playbook."

"Don't you see she's pushing your buttons? She's trying to break you down so you'll do whatever she wants."

"I know, but she's right. For years I told myself that at least I wasn't like her. What do I tell myself now?"

Damon sighed and pushed his fingers through his hair. "You tell yourself you grew up in a dysfunctional family with an alcoholic father and a sociopathic mother. The same thing I tell myself every day."

All three of them suffered growing up, but perhaps Damon the most. For the thousandth time Ben castigated himself for not protecting him.

"It's understandable you reacted the way you did. It's what we saw growing up—manipulation, ostracism, intimidation, threats. If one of us—or Peter—stepped out of line, Victoria used all those tactics, and more, to keep us in line. Do you remember when I was about twelve and I started rebelling against her? I refused to go to a political rally with the family. I screamed and cried and said I would scream at the rally, too. So she left me at home."

"I remember." She'd told everyone Damon was sick with a cold and a sitter was staying with him. In reality, he was all alone in their big, fancy, unhappy house. When they got home, he and Blair were told not to speak to him.

"I thought I'd won. But then she told me the next time I pulled a stunt like that she'd find me a sitter. She'd heard Victor Campbell was available."

Ben sucked in a breath. "She threatened to bring the man who molested you into our house when you were alone?"

"Yeah. She relished doing it, too. I'll never forget the smile on her face when she saw how scared I was." Damon paused to take a breath. "When Peter made his next speech, I didn't make a sound."

"I'm sorry, Damon."

Damon shook his head. "I didn't tell you this so you could feel sorry for me. I'm telling you so you can see the difference between your actions and Victoria's. Have you ever threatened your children?"

"No, of course not."

"Have you ever knowingly left them in the company of a child molester?"

Ben shivered at the thought. "God, no!"

"Then how can you say you're like our mother?"

They stared at each other. Damon had never shared details about his abuse. Ben knew nothing about it growing up. The truth only came out years later, when Victor Campbell was accused of sexual abuse by a child and his parents, and Damon stepped forward to make a statement to the police to back up the child's claim. Ben had been devastated for his brother.

But in discovering the truth, a whole lot of things began to make sense. Damon's self-destructive behavior as a child and teenager. His joining the military the day he turned eighteen. His inability to stay in one place for any length of time.

Ben slowly nodded. "You've made your point. I would never do to my children what Victoria did to you. But it doesn't excuse what I did to Jamie. To our family."

"No, it doesn't. If you want her in your life, you've got to get over the idea you don't deserve her." Damon gave a tired sigh. "For years, part of my therapy has been to acknowledge that what happened to me wasn't my fault. I think you need to do the same. The way we were raised made us believe we don't deserve good things to come into our lives. It has to stop."

Ben's throat closed, and all he could do was nod.

Damon got to his feet. "I'm going to try to sleep. I suggest you do the same."

He headed back down the stairs, shutting off the lights as he went. Once more Ben was enveloped in darkness.

He shook his head and chuckled grimly. *A metaphor for my life.* The only time he'd ever truly basked in the light was when he was with Jamie.

He loved her, plain and simple. He wanted light again. But he was afraid she was beyond his reach.

Chapter Thirty

Jack Garven passed a bowl of vegetables to Jamie across the dinner table. "Have you given any more thought to working with us?"

A week had passed since her parents had made their initial offer. "I've thought about it a lot, Dad."

"And?"

"I appreciate you and Zach making the offer. I've certainly enjoyed working at the clinic with you. And with the baby coming in a few months, support of family would be welcome. But I really liked working at my practice in Masonville, and I loved the people I worked with. My clients with exotic pets have come to depend on me there."

"They'll find their way to you here."

"I suppose. It's a big decision. Can you give me a little more time to think about it?"

Helen passed the mashed potatoes to her. "Of course we can. Take all the time you need."

Jamie smiled gratefully at her. Moving back to Lewiston to work with her parents and her brother-in-law seemed like the smart thing to do. When the baby came, she'd need help. In Masonville, she'd be all alone. She'd have to find a sitter to look after the baby while she was at work. She'd still need a sitter in Lewiston, but at least she'd have family to back her up. Making a permanent move to her hometown made a lot of sense.

Still, she couldn't make herself do it. She wasn't even sure why.

The doorbell rang. Helen glanced at Jack. "Were you expecting anyone?"

"No. Probably kids selling candy," he said with a grin.

Jamie laughed and got to her feet. "In that case, I'd better answer it."

"Buy two boxes," her dad called as she walked to the door, and Jamie laughed again.

The smile died on her face the moment she opened the door and found Ben on the front step. They stared at each other, and Jamie stood mutely, unable to form words.

"Hi, Jamie. You're looking well. I'm glad."

She snapped out of her stupor and wrapped her sweater around her middle to cover her expanding belly.

"What are you doing here?"

"I came to see you, to apologize."

She didn't know what to say. Jamie looked past him to his car on the street. "Are the girls with you?"

"No, they're back in Masonville. Damon is staying with them." His gaze focused on her face. "I hoped maybe we could talk."

"What is there to talk about? You made it clear our marriage is over."

"I was wrong, Jamie. Please forgive me."

He reached for her, but Jamie stepped away to avoid his touch. She was afraid if he touched her, she'd be lost.

"Please, can we talk?"

Worry lines marred his beautiful face. She felt herself weakening. Despite everything, she still loved him. She'd always love him. But how did she know he wouldn't leave her again the first time they disagreed on something?

Still, he was the father of her baby. They'd always be connected through their child. She'd need to find a way to deal with Ben.

Her dad joined her in the doorway. He stared at Ben, his face and his voice taking on an uncharacteristically menacing demeanor. "What are you doing here, Ben?"

"I was hoping to talk to Jamie, Dr. Garven."

Jamie grabbed a jacket from a hook near the door. "It's okay, Dad. I'm going for a walk with Ben. We won't be long."

"You're sure?" Jack didn't take his eyes off Ben.

"I'm sure. I'll be back soon."

Her father turned his attention to her and nodded, his eyes full of worry. "Okay. Do what you have to do."

Jamie made herself smile for him. Her father remained in the doorway, watching, as she left the house.

Ben fell into step beside her. "I don't blame your dad for hating me after what I did."

"You're the father of girls. Someday, when someone breaks their hearts, you'll know exactly how he feels."

"Yeah, I guess I will."

"The girls are really okay?"

"They are. Bella went back to school today. She'll be going half time for a while, but she's getting stronger every day."

"I'm glad to hear it."

Jamie had tried very hard not to think about Sophie and Bella. It hurt too much to know she'd never be their mother again.

"Where would you like to go?" he asked.

"There's a park a couple of blocks from here. We can talk there."

"All right."

Conversation stalled. Jamie tried to work out how she'd tell Ben about the baby. She knew for certain he'd want to be part of his child's life. She didn't want to deny him access to his child, but how could she do that without her heart breaking every time she saw him?

Like it was right now.

They reached the park, and aside from some kids on the playground equipment, there was no one around. Jamie sat at one of the picnic tables, her back against the wooden top. Ben sat next to her.

"I was ready to run away with the girls." He stared at his shoes. "I got fake IDs for the three of us and made arrangements to buy a car under my new name. Everything was in place. But you figured it out. Blair and Damon got to me in time."

Jamie struggled to keep her voice from wavering. "How long till you try it again?"

His eyes were steady on hers. "I promise you, I'll never try to disappear with the girls again. We're working things out with the Doyles. The girls deserve to know their grandparents."

Jamie exhaled in relief. "Yes, they do."

"I'm sorry I upset you. I was a little out of my mind with worry. And then my mother—" He stopped abruptly.

"What about your mother? What happened?"

He told her about his mother's attempts to blackmail him. "My siblings and I can't have anything more to do with her. Ever. Any dealings we have will be through Morley, with him acting as our lawyer."

"I'm sorry, Ben." She truly was. Not only because he was obviously in pain, but because the way he'd been brought up was at the heart of their breakup.

"I don't want to talk about my mother. I want to talk about us."

"Ben, I can't—"

"I love you, Jamie. I think I've loved you from the moment we met."

She stared at him, stunned. A declaration of love was the last thing she'd expected.

He watched the children on the playground. "I've never told anyone I love them. Not my brother and sister, or my grandparents. And not Olivia. I realize now, after loving you, what I felt for Olivia was a lot of things—gratitude, friendship—but it wasn't love. If she'd lived, I'm not sure how long our marriage would have lasted. I know for sure she didn't love me either."

Ben turned to face her. "Aside from my grandparents, no one ever told me they loved me. When I was growing up, no adults aside from them showed me love. Maybe it's why I fought so hard to keep the girls away from the Doyles. If they loved their grandparents, how could they possibly love me, too?"

"Love doesn't work that way." Jamie's heart ached for the boy, and the man.

Ben smiled his beautiful smile at her. "I'm starting to figure that out. Blair's been seeing a counselor she's come to trust in the last few months, and she recommended her to me. I talked to her for the first time yesterday." His smile faded. "I want you to know what we had was real. It meant the world to me. *You* mean the world to me. Come home to me, Jamie. Please?"

This time she couldn't stop the tears. She held up her hand when he would have touched her.

"Please, don't. Don't say anymore."

"I'm sorry. I don't want to make this any harder on you."

She wiped her eyes on the sleeve of her jacket. "There's something I need to tell you before I lose my nerve. I'm pregnant."

He stared at her, eyes wide. It took him a few moments to speak. "But you said it wasn't possible."

"Yeah, I did. But I guess miracles happen."

"Jamie." This time when he reached for her hand she didn't push him away. "This is amazing."

"I wanted to tell you. That last day, I planned to tell you. Then you came home, and you were angry, and you left with Sophie. And my whole life shattered."

He brought her fingers to his mouth for a kiss. "I'm sorry."

The gesture nearly undid Jamie, but she needed to be strong. "I believe you are. I even believe you mean it when you say you love me. But if I went back to you, would you leave me at the first sign of trouble? I can't go through that again. Especially now. I won't let my child be abandoned."

"I wouldn't do that. I swear."

"I know you mean it now, but how can I be sure?"

The pain on his face was difficult to look at. "I know you don't trust me. After what I've done, I don't deserve your trust. Is there any place for me in our child's life?"

"I want my child to know you." She made herself sit up taller and look him in the eye. "But make no mistake. I will not relinquish custody. If you fight me, I'll fight back. Hard."

He nodded in resignation. "I would never try to take the baby away from you."

She wished she could believe him. But after seeing him fight the Doyles, she wasn't sure.

"When do you plan to come back to Masonville?"

"My dad and brother-in-law have offered me a partnership in their clinic here in Lewiston. When the baby comes, I'll need support from family." It seemed she'd made her decision.

He bowed his head and made circles with his thumb on the top of her hand. "I'll support whatever you want to do. How are you feeling?"

She sniffed back tears. "I'm well, thank you. Everything is normal, my doctor tells me."

"Good, I'm glad. When—if—you want to talk more about the baby, call me." He lifted his gaze to hers. "Jamie, I was wrong about many things, but I was especially wrong about you. I wish I could take back every hurtful thing I said to you, but I can't. All I can say is 'I'm sorry.' I hope you can forgive me some day." With one last squeeze, he released her hand and rose to his feet. "I should go. Do you want to walk back with me?"

"I'm going to stay here for a while." She needed a few moments alone to compose herself.

"I'll say goodbye, then. I think I'll head back to Masonville tonight."

"You're not staying?"

"I need to go home." He closed his eyes for a moment. When he opened them she saw deep sadness. No matter how much they loved one another, they always managed to make each other sad.

"Give the girls a hug for me."

"I will. Look after yourself. And the baby."

A sob escaped her. "I will."

"I love you, Jamie."

He kissed her cheek, then walked back the way they'd come. Jamie covered her mouth to stop her cries. It was over.

It was really over.

****

The next week dragged for Ben even though he was busier than he'd been since moving to Masonville. On Monday evening he took the girls to Bismarck for their first swimming lessons. Tuesday he traveled to the reservation for a meeting with the Tribal Council. Wednesday he interviewed, and then hired, a woman to help with housecleaning. Thursday he looked at three houses with a real estate agent but didn't like any of them. On Friday he bought groceries, and on the weekend he and the girls cooked several meals they froze to use the rest of the week.

By Sunday night Ben was utterly depressed.

And alone. Damon moved back to the farm on Saturday, and with the girls in bed, the house was quiet. The oppressive silence bore down on him. His mind worked overtime, taunting him with the knowledge his controlling behavior had ruined any chance for happiness.

The desire for a drink whispered a seductive chant

in his ear.

He could slip out for a few minutes and run to a liquor store. It wouldn't take long. The girls were sleeping and wouldn't even know he'd left.

Ben hurried to the closet and pulled out his jacket. Through the open closet door he saw two pairs of little pink rain boots stacked on a shelf. A small green jacket and an even smaller lavender jacket hung side by side. If he did this, if he gave up more than five years of sobriety, he'd undermine the commitment he'd made to his daughters. And if he broke his commitment to them, what did he have left?

He wouldn't break the promise he'd made to Rob on his deathbed to look after his family.

Ben stared into the closet. Jamie's things should be there, too. And soon baby things.

His baby.

Would the baby be a boy or a girl? Would the child grow up knowing who he was, or would Ben simply be someone who sent Christmas presents once a year? Would he be a name on a card, a person he barely knew?

A father but never a dad.

Jamie said she wanted him in his child's life, but what did that mean? She lived over two hundred miles away, too far for daily contact. They should be a family. He and Jamie and the kids. It was all he wanted, all he'd ever need. Someone to love him, someone to love in return. No games, no pain. Just love.

He'd had it within his grasp and he'd let it go. He was the only one to blame.

Ben took off his jacket and hung it in the closet, then carefully closed the doors.

His phone rang, and he groaned. He didn't want to talk to anyone, to pretend he was okay when he wasn't. He ignored it and it stopped ringing. Ben breathed a sigh of relief, but then it started again. Swearing, he pulled the phone out of his pocket and saw Damon was calling. He reluctantly hit the button to accept the call.

"So I answered. Are you happy now?"

"Not particularly," Damon replied. "You don't sound happy either."

He didn't want to admit how close he'd come to leaving the house in search of booze. "This time of the evening is the hardest. The girls are asleep and the house is quiet. I've got too much time to think."

"What are you thinking about?"

Ben hadn't told his siblings about Jamie's pregnancy in the week since he'd learned the news himself. He'd brooded over it alone, mourning the loss of what could have been. It had driven him to the edge of sobriety. Perhaps now was the time to talk. Before he fell off the edge.

"There's something I need to tell you. Blair and Garrett, too."

"They're here with me. What did you need to tell us?"

Ben took a deep breath. "Jamie is pregnant."

"Oh, my goodness!" Blair exclaimed. "Ben, that's wonderful news."

"Is it? She's not coming back to me. She plans to stay in Lewiston. Her family is offering her a partnership in their vet clinic."

"Cole and Lauren haven't mentioned anything about Jamie leaving us," Blair said. "As far as I know we're not looking to hire a new vet."

"Jamie was clear she wasn't coming back to Masonville. Maybe they haven't broken the news to staff yet."

"I don't think so," she said. "Lauren and I were talking about Jamie yesterday. She said she was worried because she hadn't heard anything from her."

"Maybe Jamie isn't as sure about what she wants as she told you," Damon said.

That gave Ben pause. Was Jamie having second thoughts? What did it mean?

"Ben, the news about your baby is wonderful." Blair's voice was full of hope. "Things are uncertain now, I know, but having a child is a miracle, no matter the circumstances. We need to celebrate."

"Blair is right," Garrett added. "Congratulations, Ben."

Ben found himself smiling for the first time in days. His child *was* a miracle, especially since Jamie had believed she'd never have a baby of her own. He wished they were together to celebrate.

"Jamie is a compassionate person," Blair said. "I'm certain she'd never try to keep you from your child."

"That's what she said, but Lewiston is a three-and-a-half-hour drive away. It's not like the girls and I can pop over on a moment's notice."

"Have you told the girls?" Damon asked.

"Not yet. I didn't want to get their hopes up that Jamie was coming home."

"Have you thought about moving to Lewiston?" Garrett asked. "If you did, you'd be close by, even if you're living in separate houses."

"Moving to Lewiston?" The thought never crossed his mind.

"That's a brilliant idea," Damon said. "The two of you can co-parent all three children."

Blair laughed. "My future husband is a genius. You were planning to move anyway, right? You've already rented your house to Chris and Alison. Why not move to Lewiston?"

"What would I do for work?"

"You can open your own law office," Damon said. "Or maybe you and Morley can open a satellite office there. If you want this, you can make it happen."

He wanted it more than he could say. But there was one big obstacle in his way.

"What if Jamie doesn't want me there?"

"I guess there's only one way to find out," Damon said. "Ask her."

Ask her. He made it sound simple, but things were complicated between them right now.

So uncomplicate it.

Bella and Sophie needed him to make good decisions. So did his unborn child.

He'd do whatever it took.

****

Jamie's phone rang as she watched TV with her parents. The sight of Ben's name caused her heart to make a leap of joy she tried to quell.

But her heart wasn't obeying commands from her head.

She got to her feet and headed to the back door to speak to Ben privately in the yard, giving a wave to her mom and dad as she left.

"Hi, Jamie. Do you have a few moments to talk?"

"Sure." She closed the door behind her and walked out onto the grass. "Are the girls okay?"

323

"They're fine, but what I'd like to talk to you about concerns them."

"What is it?"

"They miss you, a lot, and they need you. I'd like to propose an arrangement where we co-parent Sophie and Bella, and eventually the new baby. Would you hear me out?"

Jamie's mind whirled in confusion. "I...okay, I'm listening."

"I rented my house to Chris and Alison Redwick. I've been looking for a new place in Masonville, but nothing suitable has come up yet. My siblings suggested since we have to move anyway, why not move to Lewiston?"

Jamie paced back and forth on the lawn. "You want to move here? To Lewiston? I don't understand."

"The girls need you, Jamie. They talk about you all the time, and they keep asking when you're coming home. You're their mother, plain and simple, and I don't want to keep you separated any longer."

She covered her mouth to muffle her sounds of distress. After a moment she inhaled deeply. "I want to be their mother again. More than anything."

"And I want to be the baby's father. I want to be part of his life right from the beginning."

She smiled at Ben's use of the male pronoun, since lately she'd been referring to the baby as a boy as well. "I want that, too. Truly. Do the girls know about the baby? Have you told them?"

"Not yet. I wanted to talk to you about this first."

"So, you and the girls would move here? What would you do for work?"

"Morley and I have figured things out. I'll open a

satellite law office in Lewiston. Every other week, I'll spend time at the Masonville office while the kids stay with you. Blair and Garrett have said I can stay with them while I'm in town."

"It sounds like you've already made your decision to move here."

"Nothing's been finalized. Logistically, I know it's doable, but if you don't want me in your town, if seeing me would be too uncomfortable for you, I won't come. I'll find a house here in Masonville for the girls and me, and if you like, you can start calling them on the phone or on Skype. Maybe they can come out to see you in Lewiston on holidays."

"You'd do that?" She was touched by his generosity.

"Of course. Like I said, the girls need you." He paused and she could hear his uneven breath. "I finally understand how much they need their grandparents, too. I spoke to the Doyles. We've been working on a visitation agreement, and I told them about our proposed move to Lewiston. They want to move to North Dakota to be closer to the girls, but they're waiting to hear which town we'll be living in."

The news astounded her. "I'm glad you worked things out with the Doyles. I know having their grandparents close by will make the girls happy."

"I was fooling myself when I said I moved to Masonville for small-town security. I moved to take the girls even farther away from the Doyles. But I'm trying to make up for all my mistakes. I want to be worthy to call myself the girls' father."

He sighed deeply, and she could almost see him rubbing his left temple the way he did when he was stressed. "I know it's too late for us. I've made too many mistakes for you to take me back. I promise you, if I move to Lewiston with the girls, I'll keep our contact to a minimum. I only want what's best for them, and I believe it's having two parents, even if we live in separate houses." His voice cracked. "And if someday you find someone new, I won't stand in your way. You deserve someone special."

Jamie closed her eyes, her voice shaking. "I don't know what to say."

"You don't have to say anything right now. Just think about it."

"I will." She likely wouldn't think of much else.

"I hope I've done the right thing by making this proposal. I don't want to cause you any additional stress, not now. I want to do what's right for you."

"I'm glad you made this offer, Ben. I miss the girls a lot." *I miss you, too.*

There was much to consider. Even though she'd told Ben she planned to stay in Lewiston and sign on as partner in the family veterinary clinic, she hadn't pulled the trigger. Nor had she put her house in Masonville up for sale. She couldn't make herself phone Lauren and Cole and give her official resignation. Making that phone call was final, the end of her life in Masonville.

The end of her life with Ben.

But now, with this proposal, he'd be in her life indefinitely. She still loved him, and if she was honest, she longed to be with him again. But she was afraid. Perhaps a clean break was best, giving her the opportunity to actually get over him. Maybe she should tell him to stay in Masonville.

Ben Greyson wasn't safe for her peace of mind.

Chapter Thirty-One

"Knock, knock. Anybody home?"

From her bedroom, Jamie heard her sister entering the house and the dogs greeting her with welcoming barks. She found Lisa in the living room playing with her dogs.

"Hi. I hope I didn't wake you."

"No, I was already awake. Just being lazy."

"You're entitled. Do you feel up to a walk? It's a gorgeous day."

"A walk would be great. These guys need to work off some energy."

In a few minutes they were out the door and heading down the street, Sammy and Rex leading the way.

Jamie lifted her face to the sun. "It feels good to be outside."

"Mom said you've been inside the house brooding the last couple of days."

"Did she send you over?"

"Nope, I made that call all on my own." Lisa turned to her. "How are you feeling, honestly?"

Jamie grinned at her sister. "So that's why you came. You want me to spill my guts."

Instead of laughing, Lisa shook her head. "No, I just wanted to talk. I know I haven't always supported you the way a sister should."

A stab of guilt speared Jamie in the heart. "I guess we're even. I haven't been the most supportive sister either."

They walked in silence for a couple of blocks, the only sounds the panting of the dogs and birds singing in the trees. Finally, Lisa spoke.

"Zach said you haven't formally accepted the partnership he and Dad offered you."

Another thing to feel guilty about. "No, I haven't."

"Mom told me about Ben's offer to move here with the kids. When are they arriving?"

"I haven't told Ben to go ahead with the move yet."

"It's not like you to be so indecisive. What's going on?" Lisa looped her arm around Jamie's shoulders. "It's just you and me here. Whatever you tell me will be between us. I promise."

Jamie shook her head, finding it difficult to put into words the emotions she'd wrestled with the last couple of days. "I...I don't know. I feel paralyzed, afraid to make a mistake."

"What do you mean?"

"Dad and Zach have made me a wonderful offer. Logically, it makes complete sense for me to stay here in Lewiston. I'll need family support once the baby comes."

"But...?" Lisa prompted.

Jamie sighed. "I loved my life in Masonville. My house, my job, my friends. I'm not sure I want to uproot and start all over again."

"You can have everything you need here. You already have a job, and you can buy another house. Eventually you'll make new friends, and you can always stay in touch with your old friends in

Masonville. It's not like Lewiston is that far away."

"No, I suppose not."

"And for what's it's worth, you have your family here, including me."

"It's worth a lot."

"If Ben and the kids move here, you'll have all the people you love close by."

Jamie didn't respond. Of course she wanted Bella and Sophie near, but they came as a package deal with Ben.

When Jamie remained silent, Lisa turned to her, her brows knit together in concern. "I'm getting the feeling you don't want them to move here."

"I do want them here. I want to be a part of Bella's and Sophie's lives, but I'm not sure what my role will be if they move here. Am I their mother? Their former stepmother? I wouldn't even know what to call myself. I don't want them to be confused."

"And Ben? What do you call him?"

The love of my life. Jamie blinked unwanted tears away.

"I don't know." Could she see Ben on a regular basis and not fall apart each time? Or did the best interests of the children outweigh what was best for her?

They reached the park, and Lisa steered her toward the picnic tables. They sat at a table, and Jamie unleashed the dogs and pulled a couple of tennis balls from her pocket. She passed one to Lisa and her sister tossed it for Rex to chase. Jamie threw her ball in another direction for Sammy.

"Jamie, what's really wrong? What are you afraid of?"

Sammy dropped his ball at Jamie's feet, and she threw it for him once more. Lisa sat quietly, waiting for her to speak. Jamie unconsciously rubbed her abdomen.

"After Carson left me, I went into a tailspin. I couldn't work. I could barely get out of bed. If it wasn't for having to look after Hector and the dogs, I wouldn't have left my bedroom.

"My clinic manager came to see me, and when she saw the shape I was in, she took me to an emergency room." She glanced at Lisa. "She was afraid I was suicidal. I had those thoughts, but I swear, I never would have acted on them. The doctors diagnosed me with severe depression, and I spent a few days in the hospital. They started me on antidepressants, and eventually I began to feel better. I saw a counselor for a while, and she helped me come to terms with my infertility and the end of my marriage."

"You kept all of this from Mom and Dad?"

"I figured they had enough to worry about with your illness. And to be honest, I didn't want to hear how disappointed they were in me."

"They wouldn't have been disappointed. None of us would have."

Jamie smiled at Lisa. "I know that now. But back then, it's what I told myself."

"Are you afraid of having a relapse?"

"It was the darkest time of my life. I felt absolutely worthless. I can't go back there."

"Of course not. But Jamie, you've already gone through a difficult breakup with Ben, and you came through it whole. You even managed to rebuild your relationships with your family. You're a lot stronger than you give yourself credit for."

"Maybe."

"You *are*," Lisa insisted. "Do you love Ben?"

Jamie answered without hesitation. "Yes, I love him. I probably always will."

"Do you trust him?"

This time her answer came more slowly. "I know he's trying to change. He's made some big strides." She told Lisa how he'd reconciled with the children's grandparents.

"But do you trust him?"

"I don't know." Jamie threw Sammy's ball again. "When it was good between us, it was very good. But the way he left me was hurtful. I can't forget."

"You're the only who can make the decision about whether you want Ben in your life. All I can say is you deserve someone who will treat you right." Lisa laced Jamie's fingers with hers. "I don't want you to have any regrets. I don't want you to look back in ten years and wonder what might have been."

"It's not what I want either, but I have to be careful." She touched her abdomen once more. "What I do affects not only me but three innocent children."

Lisa nodded. "I understand. But it sounds like you're looking for a guarantee, and there's no such thing. Maybe your family's future happiness is worth taking a risk."

"What do you mean?"

"When I was diagnosed with Lupus, I made a promise to myself. I wasn't going to let the disease define my life. I wasn't going to be Lisa, the girl with Lupus. I was going to be Lisa, the girl who graduated from college and became a teacher. The woman who's a mother to two amazing kids and wife to an incredibly sexy veterinarian."

Jamie grinned in spite of herself. "Incredibly sexy, huh?"

Lisa returned her grin, a mischievous sparkle in her eyes. "You betcha." Her grin quickly faded. "I know my attitude wasn't easy on Mom and Dad. It still isn't. They would prefer I not take on so many projects or try to do too much. They were terrified through each of my pregnancies. Zach is supportive, but I'm sure he feels the same way. But I have to live my life, and it means taking some risks. Even if I swathed myself in bubble wrap there's no guarantee my disease won't flare up."

"I wish I could be as brave as you."

Lisa gripped her hand. "You are brave. And strong and resilient and incredibly smart. Mom and Dad said you were an amazing mother to Bella and Sophie, and I know you're going to be an amazing mother to this baby. Don't let fear hold you back from making a decision. Don't let it stop you from getting everything you want in life, everything you deserve."

Jamie stared at her sister. Was she brave enough to make a leap of faith?

****

Jamie's attention wandered as she watched TV with her parents. She kept thinking about what Lisa had said about taking chances. She needed to move forward, to make good decisions for her herself and the children. And for Ben.

Finally, she couldn't sit still any longer. She got to her feet and whistled for her dogs.

"I'm going out with the boys."

"Do you need some help walking them?" Helen asked.

"No, I'm good. Thanks, Mom."

She attached their leashes and left the house, needing to move. To think.

When they reached the empty park, she unleashed the dogs and threw their tennis balls. The dogs took off on the run, Sammy with his longer legs beating the smaller terrier to one of the balls. But when he tried to steal the second ball, Rex stood up to the bigger dog. Despite his smaller size, he fearlessly demanded what was his.

Could she be that courageous?

The dogs returned with their balls and dropped them at her feet. She threw them again and again until all three of them tired of the game. Jamie sat at one of the picnic tables as the dogs lounged nearby under an elm tree, instantly falling asleep after their exertion.

She pulled the gold chain from around her neck and examined her wedding ring. The gold was warm to the touch after nestling against her skin.

It was such a lovely ring. She loved the four diamonds representing her family with Ben. Jamie touched her belly. Soon she'd need to add another diamond to the ring.

Families were funny things. The makeup of a family shaped a person for the rest of her life. Ben was a good example. His dysfunctional family had made him distrustful and suspicious and contributed to his alcoholism. Ben was working hard to overcome all the damage done to him in his youth.

The worst thing his parents had done was to withhold their love. Jamie's parents had never done that, not intentionally, but their preoccupation with Lisa made her feel like second best. The feeling stayed with her, and when she met Carson, she accepted the way he treated her because she didn't believe she deserved better.

One thing she knew for certain was that she would never again accept less than what she deserved.

She touched the two smaller diamonds on the ring. Bella and Sophie deserved a family, a whole family, with love and attention from a mother and a father. So did her unborn child. If she'd learned anything in the last few months, it was how important those childhood years were to a person's future happiness.

But without a loving relationship between her and Ben, one based on trust, mutual respect, and a willingness to work things out, there could be no marriage and no family.

She wanted a relationship like that with Ben. They'd both come a long way since they married a few months ago. But was it enough?

There are no guarantees.

No, there weren't. But there was faith. Though she'd been afraid to believe him at first, she had faith Ben meant it when he said he'd never walk away from her again. And now, she had faith in herself. She'd fight for what she wanted, for what she deserved.

Jamie opened the clasp of the gold chain and slid the ring off the end. She slipped it onto her finger once more. It sparkled like a beacon of hope.

The thought made her smile. Hope had been in short supply, but now it was back.

Jamie pulled her phone from her pocket and called Lisa. As soon as Lisa answered, she told her, "I know what I need to do."

****

Ben helped the girls load the dishwasher and wipe the table. "Do either of you have any homework?"

"Not me," Sophie replied.

"I finished mine at your office after school," Bella said. He'd been picking the girls up after school and taking them to his office for a couple of hours so he could finish his work. "My teacher says I'm almost all caught up now."

"Good for you, Bella. You were away from school for a long time."

Ben didn't like thinking about how ill she'd been. If Jamie hadn't taken her straight to the hospital...

He closed his eyes. *Jamie.* He missed her. He physically ached with the depth of his longing. He couldn't eat, couldn't sleep. The regret was overwhelming because he was the one who'd sent her away.

Three days had passed without any word from her. It likely meant she didn't want him to move to her hometown. He would see her and the baby only rarely.

Despite his melancholy mood, Ben couldn't help but smile. *Jamie is having my baby. A son.* Funny, he couldn't stop thinking of the child as a boy even though there was no proof yet. Jamie hadn't said if she already knew the gender of the child.

He was going to miss all those milestones in his child's life. Feeling the baby's first movements, being present at his birth, hearing his first cries.

All of it lost to him. Jamie lost to him. Because of his suspicion and distrust. All those years living in his parents' house and knowing he could never count on them for anything had left their mark. But he was grown now, and there were no more excuses.

"Daddy? Are you okay?"

Ben was shaken out of his reverie by Bella's question. She peered up at him, a worried expression in her blue eyes. He'd seen that look too frequently lately.

"Everything's fine, Bella. It's time for you and Sophie to get ready for your bath. You want to go in the tub first?"

"Sure." She walked off, head bowed and shoulders slumped. Her despondency hit Ben in the gut. For the sake of his children, he needed to get his act together. Tomorrow when he visited the therapist in Bismarck, he'd ask her what he could do to help the kids.

By eight o'clock both girls were tucked into bed. They'd taken to sleeping together in the same bed, and even though the twin mattress didn't give them much room, they seemed to derive comfort from their closeness. Sophie continued to suck her thumb and Ben didn't have the heart to try to stop her. As he kissed them goodnight, he vowed to do better by them.

Ben walked into the empty kitchen. He hated this time of the evening when there was too much time alone to think about all the mistakes he'd made. It drove him crazy with regret.

"Enough."

His voice echoed through the quiet room. He filled the kettle with water and set it to boil for tea, then went to work making lunches for himself and the girls for tomorrow. The busier he kept himself, the better off he'd be.

And the sooner he accepted his relationship with Jamie was over, the better off they'd all be.

His phone rang as he finished putting the lunches together. His heart made a painful thump when he saw

Jamie was calling. This was likely the call where she told him she didn't want him to move to Lewiston, and she didn't want him to have any further contact with her or the baby. With trepidation he accepted the call.

"Hi, Jamie."

"Hi, Ben. How are you?"

"I'm...I'll be fine." *Eventually.*

"I've been doing a lot of thinking," she began. He heard her pause and inhale. This wasn't any easier for her than it was for him, and it tore at his heart. He had no desire to cause her more pain.

"It's okay, Jamie." His voice was barely a whisper. "Whatever you want to say, it's okay."

"All right." She took another deep breath. "I want to say I love you."

Ben gripped his phone. Hearing her say those words now, as she was leaving him, hurt more than he could have imagined. "I love you, too."

"Do you mean it?"

"Of course I mean it. I should have told you from the beginning how much you mean to me. It took me a long time to figure it out, but I know now I wouldn't have asked you to marry me if I didn't already love you. I wanted to be with you. I wanted a life with you. A family with you. Only you."

"I need to be sure...I need your respect. And your trust."

"Jamie, I respect you more than anyone I've ever known. I can't promise we'll never disagree in the future, but I know I'll do everything I can to work things out with you. I trust you." He swallowed hard. "I'll never treat you so cruelly again. I swear."

She was crying now. "I'm happy to hear you say

that, because I'm in my car with Hector and the dogs. We're parked in my driveway. Beside your house."

It took his brain a moment to comprehend her words. "You're here? In Masonville?"

"Yes," she whispered, her voice shaking. "I'm right outside your door. I want to come home. To you. But if it's not what you want, I'll turn around and drive back to Lewiston."

"Like hell you will. Stay right there."

Gripping his phone, Ben raced out the front door. On the front step he turned toward Jamie's driveway. Sure enough, her Honda was parked there. It was the most beautiful sight he'd ever seen.

No, he amended a moment later when Jamie opened her door and stepped from the car. His wife was the most beautiful sight he'd ever seen.

His beautiful, pregnant wife. His Jamie.

They met halfway and threw their arms around each other. As he pulled her against him, Ben swore he'd never let her go again. He'd work hard to be a good husband and make her happy. To make her proud. He'd tell her every day how much he loved her.

Starting right now.

Ben held her face between his hands. "I love you, Jamie. Please stay."

"Yes." She laughed even as tears rolled down her cheeks. "I'll stay. I love you, too."

Ben kissed her, and all the pieces of his life came together in perfect harmony. Every jagged edge, every heartache and sorrow, all suddenly made sense.

He was exactly where he was meant to be, with the woman he was meant to be with.

He was home.

Epilogue

Six Weeks Later

"Mommy, we're home!"

Jamie smiled at the chorus of greetings from her stepdaughters as they arrived home with Ben. *No, my daughters,* she told herself. There were no steps anywhere to be seen, especially since all the legalities were taken care of and she and Ben had officially adopted Bella and Sophie. With the Doyles' blessings, the adoption quickly made its way through the courts.

She stepped out of the kitchen to greet them. They attached themselves to her legs and she bent awkwardly to hug them. Though she grew bigger by the day, she was proud of her expanding belly since it meant their child was growing healthy and strong.

Ben leaned over to kiss her. "How are you, sweetheart?"

Jamie reached up to touch his face. "I'm wonderful."

"Yeah, you are." Ben smiled and kissed her again. "Wonderful and beautiful."

Jamie smiled. Ben kept telling her how beautiful she was, and for the first time in her life, she believed it.

She placed a loving hand on her belly. She couldn't wait to meet the little guy. She hoped he looked exactly like Ben.

"Come on, girls," Ben said. "Let's help Mommy finish making dinner."

Ben insisted she sit at the table with her feet up while he cooked and the girls set the table. She could get used to being waited on.

"What did you do at Grandma and Grandpa's house today?" she asked.

"Bella did homework with Grandma, and I colored. And then Grandpa read us a funny story," Sophie said. "Mommy, which side does the fork go on?"

"On the left. What was Grandpa's funny story about?"

Both girls dissolved into giggles as they retold their Grandpa Doyle's story about a caterpillar who wanted to be something more beautiful than a worm. Mr. Doyle took delight in reading to them. Since they'd moved to Masonville a few weeks ago and purchased a condo close to the girls' school, Bella and Sophie spent an hour or two with them every day after school. The bond between them was growing stronger every day.

Jamie looked up at Ben and smiled. The bond between them had grown as well. She couldn't imagine ever being away from him again. She didn't like to think of how close they'd come to a permanent split.

"How was your day, Jamie?" he asked.

"Busy. But luckily I had a cancelation this afternoon, so I ran into Bismarck and found a dress to wear to Blair and Garrett's wedding this weekend."

"I can't wait to give Blair away. I've never seen her happier."

"Yeah. They're good together. Just like us."

"Yeah, just like us." Jamie's happiness was

increased by the knowledge she made Ben happy, too.

A short time later, they sat down to supper. The girls talked about school, and Ben told her about a new client. Word of his expertise in negotiating between the First Nation and the oil company had spread, and he was busier than ever. Jamie was pleased he'd found work he loved.

"I talked to Damon today. Now that Granddad's Will has passed probate, the renovations on his building have started."

"That's great news. He and Blair and Garrett are going to help a lot of veterans."

"Providing my mother doesn't throw a wrench into the works." A shadow crossed Ben's face. He'd been trying hard to put his past with his parents behind him. But every once in a while she saw the worry in his eyes.

"She can't hurt any of us ever again. We won't let her."

He glanced at the girls and then nodded, but Jamie knew a part of him might never be completely free of his mother's grip. All she could do was continue to reassure him.

"Damon was complaining about Charlotte Saunders. He said she's trying to convince him to include dogs from her rescue in his retreat. Apparently, Blair's taken her side in the debate."

"Tell him I'll be happy to help out with any veterinary care the dogs might need, free of charge."

"I'll tell him, but I don't think the dogs are the problem. I think it's Charlotte that's got him bothered," he said with a grin.

"Really? How interesting."

"My brother deserves some happiness."

"He does," Jamie said. "I want everyone to be as happy as we are."

They shared a smile, and Jamie knew she was exactly where she needed to be.

With her family.

"Daddy, why is Uncle Damon bothered by Miss Charlotte?" Sophie asked.

Jamie bit her lip to stifle her laugh. Ben rolled his eyes.

"Eat your broccoli, Sophie."

Yes, Jamie thought, *I'm exactly where I need to be.*

A word about the author...

Jana Richards has tried her hand at many writing projects over the years, from magazine articles and short stories to full-length paranormal suspense and romantic comedy. She loves to create characters with a sense of humor but also a serious side. She believes there's nothing more interesting then peeling back the layers of a character to see what makes them tick.

When not writing up a storm, working at her part-time day job as bookkeeper, or dealing with dust bunnies, Jana can be found pursuing hobbies such as golf (which she plays very badly) or reading (which she does much better).

Jana lives in Western Canada with her husband Warren. You can reach her through her website at:

http://www.janarichards.com